THE KEEPER'S CREED

I cannot stand idly in the presence of evil.
I cannot remain silent in the face of injustice.
I cannot be passive in the light of corruption.
I will act. I will strike.
And I will never give up.
I will be my sister's keeper.

MY SISTER'S KEEPER

RALPH
DELLAPIANA

ACKNOWLEDGMENTS

I COULD NEVER HAVE SUCCESSFULLY completed a book with so many female characters without the assistance of several gifted women.

The talented Isabella Arras, Editor and Story Consultant for the character of Bella, gave that gentle but resilient teenager an authentic voice amid chaos and trauma.

My dear friend Nubia Peña, who created the character of Mia Montes in my first novel, *Twice a Victim*, and inspired The Sisterhood series of novels, shared brilliantly insightful advice to make sure Mia was true to her nature in this book as well.

And my wife Rocio, whose editing and story skills would allow her to quit her day job and become a full-time editor if she wished, offered critically important analysis of the book from cover to cover.

CHAPTER 1

THIS DRESS WILL CHANGE EVERYTHING. The sparkly, red fabric contrasted stunningly with her dark complexion. Bella didn't usually wear things that were so eye-catching or, for that matter, revealing. She ran her hands over her hips to smooth out the short dress and turned to the side and bent at the waist to make sure that her rear would be completely covered. She tugged the hem a bit more then looked up and down in the mirror and couldn't help smiling.

Tonight was the prom. And she was doing it for Johnny, who should be arriving shortly. Not only did she feel beautiful, she felt *sexy*. She could only hope that Johnny would feel the same. Until this year she had hung out with the nerdy kids, sitting with them at lunch, and staying after school to study. Maybe now she could hang with the cool kids.

If Mom will just let me out of the house. The little dress violated the school dress code for sure, and maybe worse, her mother's views about what was appropriate for a sixteen-year-old child. *But I'm not a child anymore.*

Bella carefully finished applying her lipstick before stepping back from the mirror hanging on the inside of her bedroom door to take herself in. She could hardly believe it was her. Her hair and makeup were perfect, her black stilettos ideal, and her dress, well, she was so in love with it she didn't ever want to take it off.

She adjusted the pendant on the necklace her dad's friend, Mia, had lent her for the night, which featured an ornate silver ring circling a jet-black center. *I wonder why Mia told me to wear this and not to take it off?*

Her phone buzzed. A text from Johnny. "I'm here."

Bella dropped the lipstick and texted back. "Wait!" Then she added, "Don't knock on the door. I'll come 2 U."

Bella slipped her phone into the red mini purse she had selected to go with the dress and pulled the thin strap over her shoulder as she hurried out her bedroom door. Unfortunately, she had underestimated the difficulty of tiptoeing down the wooden stairs and to the front door in stilettos. She made it all the way down to the last step but stumbled on the rug. It was only a matter of moments before she heard, "Excuse me young lady. Where do you think you're going dressed like *that?*"

She sighed, cursed in her head, and turned to face her mother.

"To the prom," Bella said as innocently as she could muster.

Her mother put her hands on her hips and scrunched her eyebrows together. Bella recognized this pose all too well and braced herself for a lecture.

"You really thought you could sneak out without me noticing?"

Bella fumbled for a response. "Dad said it was okay."

Her mother gave her a hard look. "Your father, huh?"

Bella tried to keep her face neutral, but she could feel her prom slipping away from her as her mother said, "And did your father see this dress? Because I have a hard time believing he'd approve of it any more than I do."

Bella wasn't about to go down without a fight. She had been dreaming about this night for weeks and no way was she going to end up spending it in her bedroom alone. "Well, I mean he bought it for me, didn't he?"

Her mother raised an eyebrow. "So, you're saying you went shopping with *him* and not his new little girlfriend?"

Bella had no idea how her mother knew that she'd gone shopping with Mia, but Mia was kind of a sore subject and Bella knew she had to answer the question carefully if she had any hopes of finally kissing Johnny tonight.

Bella hoped to avoid confessing that she had gone shopping without her father. "I really don't think they're even dating, Mom."

Her mother rolled her eyes and said, "That's not the point, Bella. The point is that whoever she is, she let you pick out an incredibly inappropriate dress."

Peering through the windowpane on the side of the door Bella saw Johnny leaning against a shiny black sedan in the driveway. She looked back at her mother with desperation.

"Mom, *please*. I'm sorry about the dress but it's too late to get another one and Johnny is waiting for me. You know how important this is to me. And I promise to take lots of pictures and next year *you* can take me dress shopping for my *senior* prom."

Her mother was quiet for a moment. Bella felt her heart pounding in her chest.

Then finally, after what felt like forever, her mother said, "Fine, but that doesn't mean you're off the hook, young lady."

Bella squealed and rushed to give her mom a hug, "Thank you, thank you, thank you, thank you!"

Her mother couldn't help but break into a smile. "Alright, now go on before I change my mind. Just be careful and have fun." Bella giggled and hurried out the door.

Johnny pushed himself off the car and grinned at her as she approached. Once again, Bella found herself trying to control her facial expressions. Seeing him all dressed up, leaning on the car like that made him somehow even more irresistible to her than he had been before. He stared at her in awe with those big brown eyes and bit his lip before running a hand through his gorgeous thick, black hair. Bella was somehow managing to appear calm and collected but her stomach was doing flips.

She had been hardcore crushing on Johnny since middle school. Like most infatuated middle school girls, she used to figure out his class schedule just by noticing which times she saw him in the halls. She even used to walk different routes in the hopes of him noticing her and going up to talk to her, because of course she could never just go up to him. He was popular and always had half the grade crushing on him at once, and she was, well, kind of a nerd.

But that was then. Now here he was, parked in *her* driveway. He had picked her to take her to his senior prom even though she was just a junior. She excitedly hurried towards him. The awkward jog made her alarmingly aware of just how little support her minimal plunge bra provided, so she switched to a less bouncy speed walk.

Johnny opened the passenger door for her, and Bella instinctively glanced back at the house. She found herself hoping her mother was watching from the window to see what a gentleman he was being. Maybe if her mom was watching she would mention it to Bella's father and then, if the night went well, he might be okay with her dating Johnny.

She knew it was a longshot. He was her dad, and she knew it was highly likely that he would never approve of any guy she might want to date. Not only was he an overprotective father, he was also a defense attorney, which certainly didn't help how suspicious he was of everyone who came near his only daughter; well, his only child.

He had always done his best to prepare her for the darkness of the world. Of course, he had signed her up for martial arts starting when she was only six years old and constantly told Bella about the survival tips he had gleaned from his line of work. And she had taken it to heart. She had earned a black belt and heard enough horror stories for a lifetime. But now she also considered herself to be basically all grown up; she was, after all, only two years short of becoming a legal adult. She was old enough to decide if she thought a guy was dangerous or not, and she didn't think Johnny was.

"You look…fantastic," Johnny said once they were both in the car. She noticed him stare at her breasts and exposed legs brazenly before he started to pull away from the curb. "You know, that's a super sexy dress."

Bella's face flushed with heat, but she smiled. She really wasn't used to getting that kind of compliment. Physically, she had been slower to mature than her classmates, and this gave her a bit of an inferiority complex. While the other girls, including sophomores, wore short skirts and revealing tops to flaunt what Mother Nature had bestowed upon them, Bella had donned jeans and oversized tops to hide what Mother Nature seemed to have forgotten to give her.

Her mother had told her not to worry, that she was just a late bloomer—showing herself as an example of what Bella could expect. How right she was! In the last year, Bella started filling out, even more than she had expected. Now, all the boys at school turned their heads when she strolled down the hallway. Even Johnny. She really liked hearing him call her sexy.

She had barely been able to sleep the night before, unable to stop fantasizing about Johnny kissing her on the dance floor, in front of everyone. Maybe tonight her fantasy would become a reality.

"We're meeting two other couples at Olive Garden for dinner before going to the dance," he announced.

Bella snapped back to reality and nodded, pleased with the selection. She worked at Olive Garden as a server last summer. She would have stayed, but her father wanted her to focus on classes and extracurriculars once school started up again, even promising to pay for anything she needed so she wouldn't have to worry. Other teenagers may have protested, but Bella recognized how fortunate she was to be able to focus solely on school and her grades. Especially since her goal was to go to medical school and maintaining her GPA was important given how competitive the admission process was.

When they got to the restaurant, they saw that the two other couples they were meeting had already been seated. They took the two remaining seats, and a server hurried over. Bella recognized her.

"Sandy!" Bella's smile was huge.

"Bella," Sandy replied, "you look absolutely fabulous!"

Bella beamed and giggled. "Thank you."

"We miss you here," Sandy said.

"I'll be back this summer. Hopefully, I'll have the same schedule as you again."

Sandy shot a glance at Johnny and then gave Bella a look only she would understand meant she wanted the details on what was going on with her and Johnny.

Bella blushed and said, "For sure."

After Sandy had finished taking the group's orders, she turned to walk away but Johnny called her back. "Hey, Sandy, we'd also like a bottle of wine to go with dinner, okay?"

Sandy's happy demeanor changed to a more serious one. "You got ID?" She leaned in a little closer and said, "I literally go to school with you. Do you really think I don't know you're minors?"

Johnny shrugged. "No, I'm saying you could just tell them you checked our IDs, and it won't be a problem."

Bella could tell that Sandy was getting annoyed with Johnny. "I would get in a lot of trouble."

"Who's even gonna know? It's no big deal," Johnny said in a cool tone.

Sandy gave Bella a look that made Bella feel sorry for her. Not only did Sandy have to work on prom night, but *Bella's* date was trying to convince her to do something that would make her lose her job.

Embarrassed, Bella jumped in and said, "Johnny, just leave it alone. Seriously. She would get fired. Not only that but she could get in legal trouble for selling alcohol to a group of obvious minors. We're dressed for prom. No one is going to buy that she checked our IDs."

Johnny gave her a look that made her stomach drop. The table got awkwardly quiet. Sandy shot Bella an awkward smile that she couldn't quite return.

"I'm gonna go put your food in," Sandy said and walked away.

Bella couldn't believe how quickly her perfect night had gone downhill. Johnny was obviously upset with her, and she could only imagine what Sandy was thinking about her going out with him after he'd been such a jerk. She looked down at her plate, racking her brain for some way to get this night back on track.

It was quiet for a moment, but then one of the other guys at the table started asking Johnny what he thought about their new football coach and Johnny leapt at the chance to talk to someone other than Bella. The third guy excitedly joined the conversation and his date looked from Johnny to Bella and then whispered something to the other girl at the table. It was clear that Johnny was the leader of this friend group, and she was definitely maintaining her status as the outsider. Clearly, challenging Johnny wasn't her way in with him or his friends.

The football conversation between the guys went on for a long time, and none of their dates were particularly interested in it. So, Bella joined the other two girls, Sarah and McKenzie, when they got up to go to the bathroom. Bella awkwardly went into one of the stalls. She didn't even really have to go; she was just hoping a brief pause from their date would help Bella and Johnny hit refresh.

She heard Sarah, who was in the stall next to her, start telling McKenzie, who was at the mirror touching up her makeup, all about how she and Brandon had a whole plan to sneak into one of the classrooms to have sex.

McKenzie playfully replied, "Is it really prom night if you don't? It's like a rite of passage."

Bella was grateful to be in a stall by herself so that neither of them could see her reaction. She wasn't a wait-till-marriage kind of girl, but she had really thought that Sarah was. Both she and Brandon were Mormons. She thought the whole point of them being engaged all of senior year was so that they could get married and have sex as soon as possible without it being a sin. Apparently, she was wrong. Bella was utterly shocked that, of the three of them, she was likely the only virgin in the room. Not knowing how to feel about that, she flushed the toilet and tried to seem totally unphased as she exited the stall and started to wash her hands.

Sarah had come out of her stall at about the same time and turned to McKenzie. "What about you and Josh?"

McKenzie laughed. "Girl, you know we already did it in his car before we got here!"

Both the girls laughed, and Bella joined in. She was praying that they wouldn't turn to her next. It's not like they were really her friends. They started making fun of how over the top Josh was every time he came, and the weird things Brandon was into doing. Bella took the opportunity to touch up her hair and makeup.

She looked at herself in the mirror and her sexy dress took on a whole new meaning for her. It hadn't really occurred to her before that she might be losing her virginity tonight. She had hoped that she and Johnny would make out at some point, but that was all. Did Johnny think that they were going to have sex tonight? Bella thought that it was probably unrealistic to think that he was a virgin, given how popular and downright gorgeous he was.

She thought about what McKenzie had said about it being a rite of passage to have sex on prom night and considered the idea. Bella didn't particularly want to go into college as a virgin, and she was even more behind than she thought if Sarah had beaten her to it. At the same time, she had always wanted her first time to be special, or at least with someone who cared about her. She hoped that eventually Johnny would care about her, but she didn't think that's where they were now.

She'd be lying if she said she hadn't fantasized about having sex with him though. Just the thought of it got her heart beating a little faster. She couldn't figure out if that was because of the anxious feeling in her chest or the tingly feeling between her legs.

When the girls returned to the table, Johnny seemed like he was in a much better mood. He smiled at Bella as she walked in. She felt a surge of relief. Maybe tonight could be salvaged after all.

After leaving Olive Garden, Johnny turned onto State Street and headed South. Bella knew for a fact that they were not headed in the right direction to go to the school.

She asked, "Where are we going?"

Johnny smiled playfully, his face glowing a little as the last bit of sunlight glimmered on his face. "We're just making a stop before the dance."

Bella looked in the rearview mirror and saw the cars of the other two couples following behind them. To try and keep things good between Johnny and her, she decided to try and go with the flow. Johnny drove another several blocks before stopping in front of a dingy bar located between a tattoo shop and a payday loan business.

Alarms started going off in Bella's head. She turned toward Johnny in confusion, attempting to mask the concern in her voice. "Why are we stopping here?"

"To get some drinks before the dance," he said casually.

Bella did her best to hide her discomfort, remembering the look he'd given her at the restaurant when she'd told him to lay off Sandy about the wine. But her mind had started running with thoughts of all the things that could go wrong and the look on her attorney father's face when he'd have to come get her out of trouble. She had to say something, but before she could Johnny had already got out of the car. She sat there for a moment before deciding to follow.

Josh had walked over from his car and said, "Kind of a dive, isn't it?"

"Yeah," Johnny laughed. "But my older brother works here and can get us in, which is what matters."

Sarah looked at Bella and read the expression on her face. "Don't worry. Brandon and I aren't even going to drink."

Bella was confused by this "Mormon" couple who had sex and went to bars but drew the line at drinking the alcohol. Aside from that, all she could think about was how weird it would be if she asked them to drive her to the prom instead of her actual date.

Johnny came and put his arm around her. "Come on, it'll make the dance more fun if we have a little buzz."

She really liked the feeling of being held like that by him and really disliked the idea of him being upset with her again, but her anxiety level was rising rapidly. "I don't know."

Johnny's broad smile thinned into a pinched line. "Well, you don't have to come in if you don't want to, but I'm at least having one drink," Johnny said.

Blood rushed to Bella's face as all eyes fell on her. "I guess one drink couldn't hurt."

Johnny smiled and Bella's heart fluttered momentarily. He spoke to her almost tenderly. "Don't worry, my brother said he'll sneak us into a room in the back. No one will see us. It's not a big deal."

Johnny walked in and told the group to wait for him. After a couple of minutes, he came back out with a guy Bella assumed was his brother. His brother contemplated the six teenagers and then glanced up and down the street. Evidently, the coast was clear because he waved them to follow him around the building to the back door.

As the group followed him to the back of the bar, the pit of dread in Bella's stomach grew bigger with each step. With an attorney for a father, Bella had learned that every action has consequences and sometimes even having an attorney parent could not get you out of them. What if they got caught and it went on her permanent record? What if something happened and it blew her chances of getting into medical school? There was too much at stake. She couldn't just follow Johnny blindly because she thought he was hot.

After wrestling with herself for a moment, Bella finally said, "You know, I don't think I'm gonna go in." Her tone made it clear this was not up for negotiation.

Johnny's smile vanished entirely now. "Come on, are you serious?"

He walked over to her with a concerned look on his face and said in a low voice only she could hear, "Please. It's prom, this is a senior tradition. It's fun. I asked you to come with me because I thought you'd want to have some fun."

He might not have meant it that way, but all Bella heard was that he had planned for them to get drunk and hook up. She wasn't about to blow her whole future for *him*.

Bella pulled away, folded her arms, and set her jaw. "I'm staying here. Go have fun."

She could see the indecision in his eyes. She hoped that he would decide to stay out there with her or tell everyone that there had been a change of plans. She hoped that he wanted more than just a hookup with her.

"Are you coming, bro?" his brother shouted from inside the bar.

"Bella, I've gotta go inside, I promised everyone," Johnny said. "But I'll tell you what. I'll be super quick. I'll tell everyone to just pound some shots, and then we'll go. I'll only be a few minutes. Just come in."

Bella considered this. She really didn't want to be the one to cut everyone's fun short, especially since this was everyone in the group's senior year except hers. But she also refused to be a part of anything that could ruin her chances at medical school.

Bella glanced around her. The sun had already dipped below the peaks of the valley's southern mountains and the remaining light was fading fast. She didn't want Johnny to leave her all alone in the growing darkness, but he seemed committed to going inside anyway, so she quit arguing. "Don't worry. Go enjoy." The shattered remnants of broken beer bottles and cigarette butts surrounded the back door, and the smell of urine and vomit twisted her stomach. She forced herself to smile anyway. "I'll just wait out here. It'll be fine."

CHAPTER 2

ONCE JOHNNY HAD GONE into the bar and the door closed behind him, Bella realized how dark it was getting behind the bar. A light fixture hung above the door, but the bulb wasn't working. Either they hadn't thought to turn it on, or it was burned out. Either way, despite what she had just told Johnny, it made her nervous to be out there on her own. Besides, she had to get away from the stink by the back door. She decided it would be better to walk around to the front of the bar to wait.

The night started to get chilly. Bella rubbed her arms and shifted back and forth on her high heels, standing off to the side of the bar's entrance. Suddenly, the idea of a dress with a little more fabric was very appealing to her. She saw some women out on the street alone. She wondered why they were on the street. Were they waiting for someone too?

It didn't take long for her to figure out that they were prostitutes. One of them approached a car that had stopped, and she bent over the open passenger's window. After a short conversation, the girl pulled the door open and got inside the car.

Two or three of the women strolled along the sidewalks, and none of them seemed to be trying to get anywhere in particular. They watched each approaching car, waiting to pounce should any come to a stop. The drivers of the cars didn't seem to mind being their prey. At one point, a set of headlights coming toward Bella illuminated the silhouette of someone's head bobbing up and down in the front seat of a car parked around the corner.

Bella started feeling more and more uneasy. *What am I doing out here alone?* She considered how revealing her little red dress was and had the awful thought that one of these cars might mistake her for a prostitute too. The color didn't feel bold anymore, it felt like a dangerous beacon. She thought of calling her dad, but she hated the thought of the disappointed look he would give her. Instinctively, Bella nervously played with the pendant Mia had lent her for what was supposed to be her big night.

Wait. Mia!

Mia was her father's friend, and she worked as a victim advocate. He had introduced them when she went to court to go watch him in action during his last murder trial. Bella really liked Mia. They had grown close since she and her dad had been spending more time together. Bella didn't know if they were dating or not, but she liked Mia enough that she didn't care either way. If Bella called *her,* she probably wouldn't have to deal with an "I told you so" from either of her parents tonight.

She really wished that they hadn't been right about Johnny. What the hell was he thinking, leaving her out here alone? And then what was the plan? To drive her to the prom while he was drunk? *Screw the prom. Everything is going wrong.*

While considering her options, she continued fidgeting with the pendant. She noticed that the ornate silver ring moved easily when she touched it. Surprised, she twisted it as far around the stone as it would go.

"Hey, beautiful. Looking for a date?"

Bella quickly looked up to see who was talking to her. Her stomach dropped. Directly in front of her parked at the curb was a white cargo van with no windows except for the front seat. The line had to have come from the grinning idiot leaning out of the passenger's window, ogling her up and down. He was Hispanic and looked to be in his twenties. He wasn't unattractive, but he was a creep.

"No thanks." Bella looked away, hoping that the guys in the van would leave her alone.

"Come on, baby, we've got some X. I promise you'll have a good time."

She felt her heart rate pick up as she glanced back at the van again. "No. I'm not interested. I'm waiting for someone."

The guy in the passenger seat turned to the driver and said something to him but not loud enough for Bella to hear. Then he opened his door and reached into his pocket as he quickly approached her.

Her heart was now pounding in her chest. *Oh no, he's coming towards me! I should have stayed in the bar.* She flashed a glance towards the bar. *Where's Johnny?*

"If it's money you want, I can give you a hundred bucks," offered the man. Bella glanced both up and down the street, looking for a safe haven. It was dark and empty, except for the bar behind her. *I'll never outrun him in these heels.*

Bella started walking backwards toward the bar. "Leave me alone. I said *no!*" She turned so she could get away faster, but the guy was quicker. He reached from behind and grabbed her by the wrist. *Omigod. Omigod.* She staggered trying to keep her balance as she pulled against his grasp, but he was strong and holding her wrist tightly. *What is he going to do to me? Daddy told me to be careful. No. No. No!*

Bella remembered something else her father had taught her when she was just six years old right before he signed her up for a self-defense class. She twisted her wrist quickly against the thumb of the man and pulled free of his hold before pushing him away from her with both hands.

"No!" she shouted.

Bella had always wondered if with all her self-defense and martial arts training, she would be able to defend herself in a real-life situation. It seemed that her father was right to put her in all those classes. But the fight wasn't over yet.

The man frowned at her. She turned, but before she could get any safe distance from him, he reached out and grabbed her shoulders from behind with both hands.

"Bitch, you're coming with me." A burning current streaked through Bella's body as he started to pull her toward the van. She tried to pull away to run but he circled one arm all the way around her and she couldn't get loose from his grasp. As they approached the van a sliding door popped open, and someone inside pulled it all the way back. Bella twisted to try to get away, but stumbled, her footing unsure in her heels. She gasped for breath as sweat beaded on her forehead.

"Help!" she shouted frantically.

The guy turned towards her and put his hand over her mouth as he glanced up and down the street. Bella followed his gaze, hopeful for help. She couldn't see anyone. Her vision was fading. She could only focus on the man's tight arm. *I wish I had called Daddy!*

As she thought of her father, she recalled something he had told her before she started sparring in the championship round of a martial arts competition. "You can't beat someone who doesn't give up. So *never* give up." Her father wasn't here, and she wasn't a little girl. This fight wasn't over until she gave up, something she was not ready to do. *Don't quit, Bella. Fight back!*

With one hand on her mouth, the guy's grip had loosened. Bella twisted her body to face him, gripped his shirt with both hands and jerked him towards her and shouted "Hiyah!" as she jammed her knee up into his groin.

He moaned loudly, dropped his hands to his crotch, and doubled over. She swung her right elbow forward against his temple as hard as she could and then spun around and hit him even harder with the back of her left fist. All those years of martial arts training had certainly paid off as she instinctively reacted with the forms and moves she had practiced so many times before.

He tottered and landed on one knee with his hand on the ground. Seeing his dazed expression, Bella gave him a front kick to the chin that knocked him all the way back to the van door where he crumpled to the ground.

Unfortunately, Bella had never trained in high heels. They didn't give her stability and caused her to lose her balance and fall after her kick. She tried to get a leg under her so she could stand up, but another guy jumped out of the back of the van and grabbed her from behind. When he pulled Bella to her feet, she jammed the point of her stiletto heel into his foot. He yelped but hung on tightly and started to drag her into the van.

She tried to fling her head back into his nose, but he was a head taller than her, even in her heels, and her attempted headbutt had no effect. Bella reached out to grab the side of the van, but he was so big and so strong that he pulled her through the door anyway, threw her to the floor, and pulled the door closed behind them. Bella's knees hit the floor hard. She whimpered as she scanned the back of the van. *No. No. No. I gotta get out of here. Are they going to rape me?*

Bella's father had told her all kinds of horror stories about kidnappings as a child, so she knew that any number of bad things could happen to her now. *Am I going to die?*

"Go!" yelled the man.

"Wait," the driver said as the front passenger door opened and the guy she had hurt dragged himself in. Then, the driver punched the gas pedal and swerved from the curb.

Once the van was underway, the guy in the back with Bella focused his attention on the road ahead. *It's not over until I stop fighting.* She took advantage of his distraction by jumping toward the door. She might get hurt if she jumped out, but it had to be better than whatever they had in store for her.

Just as she got hold of the handle and started to pull the door open, the big guy grabbed Bella and threw her to the ground face first. She landed on Mia's pendant, causing a sharp pain in her chest. The guy dragged her away from the door across the metal floor, and the pendant scraped along it. Then he landed heavily with his knee on her back.

Bella couldn't move and could barely breathe. Summoning all her energy, she shouted as loudly as she could, "HELP!"

The big guy pushed a pillow on top of her head, presumably to muffle her screams. Then a sharp object stung her neck. She struggled, but within a matter of seconds, a warm wave slowly swept through her, and soon after that, everything faded away.

CHAPTER 3

MIA MONTES SWUNG OPEN her front door and saw Frank Bravo standing in a relaxed posture with a plastic container in his hand.

"Hi, Frank. Welcome to my humble abode. Please come in." Mia noticed that Frank paused to gaze at the short summer dress that clung to her small but athletic frame. He looked up at the long black hair Mia let hang loosely today then directly into her dark brown eyes. He smiled. "You look great."

"Thank you." Mia smiled back, stepped aside, and waved him forward.

Frank followed her inside toward the kitchen where he handed her a medium-sized Tupperware container. "I brought my homemade Bolognese sauce. It's my grandma's recipe. I think you'll love it."

"Wonderful." Mia took the sauce and sat it on the counter by the stove. "Please make yourself at home." Mia glanced at Frank over her shoulder. Mia appreciated that Frank made the effort to shave his balding head and trim his goatee. He was a bit older than her, but she was impressed at how fit and tanned he was.

Frank looked around and sat on the brown leather couch.

"And kick off your shoes if you want." Mia lifted her foot to show off her house slippers. She had considered wearing a nice pair of shoes for the occasion, but then she chose to look both casual and homey. That way, if this was just a friendly get-together, she wouldn't look awkward. If it turned out to be something else, well…

Frank nodded and put the toe of one shoe against the back of the other and pulled his foot out and repeated the same process for the other foot. After laying his shoes along the side of the couch, he followed Mia into the kitchen.

Mia walked behind the island, and Frank sat down on one of the stools opposite her. Her eyes met his. "It's been a long time since I've had a guest…a male guest anyway," she admitted, feeling blood rushing to her face.

Why am I so nervous? God, I'm blushing! I hope Frank doesn't take it the wrong way and think this is a date or something. I can't believe he's here, in my home.

She quickly tried to fix any misunderstandings that she may have given him about her intent. "I'm glad you agreed to come. I don't think we ever properly celebrated our success in Kala Tausinga's case. I loved the way you defended her at the trial. I was particularly impressed when you told the jury that she was *twice a victim*, first victimized by an abusive husband and then by the legal system that tried to prosecute her for a murder she didn't commit. Brilliant!"

It had been a couple of months since she and Frank worked on the case that involved a Tongan woman falsely accused of killing her own toddler. At the beginning, Mia was the victim advocate for the family of the deceased child, so she worked with and for the prosecutor. As the case went on, however, she came to believe the mother was innocent and that it was her husband who had killed the child. Consequently, she switched sides and helped Frank, the accused woman's legal defender, to win the case.

Frank placed his lower arms on the island countertop and leaned forward on them. As she spoke, Mia noticed that his gaze wandered to her lips.

"You're too kind," Frank responded. "I couldn't have done it without you. It was you who saved the day in the end. You gave Kala the courage to testify against her husband." He looked at her in apparent admiration for what she had done during the trial.

But Mia had never told Frank exactly what happened *after* the trial. How Kala had called to tell Mia that her angry husband, Afa, tracked her down by the address on her divorce petition. Mia didn't divulge how she had rushed to Kala's apartment, and when she arrived, she found Afa strangling Kala and had used her martial arts skills to knock him off Kala. Mia wondered if Frank would still feel the same admiration for her if he knew that instead of calling the police, she had kicked Afa in the face hard enough to break his jaw before crushing his windpipe, and in furious revenge choked whatever life was left out of him.

Killing someone, even under those circumstances, had affected Mia profoundly. As a victim advocate, she spent a decade working *within* the law, helping the prosecutors hold people accountable for their bad acts. At the time she killed Afa though, she had just adopted the mission of The Sisterhood, to get justice for abused women when the legal system failed to protect them. But now, almost daily she wondered if she had committed murder. She didn't *have* to kill him, but she did it anyway. Purposefully. The memory weighed like a backpack of stones on her conscience.

Not wanting to broach that topic now, or probably ever, Mia forced a smile and simply said, "Let's put your sauce on the stove to warm it up. I made penne pasta and grilled some sliced zucchini and eggplant as you suggested. I wasn't quite sure which wine to get to go with a celebration dinner, but since you're Italian, I picked out two: a bottle of Chianti and a Prosecco."

"That's perfect," Frank said, grinning.

Once the food started warming, Mia walked to the couch and slid into one corner of it with her legs folded under her. She patted next to her on the couch. "Come. Sit with me, and let's catch up."

"You first," Frank said as he eased down on the other end of the couch and brought one bent leg up onto the couch to make it easier to face her. "What have you been doing for work since you left the District Attorney's Office?"

"Well, *left* doesn't quite do justice to what happened," Mia said. That prosecutor *fired* me."

Frank grimaced. "Yeah, I remember. But did they ever give you any official reason for that?"

"Just for helping Kala. After all, the prosecutor told me that she was the one he was trying to convict. He said I was supposed to be helping *him*, not helping her."

Frank sat up straight. "But you were being a true advocate for the *real* victim. What you did may have been difficult, but it was the right thing to do. I admire your courage."

Mia smiled. She had disliked Frank when she first met him. Truth be told, she disliked all criminal defense attorneys. But Frank had proved that he truly cared about Kala, and he had fought hard to help her.

In addition, he had raised a confident, kind, and intelligent daughter, who Mia had met during Kala's trial. There was something sweet about men who were loving fathers. Having been an orphan most of her childhood after the tragic death of her parents, Mia felt a deep tenderness mixed with a bit of envy toward men who were good role models to their kids. Over the years, Mia had learned that you can tell quite a bit about a man from the daughters he raised. And Frank's daughter Bella was an extraordinary young woman. So Frank was growing on her.

Frank shifted his position. "So, what are you doing now?"

"I'm a private investigator, working mostly on criminal cases. But occasionally, I'll have someone ask me to check out a spouse, you know, to see if they're cheating. That's sort of fun."

Frank nodded. "Does that keep you busy full time?"

"Not quite. In my spare time I've started a training program for that women's group I'm involved with."

"Oh yeah," he said. "Do you mean the group led by the mysterious Middle Eastern woman? The ones who get justice for abused women who can't get it in a court of law. What's it called? The Sisterhood?"

Mia leaned forward but hesitated. When she had killed Afa, she had done so with the blessing of The Sisterhood. She was not a formal agent but had acted on their behalf in an emergency. She was still affiliated with them, and they had spoken of conducting the ritual to make her a blood-oath member, but she was having second thoughts about whether she could do what they did. What they now expected her to do.

"Frank! I told you not to say that name. It's a *secret* group."

He frowned. "Oops. Sorry. But I promise I don't talk about it with anyone else. I just thought I could talk about it with you."

Mia took a breath and stared into Frank's brown eyes, pondering whether that was his first slip in mentioning The Sisterhood or merely the first one brought to his attention. He was pouting like a scolded puppy. She caught herself staring at his full lips.

"That's okay. Yes, you can talk to me about it." She decided she trusted Frank. "But to no one else."

Frank's muscles relaxed as a warm smile spread across his face.

"Let's get the food on the table," Mia said. "I'll make the plates. You open the wine."

"Don't forget the parmesan," Frank added as he grabbed the bottle and bottle opener. "Hey, this is a *molto buono* brand of Chianti. Good job picking it."

After they settled in at the table, Mia asked, "What are *you* working on lately? Do you have any big cases?"

"Always." He shook the small glass container of parmesan cheese until a big pile of it fell onto his pasta. "But one case is keeping me up at night. It's another murder. Maybe a cartel hit. I think my client may be innocent, but he isn't talking. Something about a code of silence."

Mia held up a finger as she closed her eyes and slowly savored Frank's meat sauce on her tongue. "Mmm, that's good." She sipped a bit of her wine. "Especially with the Chianti."

Frank smiled at the compliment. Then he picked up his wine glass and lifted it for a toast. "To good food, good wine, and…good friends."

"Cheers." Mia met Frank's gaze as she clinked her glass against his.

"Now, sorry I interrupted you," Mia said. "I want to hear more about your murder case. Another innocent client you say?" She took her eyes off him long enough to take a bite of her pasta.

Frank swirled the wine in his glass. "Maybe that's enough shop talk for tonight." He took a sip, put his own glass down and picked up the bottle. With a twinkle in his eye he said, "Here, let me top off your drink."

Mia scooped up a large forkful of pasta and opened her mouth wide to try to fit it all in at once. She got most of it. She chewed slowly, savoring the flavor. After a while, she asked, "How's Bella? Isn't the senior prom tonight?"

"Yes, it is. She must be going to the dance as we speak. By the way, thank you for helping Bella pick her dress. She wouldn't let me have anything to do with it." He smiled with a mischievous twinkle in his eyes.

"Well, she told me that you wanted to buy her a long-sleeved gown that extended past her ankles." Mia laughed. "Of course, she wouldn't let you help."

Frank shrugged and smiled. "Also, thank you for that 'special pendant' you loaned her. She's going to the prom with a football player I don't know. I remember my senior prom—booze, sex, or so I'm told." The mischievous twinkle returned with a wink. He paused in thought, and his forehead wrinkled. "Anyway, I'm worried about her."

"Don't worry." Mia found Frank's worry for his daughter endearing. "I turned on the transponder when I gave it to her, and she promised to call if there was trouble."

Frank said, "I looked at the pendant and couldn't see an on-off button."

"It's that ornate, silver ring around the stone. You turn it one centimeter to turn on the transponder and one more centimeter to turn on the video recorder, and then just backwards to turn them both off."

Frank nodded. "Okay. Thanks. That's sweet of you to do all that you've done for Bella."

"For Bella and for you too, Frank. It was no problem."

Mia picked up the dinner plates and took them to the kitchen. Glancing back over her shoulder, she said, "Hey, the Chianti's gone, but we still have the Prosecco. Do you want some for dessert?"

Frank nodded. "Yes, I believe I do. I love Prosecco. But…I probably shouldn't have any more or…I won't be able to drive home safely."

Mia turned to study Frank. Something about the way he hesitated, the way he raised an eyebrow when she caught his eye, made her wonder what he was thinking.

Mia's heart started beating harder. She had sworn off men after her ex-husband tried to kill her. But that was ten years ago now. She had never been able to bring herself to trust anyone since. Over the years, her friends had encouraged her to try again, and she had accepted the offer of an occasional date. But none of them went anywhere. Afterward, she would declare again that she was done with men forever.

She snuck another look at Frank from the kitchen and found him watching her openly. He was unfailingly kind to her, recognized her abilities, and applauded her accomplishments. Plus, he wasn't bad looking either.

Mia hadn't planned it like this when she and Frank set up this dinner. But now, in the warmth of his company, she believed that maybe, just maybe she could trust another man again. She turned to go get the bottle of Prosecco from the fridge.

CHAPTER 4

IN A CLANDESTINE FACILITY HALFWAY down Interstate 80 between Salt Lake City and Wendover, the executive director of the secretive vigilante women's group known as The Sisterhood met with its founder to try to answer the critical question of what to do with Mia Montes.

The building was tucked behind a rock formation off a side road and could have passed for a maintenance building or a small storage facility. It was gray and white. No signs announced its purpose. Only one floor was visible above ground. A small doorway was visible at the front and there was a large garage sized door around the side. The two women met on the sixth subfloor.

Victoria, a tall, attractive blond, was the Executive Director of The Sisterhood's North American Division. Having been rescued by The Sisterhood from an abusive man when she was young, she had found a home among women who cared deeply for each other and fought to protect others. Now, among her many duties was to nominate extraordinary women to become members of the organization.

Xtina, the founder of The Sisterhood, was a mature woman from Israel. She had long black hair and emerald green eyes that sparkled from within. She had directed The Sisterhood for longer than anyone knew and was reputed to be able to see future events.

Xtina appeared in the doorway of Victoria's office. Once Victoria met her gaze, Xtina asked, "Have you decided whether to nominate Mia Montes to become a member of our organization?"

Victoria cocked her head to the side in thought. "Frankly, I'm not sure. What do *you* think?"

Xtina clasped her chin and took a deep breath, her eyes fixed on Victoria's face. Let's work through the decision together, my dear sister."

Victoria smiled. "You are wise, as always."

Xtina tilted her head to the side. "Let's go take a seat in the boardroom."

Victoria picked up her laptop and followed Xtina down the hallway into a dimly lit room. Xtina flipped a switch on the wall that illuminated an ancient oak table with obsidian inserts in front of each of several black leather and wood chairs. Swords, helmets, spears, bows, and shields selected from Xtina's vast collection of ancient artifacts hung on the walls and occupied shelves around the perimeter of the room.

Xtina pointed to a seat for Victoria and then took one herself. "Let's consider Mia's qualifications. First, what can we say of her commitment to The Sisterhood's mission to get justice for women who are victims of abuse when the legal system fails?"

Victoria flipped open her laptop and tucked a loose strand of her long blond hair behind her ear as she considered the matter. "At her interview, the board was not convinced that she was up to the task."

Xtina nodded. "It's true that her long service as a victim advocate at the District Attorney's Office had made her feel a strong commitment to the criminal justice system. I recall that she hesitated when asked if she could work outside the legal system to get justice for victims."

Seeing that Xtina had not only paused but also appeared to be waiting for her input, Victoria replied, "But that was before her work to clear the Kala Tausinga case. When Kala's husband found her and attacked her, and Zena was too far away to respond, Mia stepped up without hesitation, saved Kala, and carried out the demands of justice against her husband where the legal system had failed. Mia told me later that she was afraid at the time, but courage is action in the face of fear. And Mia acted courageously. Heroically. So, I would conclude that yes, she is, to use the board's language, up to the task."

"I agree," said Xtina, nodding. "Now, let's look at the second qualification—experience and training. Mia started martial arts instruction living here in The Garden when we took her in after her parents were killed in a car accident. I know that she has continued training on her own ever since then. Plus, at my request, Sally opened the armory and provided some firearms training and showed Mia some of our advanced weapons."

"Yes, but Sally has made it clear that Mia's training is far from complete," Victoria pointed out. "So, wouldn't that fact alone bar her from eligibility to participate in the Rose Ceremony?"

Xtina paused before answering. "I admit that Mia's lack of training is a concern. But throughout the history of The Sisterhood, the women who have stepped up to the challenge of defending other women didn't have the benefit of Sally's special ops training. They've had only their wits and the determination to fight to protect their sisters."

Victoria frowned. "But the board has determined that it is mandatory to complete the training."

"Yes, my hand-picked board did say that." Xtina allowed her eyes to focus somewhere well beyond the walls of the conference room. "But it is a courageous heart and a commitment to serve that are the true requirements. And when I placed my hands on Mia's head, I sensed her great strength of spirit and will, and I perceived that it is her calling, her destiny, to fight injustice and evil."

"Then I will accelerate her training schedule," Victoria said, "to remove that hurdle as an obstacle to her progress as quickly as possible, and to prepare her for what's to come."

Xtina nodded. "Perfect. Now let's look at the third qualification."

Victoria held up her hand. "Hold that thought. I have a signal coming in on my security system monitor. Let me check it out."

"What is it?" Xtina asked.

Victoria tapped a few keys on her computer. "The GPS pendant Sally signed out to Mia has just uploaded a video."

Xtina stretched her neck toward Victoria's monitor.

"I haven't opened it yet," Victoria said. She turned to face Xtina. "Yesterday, I had lunch with Mia. She said she had invited Frank Bravo to her house for dinner tonight. You remember. He's the lawyer who represented Kala Tausinga."

Victoria looked at her watch. "It's about ten p.m. They've probably finished dinner by now. The video is activated by twisting the silver frame of the stone one centimeter clockwise. That small of a change *could* happen just by the friction of certain body parts moving. I wouldn't want to intrude on—"

"I see where you're going with this." Xtina's eyebrows furrowed with concern. "But I have a bad feeling about it." She put her hand on Victoria's shoulder. "Open it. Now."

CHAPTER 5

MIA SMILED AT FRANK as he popped the cork of the Prosecco and then slowly filled her champagne flute with bubbly liquid. He set the bottle down and scooted his chair around the edge of the table, closer to her, then picked the bottle up again, filled his own glass and lifted it to her. They clinked their glasses together and took a long sip, their eyes locked on each other.

Opening the extra bottle must have made it clear to Frank that Mia wanted him to stay the night. Her heart pattered faster in her chest at the thought. But she wondered for just a moment whether she should have sent him those signals. This wasn't even an official date. And it had been so many years since she had given herself to a man. Uncertain about what she should do, she leaned back into her chair.

Then Frank touched her. He had leaned forward and stroked her shoulder softly and caressed her arm gently. She liked it. Her remaining doubts fell aside, and the high wall she had spent a decade building around her heart crumbled to dust in an instant. She knew she wanted more. She reached out and took hold of Frank's arm above the elbow and pulled him toward her.

They both set down their glasses on the table and turned back to each other. Slowly, they drew closer together, gazing into each other's eyes and glancing at each other's lips. Then they pulled each other even closer.

Frank's knee pushed between her legs, grazing her thigh, and sending a tingling sensation up her leg. Just before their lips touched, he paused again for just a moment. Then he pulled her decisively to him, his kiss crushing her lips, but she didn't protest.

The intense warmth rushed from her lips to her chest, sending shivers down her spine and ripples that tingled her tummy and the softness between her legs. After the passionate moment, Frank pulled back slightly. Maybe he was hesitant to go further without her consent.

But Mia didn't let go, didn't dare pull away.

Frank leaned forward, capturing her mouth, his tongue parting her lips as she welcomed the kiss. She wrapped her arms around him, tugging him tighter against her, certain he could feel her quickened heartbeat and pulsing need. He grasped her waist, his free hand sliding up her thigh, inching its way up her side. He trailed the soft curve of her breast with a knuckle and her breath caught.

She didn't move, but closed her eyes instead, savoring his touch and the heat now claiming her middle. No way she'd allow him to leave tonight. After a moment, she stood and took his hand, urging him to his feet. Their eyes met. Mia paused, trying to gauge Frank's intentions in the depths of his brown eyes. He raised an eyebrow. Still grasping his hand, she grinned and turned towards her bedroom.

Right at that moment, Mia's phone rang and interrupted the vision in her head of bodies intertwined in a passionate embrace. She was determined to ignore her phone and continued pulling Frank along behind her. He quickened his pace to keep up. But on the second ring, it registered in her mind that this ringtone was one she had specially designated for emergency calls from The Sisterhood. She stopped in her tracks.

Mia glanced back at Frank. "I'm sorry. I have to take this call. It's an emergency." Mia picked up the phone, but before pushing the button to answer it, she smiled at Frank. "But don't go anywhere."

"Mia here."

"Mia!" It was Victoria, speaking quickly. "I just received an alert from your GPS pendant. Where are you? Can you talk?"

"I'm at home. Frank's with me. If it's about the pendant, I loaned it to Frank's daughter Bella to take to her senior prom just in case—"

Victoria interrupted. "If Bella has your pendant, then she's just been kidnapped."

Mia started shaking. She couldn't believe what she was hearing. When she loaned the pendant to Bella, she couldn't imagine that she was going to be in any danger. It was just the prom.

"Oh my god." Mia turned quickly back to Frank. He looked interested in her side of the conversation but not alarmed. *What words? How do you tell someone something that will turn their life upside down?* She decided to just blurt it out. "It's Bella. She's been kidnapped."

Frank's jaw dropped open. "What?" His face morphed into a gruesome grimace. "Noooooooo!" He gripped the top of a nearby chair to steady himself. Mia watched as his knuckles turned white. "She's just a child," he murmured. "Where? When?" Then, he shook himself and spoke louder and faster. "How? Do they know who took her? Are they looking for her? Do they know where she is?"

Mia hit the speaker function on her phone. "Victoria, I've put you on speaker. Frank needs to hear this. Tell us what you know."

Frank moved forward quickly and leaned over the phone. Mia heard his quick breathing and saw his eyes tearing up.

"Okay. The alert came from a video that was uploaded automatically from the pendant. Bella must have turned it on. It appears that she was grabbed on the street. She fought hard, but there were at least two of them and they overpowered her and took her into a van. After more of a struggle, the video just stopped.

"You can track her, right?" Mia blurted. "Where is she?"

"We know where they grabbed her—in front of a bar on State Street. We also know the direction they started out, but the GPS signal stopped. So, we don't have a location. It's been several minutes now. Maybe they took her underground. Maybe they figured out how to turn it off, or they destroyed it. I don't know. But we need the GPS signal to track her. I'm trying to reach Zena, our best field agent, so she can take the lead on the rescue. It would help if we had Bella's phone number. We can try to track her by her phone."

"I'll text that to you now," Mia replied.

• • •

Frank paced back and forth while the women started mobilizing their rescue of his child. But who were they, really?

"What about the police?" Frank asked, his level of concern increasing with each passing second.

"I'm monitoring the police dispatch frequency," said Victoria. "The police are just arriving at the bar now."

"I'm going there now," Frank yelled over his shoulder as he started grabbing his shoes and car keys.

"Go," Mia encouraged. "I'll get the exact address from Victoria and text it to you. I'll coordinate with The Sisterhood. We'll find her. I promise."

Frank didn't know whether to accept the leadership of these strange women, but he trusted Mia. So, he nodded, grabbed his phone, and rushed to the door. Just before pulling it open, he turned back to Mia. "Listen to me. I'm hoping the police can catch the bastards that took my baby."

Mia could see Frank's jaw set and tears welling in his eyes. "You told me that The Sisterhood gets justice for abused women when the police and the system fail them, right?" His voice was now husky with emotion.

"Yes, that's right." Mia thought she knew what he was going to say. He was going to ask that The Sisterhood hunt down the kidnappers and make them pay. But she wanted to be sure. "What is it?"

"Do you think The Sisterhood can help the police find Bella?"

Mia let out a big sigh of relief. She hadn't realized she had been holding her breath. She had thought Frank was about to ask her to use her connections with The Sisterhood to go outside the law, not just to find Bella, but to also take vengeance on her captors. She hadn't told him about the organization's full capabilities and the realities of what its members were willing to do.

"Sure. I'll ask my people to try to help the police."

He nodded and rushed outside to his car. As he pulled his car door closed, he saw Mia's text with the address of the bar. About two miles. He fired up his Jeep and pushed the accelerator to the floor.

CHAPTER 6

SPEEDING THROUGH THE DARKNESS towards the bar, Frank couldn't help but think about the fear his poor Bella must be experiencing. Sure, he started her self-defense training when she was six years old. He had wanted to protect her from the harsh world that he had come to know as a public defender. With his support, she had stuck to her training, and at just twelve years old, passed her black belt exam. He had just hoped that she would be able to defend herself against unwanted sexual advances by boys. But the perverts who had taken her were obviously not just boys.

The traffic light turned red just as Frank reached it, causing him to screech to a halt at the busy intersection. He wanted to push through and keep going, but there were too many cars. His toe tapped at the side of his accelerator, and he wiped tears from his eyes so he could see the light as soon as it changed.

Frank remembered that black belt exam well. The master had pressed the students to complete a full hour of exercise at maximum effort before another hour of forms competition where they were required to demonstrate competence in all the basic karate techniques. Afterward, they sparred with each other to show that they could apply those forms in active combat. Finally, they had to exhibit their board-breaking skills. A straight punch. A forward kick. Spinning back kick. Jumping double kick breaks. And last, the breaking of a board by the knife-hand technique while the master held the top inch of it.

Frank watched as some of the other candidates tried and failed to complete that last break. Admittedly, it was challenging. Holding only the edge of one side of a board caused it to flip back when struck.

He remembered how the master had Bella perform this break right in front of where he was sitting on the mat with his back against the wall. On Bella's first try, she seemed to stop her hand right at the board. She didn't follow through. He observed quietly as the wise master patiently told her to concentrate all her focus on the center of the board, snap her hand just as she hit the board and then follow all the way through the board.

Frank remembered vividly the determination on Bella's twelve-year-old face. How she set her feet firmly on the ground, turned her body at ninety degrees, and then suddenly and fiercely, whipped her hand through the middle of the free-hanging board, sending it flying in splinters against the wall.

The light finally changed. He gripped the steering wheel and stomped the gas pedal to the floor again. As he raced to the bar, he remembered how all of Bella's competitions had been in air-conditioned gyms with referees to stop the fight or issue warnings for unnecessarily hard contact.

Frank bit his lip as he imagined the fright his daughter must be suffering upon being taken. Dark memories of horrific kidnapping cases he had been obliged to handle as a public defender filled his mind. Some cases were just one angry parent who had lost custody when a judge deemed them unfit who had disappeared with a child. Those typically resulted in some brief jail time and counseling if the harm to the child was no more than emotional trauma. But then there were others, like those two teenage girls who were hitchhiking and found later at a remote cabin, raped and murdered. He wiped his eyes again but couldn't stop the tears as he sped through the streets.

Finally arriving at the bar, he screeched to a stop near the curb and jumped out of his car. It didn't seem as if his feet hit the pavement before he took off running.

"What the hell is going on here?" he shouted at the first cop he could find, a young officer standing outside of the bar. The officer glared at him as if he were a madman and put his hand on his holster. Frank shouted, "Why the hell are you just standing here? Why aren't you out looking for my baby, godammit!"

The officer raised a hand to stop Frank and pulled his gun out of his holster. He pointed the gun at Frank and said in a loud voice, "Take a step back, sir, and raise both your hands over your head."

Frank took a step back and took a deep breath. He just came to the realization that a police officer was pointing his duty weapon directly at his chest, so he complied and raised his hands. He recalled that over the years, more than one of his clients was shot after acting out and shouting in front of a cop. Even worse, if they survived, then they were charged with assaulting the officer. Frank stood still.

After a moment, he decided to speak slowly and as calmly as he could muster with his heart pounding so fast, "Sorry, officer. I apologize. It's just that I'm the father of the girl who was kidnapped. I'm upset and trying to find out what's going on." The officer's grim glare started to soften. The gun was still pointed at him though, so Frank kept his hands up. "Have you found out who took her or where she is?"

Frank stopped speaking and waited. Slowly, the young officer lowered his weapon to his side. After obviously considering Frank's words, credibility, and threat level, he put it back in his holster.

Frank took another deep breath and cautiously brought his hands down to his sides. "Can you please direct me to the officer in charge?"

"I'm the first one on the scene," the officer replied. "I was just around the corner. No backup has arrived yet."

"Well, what are you doing? Can't you start investigating?"

The officer's face morphed into a deep frown. "That's exactly what I was doing. I was just trying to get a statement from the doorman when you ran up on me shouting."

Frank's head pivoted until his eyes locked on a large young man standing in front of the bar. "Well let's go talk to him."

The officer clipped the strap over his weapon and pulled a notepad out of his shirt pocket. "That's my job. Don't interfere."

Frank did not want to aggravate the officer any more than he already had, so he bit his tongue and raised his hands in acquiescence. He waited for the officer to walk back to the young man and followed a few steps behind him so that he hear the questioning.

Clicking the top of his ballpoint pen the officer asked, "You're the one who called 911 right?"

The doorman nodded. "Yes. I was sitting on a stool near the entrance when I heard a scream for help. I came out just in time to see a white van speeding away." The doorman pointed down the road.

"Did you get the plate?" asked the officer, ready with his pen on the paper.

"Sorry, I didn't see one. I looked, but I don't think the van had a license plate at all."

"Can you give me a description of the driver?"

"I can't. But after I made the call, one of the girls came up to me and said she recognized the passenger. She said he's the one who got out and grabbed the girl who was standing in front of the bar." The doorman shot a worried look at the officer. "Now, we don't tolerate the pros trying to work the customers here at the bar—"

Frank spit a gruff interruption. "She's not a prostitute. She's my daughter and—"

The officer raised his hand. "Stop it." Glaring first at Frank and then at the doorman and waiting until he saw that they both appeared willing to obey his command, he turned back to the doorman. "You said one of the girls can identify the passenger. Where is she?"

The doorman pointed down the sidewalk towards the far corner of the bar, where a girl in a tight dress and long eyelash extensions stood on the sidewalk, shifting back and forth on her high heels. She tentatively raised a hand towards the three men.

"I'm going to get her statement now so I can broadcast it asap," the officer said. "You two stay right there. A detective is on the way to take lead. He'll have more questions for you. Don't move!"

Frank sighed and leaned against the front wall of the bar. He wanted to do something, but he understood that getting a description of the vehicle and of any kidnappers to be communicated to other police was the priority. And the officer was doing just that.

The doorman stepped inside the bar and brought a stool out front and sat on it. As predicted, another police car pulled up and an older officer got out and approached the first officer who was still questioning the girl and appeared to take over the questioning. Frank could see the girl gesturing and pointing but couldn't quite make out what she was saying.

Frank watched and waited for a few minutes. He checked his watch about every thirty seconds. Things were moving too slowly. He had to do something. He turned to the doorman. "My daughter was with a boy named Johnny. Her prom date. Do you have any idea where he is?"

The doorman looked over his shoulder into to the bar and then glanced towards the officers. "It wasn't my idea to let them in. His brother was the one that let them in. I didn't have anything to do with it."

Frank suppressed an urge to punch the doorman in the face. "Didn't have anything to do with it my ass. You're the doorman." The kid looked away and seemed contrite. "Well shit, tell me what happened."

The doorman swallowed hard. "I saw them come in. There were three couples. Your daughter wouldn't go in. She said she was afraid you'd be mad at her if she did."

Frank's throat tightened with emotion. He could barely choke out any words. "And they went in without her?"

The doorman nodded. "Yeah. I'm sorry, man."

Frank and the doorman both turned as the older officer approached them.

"Who are you two?"

The doorman seemed lukewarm about the prospect of chatting with the police, so Frank took the lead. 'Pointing at the doorman, he said, "This is the guy who called 911." Nodding towards the other officer, he added, "He told your responding officer that the girl over there was an eyewitness and asked us, well, *told* us to wait here. I'm the father of the kidnapped girl. Bella Bravo is her name. My name is Frank Bravo."

The officer studied Frank's face. "I know you," he said. "Bravo. Yeah. I've seen you in court. You cross-examined me once about a search warrant I submitted."

Frank tried to remember the case where he had cross-examined this officer, but there were so many such cases. He drew a blank. Finally, Frank shrugged. "So, I hope I wasn't too hard on you?"

"Yeah, you were tough on me. You made me justify my probable cause for the warrant. You challenged every detail I relied on."

Frank still couldn't tell what the officer was feeling towards him. Couldn't tell if it was good or bad. So, he just waited.

Finally, the officer said, "But you were polite. You were professional. And after you finished your questions and I was leaving the courtroom, you approached me to thank me for my service and for the work I do."

Frank relaxed. He reflected on the fact that he didn't always behave that way with officers on cross-examination. Sure, on the street, he was all, "Yes sir, Officer," and "No sir, Officer" because, after all, on the street, the police approached you with their hand on a gun. However, in the courtroom… Frank knew *he* had the power.

Frank shook himself and got back to the issue at hand. Taking advantage of the good luck to find one of the few officers that he had not offended, he looked at the officer's name tag. "Well, Detective Gooden, I *am* grateful for what you do. I'm not sure I'd be willing or able to do your job. What can you tell me about what happened to my daughter? What do you know?"

Detective Gooden contemplated his question as if deciding whether to answer it or how much to say. Frank knew that officers usually didn't share the details of an ongoing investigation.

Frank pleaded, "Please. Just tell me what you know."

"Okay. All right," Gooden said, nodding. "Here's what we know so far. The girl over there hangs out on this block and she heard a shout and then saw your daughter being pulled into a white van. She tried to get a license plate number but didn't see any plates on the van at all. She said your daughter fought back, but they overpowered her and took her."

Frank clenched his jaw and fought back his tears. "Could she give a description of the kidnappers?"

"The girl had seen the guy in the passenger seat before. Said he comes around occasionally. She knows him to be a pimp, maybe affiliated with a gang."

"Did she know his name?" Frank asked.

"No. She knows him only as Chacho. She said that one of her friends went with him a while ago and never came back. So, she and the other girls around here avoid him."

Frank asked, "Does this Chacho have a record? Do you have any address or something for him?"

"We're looking into it. We'll search for any addresses on file associated with the name Chacho. Check criminal histories. The usual. But that all takes time. We don't have much to go on."

Although Frank knew the investigation had just started, it wasn't going fast enough. "What about the kid my daughter was with? Johnny. Apparently, he's in the bar right now. She was supposed to be on a date with him, but he left her out on the street."

Frank processed this information for a moment, and then asked, "Detective, you got any kids?"

Gooden paused as if assessing Frank's intentions. "Yes, I have two daughters."

Frank looked the officer in the eye and then said something he instinctively knew was the type of thing no one should ever say to a cop. But he said it anyway. "Then you know that you should keep Johnny in protective custody, right?"

Gooden, to his credit, didn't challenge Frank over the thinly veiled threat against Johnny. Maybe he was thinking about what he might do under similar circumstances.

Just then Johnny and the other kids walked out front from the side of the bar. Frank grimaced and started striding towards Johnny. "You little shithead, how could you leave her out in the dark like that? I should—"

"Bravo!" the detective shouted as he grabbed Frank hard by the arm. Frank tried to pull away, but the detective squeezed harder and pulled Frank to a standstill. Frank turned and met the detective's grim gaze. "Don't!" the detective added.

Frank set his jaw and the two men glared at each other for a long moment. Finally, the detective spoke, quietly, but firmly. "I'll question him thoroughly. You can leave that to me."

Frank shot a hard glare at Johnny, but then nodded, satisfied for the moment, and thinking twice about committing an assault in plain view of two police officers. Although at some point he would have his own words with Johnny.

Then he rummaged through his mind, making sure everything he knew could be done was being done. "Have you put an ATL on the van at least?"

"Of course," answered Gooden. "First thing we did was send out a call to attempt to locate the van. We also have a couple of officers who'll stake out the bar just in case they come back. But there's nothing else I can do unless we get a new lead."

"And will you call me if you do?" Frank asked while staring him directly in the eyes.

"Yes, of course."

Frank handed the officer his business card, nodded, and turned to walk away. As he approached his car, he heard the first officer say something like "How'd the father get here so quick?" Frank realized the information Mia had trusted him with was from her secret women's group, and he figured he couldn't, or at least shouldn't, disclose that to the police. Not wanting to have to face the possibility he ducked into his Jeep without looking back and drove quickly away.

Once he had put about two blocks between himself and the bar, he pulled over to the side of the road and pulled his phone out of his pocket. With his fingers poised to type in her phone number, he wondered how he could tell his ex-wife Janelle that their daughter had been taken.

CHAPTER 7

VICTORIA STARED AT THE SCREEN of her video conferencing app and realized that she was tapping her toe and needed to pee. As soon as she and Xtina discovered that Bella Bravo had been kidnapped, they had discussed options and agreed to call on The Sisterhood's most competent agent to lead the search and rescue op. But she wasn't logging in. Victoria had texted, called, and emailed her asking her to please log on for a video chat, indicating that it was urgent. *Where are you, my friend?* Victoria was just about to call Xtina and make a new plan.

"Hi, Zena," Victoria said, sighing with relief, when Zena's face finally appeared on the screen. "I've been trying to get in touch with you for hours. I've got a job for you. It's urgent."

"Not now, Victoria," Zena said, gesturing behind her. "I'm packing my bags. I've been doing a lot of heavy lifting for The Sisterhood lately. And the jobs are always *urgent*. I need a break. I've got a ticket to Bora Bora, a one-way ticket. And I don't know when I'll be back. You know as well as anyone that I've upheld my responsibilities and never complained. But I *really* need a break right now."

Victoria paused before responding to Zena. It was true. Zena was the Western division's go-to girl when The Sisterhood needed to get justice for an abused woman where the system failed to do so. She was a muscular six foot two and an expert in martial arts. Although she had mastered many weapons, she preferred brute force. When an abusive husband wasn't arrested, Zena was the first they called to find him and make him pay. If a rapist got off without a severe penalty, they would send Zena to punish him. If a murderer walked free, Zena was the one who made him disappear. When the scales of justice needed to be balanced—not always—but perhaps too often, it was Zena who was called on to do it. She had resolved dozens of cases, most of them by herself, and was invincible in the field. The Sisterhood counted on her, and used her, maybe too much.

"I hear you, Zena," Victoria said, waving her hand as if she were throwing something away. *Ugh. She's right. I have been leaning on her too much. I need her. I want her. But... I shouldn't. I can't this time.* "Forget about it. I won't pressure you to help with this one. Like you said, you've done your part, and then some. Don't even worry about it. I'll get someone else to handle this one. I was just about to do that anyway."

"Good," Zena said, "because I've reserved a bungalow right on the most beautiful beach in the world. The water's clean and clear. The beach has soft white sand that extends out at a gentle angle into a cove that keeps the waves from crashing onto the beach. The resort is all-inclusive and has beautiful and cultured servers that they say will wait on me hand and foot and serve my every need. Do you know how long it's been since someone served me instead of me serving them?"

Victoria considered Zena's words for a moment. She had never heard Zena complain before. Nor turn down any assignment. They turned to her when needed because she was reliable. Because she never failed. Apparently, the accumulated effect of doing the difficult work of The Sisterhood had finally caught up with even Zena.

"My dearest sister," Victoria said, "it's true that you, among all of us, most deserve a break. In fact, I'm quite jealous. I wish I could go with you. We would have so much fun. But at least send me a picture of you in a bikini lying on a lounge chair and holding a drink with an umbrella in it."

Zena's eyes softened and her facial muscles relaxed. "Thank you, dear sister. Thank you." Finally, she smiled. "I'll send you some pictures." She winked. "And then you can send me some selfies of your sexy self in a bikini too."

Victoria smiled at Zena's playful gesture. Although Victoria knew that Zena didn't share Victoria's preference for women, she did consider her a dear friend and had discussed the intimate details of her life with her previously. Zena was, after all, like a sister to her.

Zena became quiet, staring off into the distance. After a long moment she looked back into the screen at Victoria. "But at least tell me why you called."

Victoria waved at the screen dismissively. "Don't worry, my friend. I'll find someone else. It's someone else's turn."

Zena stared directly into the screen. Victoria wondered if Zena had sensed her distress, despite her attempts to let her off the hook for this one.

"Tell me, Victoria."

Victoria took a deep breath. "It's Mia's friend, Bella. The daughter of Frank Bravo, the lawyer who helped Kala." Victoria couldn't hold in her desperation any longer. She broke down in tears and cried out, "Someone kidnapped Bella! I have it on video."

Zena's face morphed from calm to anger in front of Victoria's eyes. Anger and determination. Victoria had seen that look in Zena's eyes before, just before she charged forward and relentlessly waged whatever war was necessary to get justice for a victim of abuse. Victoria knew that now there was nothing anyone could say or do to dissuade Zena from her goal.

"Mia used to tag along behind me like a puppy when she was a kid at The Refuge," Zena said, her gaze straying downward. We grew close. "She must be suffering horribly right now." Zena lifted her head. "I'll come, Sister. I'm at my cabin in the canyon so it'll take me a while if you need me to come to the office out at The Refuge."

"No, I want you to meet up with Sally to make plans at the warehouse in Salt Lake."

"Okay, I'll grab some gear and head out asap." Zena locked eyes with Victoria. "I'll find them. Those fucking bastards are going to pay."

CHAPTER 8

BELLA WOKE UP. *Ugh.* She was sick to her stomach. *I feel like shit.* Groggy, she noticed her right hand dangling from a handcuff attached to a side railing behind the driver's seat of the van. *Omigod. Omigod!* Bella jerked her hand several times to see if she could get loose without success but stopped because she was making noise and did not want to draw attention to herself. *What the hell are they going to do to me? I've gotta get out of here.*

It all started coming back to her. They must have injected something into her neck because she had evidently been out for a while. How long, she wasn't sure.

The nausea made her want to sit up, but she was afraid to move, afraid of getting stabbed with another needle. She pretended to still be asleep and peeked through the slits of her eyes to take in her surroundings and try to figure out where she was.

The van was moving. But she had no idea how long they had been driving. No one else was in the back of the van, so she opened her eyes all the way but remained still, fighting the nausea that overwhelmed her again. *What did they drug me with anyway?* Bella had never used drugs except for a puff of marijuana at a party once, and it wasn't like her school provided an in-depth education about weed or anything harder, but she had heard kids talking about drugs. *Could it be heroin?*

She looked around. There were two seats up front, and the rest of the van opened all the way to the back. A bottle of water was under the front seat just within reach.

The same Mexican she beat up was sitting in the passenger seat, staring forward. There were three guys before, but now there were two. The biggest guy was gone. Better odds for her, but still not great ones.

The back of the van didn't have any windows, but she tried to find out if they were still in the city or not. They weren't stopping, so there were no stop signs or stop lights. They must be out on the highway. So, no one would hear her if she screamed now. The handcuff prevented her from running. She didn't want to start a fight she couldn't win. Basically, she couldn't do anything but be quiet and hope—and wait for an opportunity.

After a while, the van slowed.

"Why're you stopping?" the passenger asked.

"We need gas, *cabrón*. And I've gotta take a piss."

"Yeah, yeah. Me too."

"What about her?" the driver asked.

Bella closed her eyes and stayed as still as possible.

The passenger glanced back at their abductee. "Looks like she's still out. How much did you give her?"

"Not that much. Well, it could be a lot for a first timer, especially someone as small as her."

"Check her," ordered the passenger. "And get another dose ready, just in case."

Bella relaxed her body. One of them shook her by the shoulder but she stayed limp.

"Looks like she's still out. And she's not going anywhere anyway. She's chained up."

Bella heard the doors of the van open and close and the two voices moving away. *Now's my chance.* She grabbed at the railing with both hands to see if she could pull it loose so she could slide the handcuff to the end and get free. She couldn't budge it, so she turned and tried to kick it loose. Someone had taken her shoes off. It hurt her foot to even try. But she kicked several times anyway, until she was sure she couldn't break it.

Maybe her hand could be pulled through the handcuff. She pushed her thumb into the middle of her palm, squeezed her fingers together, and wrenched against the handcuff. The metal cut against her hand. She tried to spit onto her hand to lubricate it a bit, but her mouth was dry. She pursed her mouth and squeezed her salivary glands as hard as she could and finally generated some spit and spat it between her wrist and the handcuff. Gritting her teeth against the pain, she made her hand as small as possible and tugged as hard as she could. Her hand caught on the bolt of the cuff's hinge and started to bleed but she grit her teeth against the pain and kept trying. The blood seemed to help make the cuff slide. She twisted and pulled. Twisted and pulled. Pulled and pulled until she popped her hand through the cuff. *Yes!*

Just as Bella got to her knees to crawl to the door behind the passenger seat, the driver opened his door. Bella dropped back to the ground, unsure what she should do. She heard the passenger shove what sounded like a gas nozzle into the side of the van. Bad luck. Both were now back, but she was so close to getting free. She decided that the only option was to run for it.

She quietly moved to the back of the van and then quickly grabbed the rear door handle and jerked it. It was locked. The sound had startled the driver and Bella's stomach dropped. He moved quickly between the two front seats to stop her.

Bella got out a short scream for help just as the driver grabbed her and put his arm around her neck. She jammed her chin down against her chest to stop herself from being choked and then remembered another self-defense move. Four fingers are stronger than one finger. Bella grabbed the driver's little finger and pulled it down as hard as she could.

"*Pinche perra!*" the driver bellowed, but she kept pulling and twisting until she heard it crack. Finally, he let go, and Bella flashed a quick knife hand strike into his throat that brought him to his knees. As he tried to choke some air into his lungs, she scrambled past him toward the front of the van. Bella was woozy and weak, but if she could just get to the door and get out, she would have a chance. They were at a gas station. There would be people. *Gotta go. Gotta go.* The side door to the van opened as Bella was almost at the front of the van. She glanced and saw that it was the passenger. Now both were there. Desperate, she tried to jump into the front seat, but a strong hand grabbed her by the ankle, pulled her feet out from under her, and dragged her backwards. The driver had recovered and grimaced at her. He pulled his fist back to punch her in the face, but the passenger hooked the driver's arm at the elbow with his own arm just in time to stop him.

"No. Big D said not to hurt her."

The driver emitted a low growl and said something that Bella didn't understand but slowly unhooked his arm from the passenger's hold.

The passenger added, "I texted a picture of her to Big D. He said she's worth a lot of money if she's clean and pretty, but less if she's beat up."

Bella's heart was racing, and her mind went reeling with the snippets of information she was gathering from their short conversation. *Worth money? For what?* She was cornered in the back of the van. Both the men glared at her with grim frowns. Bella was afraid to act out now that they had her surrounded again, especially after the driver came so close to punching her in the face.

But then again, their boss had ordered them not to hurt her. Maybe she still had a chance to get someone at this gas station's attention before they drove her away again. She was scared but she had to try. She drew in a big breath to scream, but just as she started, the driver shoved the pillow into her face and pinned her head on the floor of the van.

Her heart dropped.

She anticipated the needle this time. Sharp pain penetrated her neck as the darkness overtook her.

• • •

When she woke up again, the van was bouncing along what must have been a dirt road. She noticed it was starting to get light outside. They must have been driving all night.

What's that smell? Manure?

The van rumbled to a stop. The driver shut off the engine and got out. A couple of seconds later, the side door of the van slid open. Bella saw a horse.

It's a farm. Bella had grown up in the city and had only been to a farm once. When she was about thirteen, her father had taken her to visit the farm where his mother grew up. Now, some of Bella's cousins ran it. They planted potatoes and raised cows and sold the milk. Bella remembered her cousins waking her up before dawn one day to go milk the cows. They showed her how to pinch the cow's teat at the top and then pull and squeeze it to get the milk to squirt out. They told her to fill the bucket. She tried, but after a few minutes of watching her fail horribly at the task, they laughed and showed her the mechanical pumps they used to milk the cows.

Bella also remembered getting a lot of stares when they went to the local store. Her dad was second-generation Italian, and her mother was half-black. Bella had deep green eyes, dark, olive-toned skin and long, dark hair that was thick and curly. With the name Bravo and her looks, most people assumed she was pure Italian. But not in a small farm town. There, she stood out. One day, at the small grocery store, a blond boy pointed at her and asked his mother, "Why does that girl have dark skin?"

Bella didn't like farms.

The sharp jerk on her arm brought her back to the present. Someone had unhooked her handcuffs while she was still out. Now, the driver had reached into the van with his left hand, grabbed her arm, and pulled her hard to the door, cradling his right hand, the one with the broken finger, against his stomach.

"No. Get some shoes on that mare first," yelled a tall blond man with a cowboy hat. He stared directly at her as he approached the van.

Bella realized the man in the hat was talking about her, like she was an animal. It made her sick. The driver scowled at her and nodded towards her shoes. Even though she felt anger building in her throat, the fear in her stomach was stronger. She sat on the floor of the van and pulled her black stilettos onto her dirty feet, turning to the side so her underwear wouldn't show.

She slid out of the van and onto the hard-packed dirt road, blinking in the sunlight as she looked around. A cornfield was to her left and a large house to the right. To get a fix on where she was, she turned around and saw a large barn with some big trucks behind her. Yes. It was definitely a farm. But where?

The fear in her stomach grew into panic. *I've got to get away from here. But there's too many of them. And nowhere to run.* She had no idea how long she had been out. She wouldn't be surprised if they had drugged her multiple times after her attempt to escape at the gas station. Was it the morning after the prom or could it have been longer? The only thing calming her down was that she had gotten out of the same van as far as she could tell, so at least she was within driving distance of home. *Home.* Bella felt tears pricking in her eyes at the thought of it and her parents. But she couldn't linger on that thought for long.

"Hey, Big D. What do we have here?" asked a voice Bella hadn't heard before.

She turned around to find another man staring at her intently.

A fat Mexican with a Fu Manchu mustache walked over to the van. He hooked a thumb into his belt. "*Bonita.* But is she clean, *guero*?"

"My guys tell me they haven't touched her," the man in the cowboy hat said. "She's young, looks clean, not even a tattoo."

Big D frowned as he directed his attention onto the driver of the van. "Where'd you get her? I got yer call sayin' you was bringing a new girl and the picture of her standing in front of the bar. But she don't look like no pro."

The driver looked down at his feet for a minute, seemingly hesitant to answer Big D while he was so mad. He pointed a thumb at the passenger. "Chacho here grabbed her off the street. Dragged her into the van. I didn't know what to do. So, I just drove…drove her here."

Big D strolled over to stand in front of Chacho. He drew his fist back, and Chacho stepped backward but not far enough before he received a deep punch to the gut. He bellowed and fell to one knee.

Bella couldn't help flinching a little.

"You idiot!" Big D screamed. "There's a reason we take runaways, stranded immigrants, and streetwalkers. It's because no one *cares* about them. No one fucking *looks* for them!"

"Sorry, boss," said Chacho looking up sheepishly. He didn't get up though.

"You think you're sorry now?" Big D glared at him menacingly. "You'd better pray the cops don't show up."

The fact that Big D was so worried about the cops coming gave Bella a glimmer of hope. She didn't just have people who cared about her, her dad was an attorney, and he would know who to call to start the search.

"No way," Chacho said, as he cautiously stood up and took another small step back from Big D. "The cops wouldn't even think to look for her way the hell out here. Besides, we took her phone and tossed it into the payload of an eighteen-wheeler at a gas station that was headed in the other direction so the cops couldn't use it to track her."

Big D nodded but didn't say anything.

Bella felt her spirit break a little hearing that, but she still had a chance.

Right then Bella noticed the Mexican with the mustache coming up behind her. He reached out and suddenly jerked the back of Bella's dress up to her waist with one hand. She immediately pulled away from him.

"High and tight butt cheeks, just the way I like them," said the Mexican. He started rubbing the front of his jeans with his free hand.

"Don't touch me, asshole!" she yelled. "HELP! Someone help me!"

Big D turned away from the driver and fixed his glare onto Bella. "You're wasting your breath, you stupid bitch. We're on a farm, more'n a mile from our nearest neighbor. No one'll hear you."

Before Bella could react before she heard, "Yeah man, I like her." The Mexican grabbed her arm and pulled her roughly to him. "*Guapa* too." She struggled against him.

"Careful with the merchandise," warned Big D with a laugh. "You break it, you buy it."

"Oh, yeah, I'll break her all right," the Mexican said. "I'll brand her ass. When I'm done with her, she'll do anything I say. What's her name?"

The man's effortless strength made Bella's level of fear rise exponentially. She was doing everything she could to get free of him and the man wasn't even fazed.

"Call her what the fuck you want, man." Big D shrugged nonchalantly. "You buy her, she's yours. You can do whatever you want."

The man's grip relaxed a little and Bella finally twisted free from the fat Mexican's grasp. "Let me go!"

The fat Mexican and Big D looked at each other and laughed.

The Mexican scowled at Bella. "You won't be acting tough for long, you little bitch." Turning to Big D, he asked, "How much do you want for her?"

"Now that I seen her, she ain't for sale. She's young, pretty, and clean. I'm gonna put her up for auction," he said. "I can add her to the one I got set up for tonight."

Auction? Do they mean to sell me? To whom? For what?

"Bullshit," snapped the Mexican. "You said you would sell me some girls."

"And I will, just not this one."

"I'll give you five thousand," the Mexican offered.

"No deal."

"How about ten?"

"Dude, multiply that by five. Bidding starts at fifty thousand."

Bella grew cold. This had to be a nightmare. How was it possible that she was listening to these two men negotiating over her as if she were livestock, an object? The whole time she had been running on adrenaline, but now it was hitting her that she was being sex trafficked. She had been kidnapped, and she was going to be sold as a sex slave to the highest bidder. Bella felt like she had floated out of her body and was watching herself in some kind of twisted movie because it just didn't seem possible that this could be her life.

In a daze, Bella saw Big D point at the driver of the van. "Take her to Nita."

The driver took Bella by the arm and pulled her toward the big farmhouse. *Oh no. What new horror is waiting for me in there?* She tried to pull her arm free, but he held her too tightly. The dirt road was bumpy, and she was weak, so it was all she could do to stay on her feet.

Once inside the farmhouse, the driver led her over to an attractive Hispanic woman wearing black leather pants and a sequined tank top that showed off a skull and crossbones tattoo on her shoulder. Something about her felt familiar to Bella.

"Big D said to hold her for auction," the driver said.

"Let go of her," the woman demanded. "I've got her now."

The driver immediately deferred to the woman and let go of Bella.

Turning to Bella, the woman plainly said, "You can call me Nita. I'll be taking care of you while you're here, helping you adjust to your new home."

Bella finally figured out why the woman looked so familiar. "Mia?"

Nita took a step back and regarded Bella cautiously. "What did you call me?"

Bella shook her head. *No. It's not Mia.* Puzzled, and momentarily forgetting about her current situation, she asked, "Do you have a sister?"

Nita frowned and stared hard at Bella for what seemed a long time before speaking. "My family's all dead. You're mistaking me for someone else."

The look she had given Bella jolted her back to reality. She got the feeling that she would want to stay on Nita's good side. "Oh, sorry."

"What's your name, sweetheart?"

"Bella."

"Bella, I'd like us to be friends. But we have some rules here. Not many. And they're simple. You cooperate, and your life will be better. In fact, some of our girls have met guys who have bought their way out of here. Some of the girls like to fuck the guys. And believe me, most of our girls fuck a lot of guys. But if Big D said he wants to auction you…it's not guaranteed by any means, but chances are, you'll go to a wealthy guy who'll leave you alone in his mansion or on his yacht most of the time and only fuck you on occasion and maybe give you to his friends at parties. That sort of thing. So, life can be good."

Bella listened to Nita, wide eyed. *Good* was a relative term.

"Some guys are just assholes of course, but you have a much better chance at the good life if you cooperate."

A good life? There was nothing good about anything this Nita had said.

"And you don't want to know what happens to the girls who don't cooperate, honey. Got it?" Nita gave her a threatening look.

Bella's throat was tight, and she felt herself shaking. She swallowed hard and forced a small nod.

CHAPTER 9

"COME WITH ME, BELLA," Nita said as she turned and walked from the entryway of the farmhouse through a dusty living room that had a wooden floor and lamps and chairs that seemed to Bella to be old enough to be antiques. Then they turned into the kitchen, which had a large island with drawers in the middle and a restaurant-sized refrigerator. Cans and boxes of food were stacked on the counters. Pans were on the stove. The kitchen was well-used.

At the back of the kitchen was a large door with a metal frame. Nita pointed at it. "This goes to the basement. In about an hour, lunch will be served. Later, I'll help you get cleaned up. The auction Big D mentioned is tonight."

Nita pulled a key card from her pocket and waved it in front of a sensor next to the door. Bella heard a click, and Nita pushed the door open.

It opened to a stairway. Bella followed Nita down it into a basement that had been finished and furnished with several tables with chairs around them. Couches were pushed against two walls, and a giant screen TV covered most of the other wall. Several doorways on the opposite side led to other rooms. One was open, and Bella saw a set of bunk beds.

"Felicia," said Nita to a girl nearby. "Come here."

A tall girl with long blond hair sauntered over to them. Bella was struck by how comfortable she seemed to be in their environment.

"This is Bella," said Nita.

Felicia looked Bella up and down. "Where's she going? It's payday at the construction site. Shall I send her out there with the other girls tonight?"

"Don't you worry about that for now," Nita firmly stated.

"But what do you want me to do with her?" Felicia asked, her face showing confusion as she glanced back at Bella.

"Just show her around for now. Get her a bed. Big D wants to save her for the auction tonight," Nita said.

Felicia's eyes darted back and forth between Nita and Bella. "But she doesn't look—

"That's what Big D wants," Nita interrupted. "We'll clean her up later."

Bella wondered what the girl was going to say before Nita had cut her off. Her dress was dirty from being on the floor in the back of the van and she had a bruise on her knee from when she was thrown into the van. She self-consciously pulled her fingers through her thick hair. Normally, her hair fell to her shoulders in natural ringlets. But now, it was dry and scrunched up where a rubber band had been used to pile her hair on top of her head for the prom. That seemed like a lifetime ago.

Nita frowned, turned, and started to walk back to the door, but then stopped. Over her shoulder, she said, "And Felicia, take that pendant she's wearing and put it with the other jewelry."

Then Nita left. Bella heard the electronic lock click as the door closed behind her. That sound made her stomach drop. She was trapped in a basement, who knows where. *I can't be here.* Then tonight, she was going to be sold off as if she were just a farm animal or something and forced to… She didn't even want to think about that right now.

Once Nita was gone, Felicia turned to Bella. "Rough night?"

Bella took in the girl, unsure of how to feel about her and then nodded.

Felicia put out the palm of her hand to Bella. "Here, give me that pendant."

Bella grasped the pendant protectively. She had completely forgotten about it in all the chaos. Mia had told her to be sure to keep the pendant with her because it would help someone find her if she had it with her. Bella had thought that it was a bit excessive when she thought that she'd just be going to the prom, but now it was her last hope. She rubbed the pendant and the silver ring that encompassed the stone and twisted it in her hand again.

"Do I have to? It belongs to a friend. It's not mine to give you." *And if I do, how will they ever find me?*

Felicia shook her head. "I'm sorry, but Nita said you've gotta give it up, and around here, what Nita says goes. Besides, I doubt you'll be seeing your friend again anyway." Bella's forehead pinched tightly, and she felt her eyes tear up.

The girl gave her an almost pitiful look and Bella considered telling her that the pendant could get them both out of here, but she wasn't sure if she could trust Felicia yet. She figured her odds were better if she just stayed quiet about it. She reluctantly reached behind her neck, disconnected the link, and placed the pendant on Felicia's open palm.

Felicia nodded at the couch. "You can sit down over there."

Bella timidly sat down and when her body touched the couch her body instantly relaxed a little bit. She may not have been sure that she could trust Felicia, but she at least didn't get the feeling that she had to worry about being sexually assaulted by her. Felicia casually sat on the other end of the couch. Bella pulled off her stilettos, her feet aching.

Felicia seemed to be studying her. "Where're you from?"

"Salt Lake City," Bella said. Then it occurred to her that Felicia might be able to tell her where she was. "Where are we now?"

"Podunk, Nebraska. We're on a farm out in the boondocks somewhere between North Platte and Grand Island. I'm not sure exactly where. In the southern part of the state, I think."

Nebraska! Bella wondered how the police or Mia would find her and prayed that they were tracking the pendant as they spoke. She was surprised by how freely Felicia had told her all of this since Nita seemed to trust her. Maybe she would be an ally to her in this place and she could get some more information out of her.

"How about you? I mean, where are you from?"

"I don't know where to call home. I've been around. We moved a lot when I was little, and then when I was thirteen, I ran away from home. My mother OD'd on heroin laced with fentanyl, and my father pimped me out to get enough money so that he could stay high." Felicia fell silent for a long moment, her eyes darted back and forth as if she were reliving old memories. She hugged her arms tightly to her chest and took a deep breath. "Eventually, a guy who worked for Big D found me and offered me a place to stay. I had no idea it would be like this." Felicia's lips twisted into a deep frown. She sighed. "At the time, though, it seemed like it would be better than where I was, just out on the street."

She said it all so casually, like it was just normal. Bella's first thought was to say, "Sorry," but realized that it might come off as more offensive than kind. Bella had led a very privileged life, and she'd gathered from the conversations the men had had in front of her that she wasn't the type of girl that usually ended up here. She wondered if there was anyone else who'd been taken by mistake.

"How about the other girls," asked Bella. "How did they get here?"

"Everyone has their own story," answered Felicia. "Over the last four years, I've seen girls end up with Big D in a lot of different ways. A lot of them are like me—runways, streetwalkers. They're used to fucking for money anyway. So, this is just a job to them. No big deal. But many are illegal immigrants, mostly from Honduras. They're brought across the border with promises of jobs, like working as maids or in other cleaning services or restaurants. Some do get those jobs, but the pretty ones…they bring them here."

Bella asked, "But why do they stay?"

"They can't get other work. They have no papers. If they complain, they're threatened with deportation. Most already gave all their money to coyotes to get here in the first place. I've also heard Big D threaten that if anyone tried to leave, he would send gangs back to kill their families. So…they stay.

"And sometimes, very young girls are brought here. Children really. They don't stay here though. They're moved out quickly. We never see them again. One night, Nita was drunk and said something to me about a billionaire who liked underage girls. She said he'd tempt them with money to have sex with him and would also provide them to other rich and famous celebrities. And if that wasn't bad enough, he sometimes blackmailed those men and women he gave the kids to by threatening to release photos and recordings he secretly made of them having sex with the children. Nita told me she wished she had thought of it because it was a great scam."

Bella felt sick. Her body had gone cold, and the blood had drained from her face. Her eyes fixed on the floor. If these people could so easily do those unspeakable things to small children, she could only imagine the things that they would do to her. Involuntary tears swelled in her eyes.

She noticed Felicia studying her out of the corner of her eye. "You don't look like someone who has one of those stories. You're pretty clean cut. Bet someone got in trouble for picking you up."

A tear escaped and ran down her cheek. Bella wiped it away quickly and sat up a little straighter. This was not the time to break down, if she did that would mean that she was accepting this reality, and she wasn't giving up yet. She had to escape, as soon as possible. She figured the best way to do that was to get as much information as she could from Felicia and maybe even create a plan with her.

"How long have you been here?" she asked.

"On the farm? Almost two years. We move around, like when a place gets too hot. I mean like when too many police come around. We just move to a new place. We also travel for jobs. That's what they mostly use those big trucks for, hauling the girls around. Otherwise, they're used to transport corn at harvest time. Then we live here in between jobs."

They are treated like livestock, literally like animals. "And you're planning to stay here? Why don't you try to escape?"

Felicia frantically looked around before leaning in and giving Bella a look that sent shivers down her spine. She lowered her voice to almost a whisper, "Don't let *anyone* hear you talking like that. There are very few girls I trust to talk to about that. One or two of the others sometimes talk about trying to escape. But I'm warning you, keep your mouth shut and don't trust anyone."

"Okay," Bella said solemnly, glancing at the pendant in Felicia's hand. *If only…*

"I mean it, don't talk to anyone else about this. Someone might snitch you out to Big D. I don't even wanna tell you the things that happen to girls who try to run."

Felicia gave her a stern look as if to make sure that her words really sunk in. Bella gave a small nod. "I won't."

"Good," Felicia added.

Felicia leaned back and took a deep breath before releasing a small sigh. She checked to make sure the coast was clear again. "But yeah, of course," she said in an extremely low voice. "I think about getting out of here all the time. I'm so fucking tired of this shit. You're always in survival mode. It's exhausting."

Seeing Felicia relax, Bella's own stress faded a bit too. She looked at Felicia in a new light. This was the first time she'd seen any kind of softness in her. She committed herself to remember Felicia and her kindness.

Felicia's tone changed slightly. "But I try not to think about it. It's hard to get out, to get away. And even if I could, I'd have nowhere to go anyway."

"Well, maybe I could help you," Bella offered.

Felicia laughed. "I'm not sure you understand your situation, Bella. I have more freedom than you do as it stands."

"What do you mean?"

"Nita trusts me more than the other girls. She has me get the girls ready for jobs or to go to their next stop. In return, she lets me choose what jobs I want to do. It's not much, but it's better than what the other girls get. They have to go where they're told, do what they're told, and fuck who they're told."

"That's not gonna happen to me," Bella said. "I have people who will come for me. Or I'll find my own way out."

Felicia gave her a look that Bella could only read as pity. "I hope you're right. But don't let Nita hear you talk like that. I'm serious, she will…" Felicia locked her eyes on the ground as if remembering something and swallowed hard. "She'll really hurt you."

CHAPTER 10

ZENA SPED IN HER BLACK SUV to The Sisterhood's secluded Salt Lake headquarters in a warehouse on the west side of town, knowing that the vehicle's radar detection and police car location systems would allow her to avoid being stopped and ticketed. She weaved her way to the dead end at the far corner of the park and skidded to a stop in the gravel in front of the building. The large warehouse's old and dilapidated appearance deceived anyone who happened to come across it, which was possible, even with it being so well-hidden. The Sisterhood made sure it possessed the most progressive, state-of-the-art technology available. Zena touched her ring to a sensor, and a metal door opened and then automatically slammed behind her once she entered. She strode briskly to a large office with glass windows where she could see Sally speaking with Mia.

"Catch me up," Zena said as she entered the office.

Sally took her eyes off Mia and put them on Zena. "We're trying to locate Bella by tracking her phone. It was heading west on Interstate 15 but then stopped. Google Maps shows it's at a large truck stop in California not far from Los Angeles."

Zena nodded. "I'll take the helicopter, catch up quickly. It'll be easier to stop them on the highway than it would be if they get into the city." She rushed to the metal cabinet against the wall where the key to the helicopter was stored.

Mia held up a hand. "Wait. There's more. I loaned Bella the pendant that Sally gave me from her stash of spy toys."

Mia saw Sally smile at the "spy" reference. She had learned that Sally's background was with the CIA and knew that she had collected and manufactured quite an assortment of weapons and gadgets over the years, from guns, explosives, and poisons to electronic devices such as the GPS pendant with video recording capabilities that she had given Mia after her initial training.

Mia turned to Sally with a quick nod, signaling to her to explain what she had discovered about the pendant. Sally said, "The first signal we got from the pendant was heading east. But it shut off quickly, and we lost the signal. But then I tapped into a GPS tracking satellite focused on major routes heading out of Salt Lake City and this morning we got a hit on the pendant's signal in Nebraska."

"What the hell?" Zena exclaimed. "What do you think's going on?"

Sally replied, "It's hard to know for sure. They may have taken the phone from her and sent it West in a misdirection. Or, she may be going West, and someone took that pendant from her, and now that person just happens to be going East."

"Everyone knows phones can be tracked," Zena said. "It would make sense for a kidnapper to try to throw any cops investigating the case off the trail by ditching the phone or sending it in another direction. But the guys who took Bella would have no reason to suspect that a high school girl's necklace had a tracker in it. I think we should track the pendant."

"That's just what I was thinking," Sally replied. "From the pendant's uploaded video, it's obvious to me that this was not a professional job. Sloppy. It looks like some kids just grabbed her. They wouldn't think to check for a tracking device. But just to make sure, I've contacted one of our sisters based in L.A. to find the phone and then check back in with me. Meanwhile, Zena, you follow the pendant."

"I'll need some supplies."

Sally walked to what looked like a large storage cabinet at the edge of the office and waved her ring near a sensor on its side. Machinery whirred, and the steel cabinet doors slowly opened to reveal a short hallway leading to another room.

Sally stepped back and motioned with her hand to the opening. "You can find everything you need back there."

Zena assessed the entrance and then walked quickly into the back room.

"I'm going too," Mia proclaimed and turned to follow Zena.

Sally stretched her arm in front of Mia to stop her. "No way. You haven't finished your training yet, Mia. And you're still not actually an agent of The Sisterhood yet. You're only here with us now because Xtina told me to start training you."

"You can't stop me. I have to go. Bella's my friend. And her father Frank is…a friend too."

Sally paused, took a step back and shook her head. "I won't stop you from going. Just before you arrived, Xtina called me. And she told me that you would say…exactly what you just said."

Mia took a deep breath. Xtina was an ageless woman from Israel. Xtina not only directed The Sisterhood, but she also ran a home called The Garden for children who had been orphaned or abandoned, and refugees, and another residence called The Refuge, a place for women and girls who had been victimized and had come to find safety. Mia was taken into The Garden as a child when the rest of her family died in a car crash. Later, Mia returned briefly to The Refuge after her husband tried to murder her.

Mia stared into Sally's eyes. "What else did Xtina say?"

"She only said to tell you to wait until she got here, that she had something she needed to tell you."

Over the years, Mia had heard Xtina accurately describe future events on many occasions. Everyone called her the oracle of The Sisterhood. So, if Xtina had news for her, Mia wanted to hear it. "I'll just call her," Mia said.

"No. She said she needs to see you. In person."

Mia was frustrated. They had to hurry to go and try to save Bella. Who knows what the kidnappers had done to her by now or what they might do to her if they didn't get to her quickly. It sounded like she was hours away, somewhere in Nebraska. There was no time to wait. Mia raised her voice, "But when will she—?"

"Now," Xtina said as she entered the office smiling and moving gracefully toward Mia.

"But how, how did you…?" Mia stammered.

Xtina lightly touched Mia on the shoulder. "My dear Mia."

A warm wave of peace and love washed through Mia. Her heart rate slowed, and her shoulders relaxed.

Xtina allowed Mia a moment to let those positive emotions overcome the anxiety and fear she had been swathed in since learning of Bella's kidnapping. "I know you'll go to help Bella," she said. "I sense that your will to do so is strong." Xtina put her left hand on Mia's other shoulder and turned to her so they were face to face. "But there are a couple of things I need to tell you before you go, and I probably should've told you one of those things a long time ago."

Xtina paused before adding, "And the other thing I wish I did not have to tell you now at all."

Stunned by what Xtina said. She wondered what things Xtina could be talking about. Her mind raced with imagined possibilities.

Xtina sighed. "Come. Sit with me." She took Mia by the elbow to a black leather couch at the far end of the office.

She smiled. "You don't have much time, so I'll get right to the point. You have a sister."

Mia returned Xtina's smile. "Yes, I feel like everyone at The Sisterhood—"

"No, I mean *your* sister, your twin sister. She's alive."

"Nita? But I thought she died in the car crash with my parents. I thought they were all killed."

Xtina explained, "Because you were only twelve and just lost your parents, the social worker assigned your case at the Department of Child and Family Services thought it would be easier for you not to know that it was Nita who caused the car crash. She caused your parents' deaths. I guess she thought that you wouldn't be seeing her because she was put in juvenile detention. So, she told you that Nita died too."

Mia shook her head, trying to take in Xtina's shocking revelation about her past.

"I believe it was a mistake on her part to lie to you," Xtina continued, "because after all, there would always be a chance you would find each other again later."

Mia put her hand on her forehead. Her mind raced back in time. When she and Nita were about twelve, she suspected that Nita might hurt their parents, but she never told anyone. Around the time they entered puberty, Nita changed. She seemed depressed, and occasionally, she was angry. Once, their mother yelled at her for coming home late from school. Then their father punished her by grounding her and not letting her leave their home for a month. Nita told Mia she wished their father was dead. Kids say things like that out of emotion, but they don't do anything. They just… *Oh my god, Mom's cat! It was stabbed to death. Maybe it was Nita. It must've been Nita.*

Xtina let Mia process this news. When Mia raised her eyes again, she continued. "On the day of the crash, your parents left you at home. They were taking Nita to a child psychiatrist. Your father was driving. Nita was in the back seat. The car swerved into oncoming traffic and hit another car head-on." *Oh no no no….* A wave of dark emotion surged through Mia. Long-hidden memories about what she was told of her family's death flashed through her mind. *Nita, how could you?*

Mia started crying, so Xtina put her hand back on Mia's shoulder and waited for her to calm down. Unfortunately, she wasn't done.

After Mia's cries became whimpers, she said, "One of our sisters was working for the police department at the time. She told us that the officers who investigated the crash found your father's throat cut with a knife that matched a set from your kitchen. It had his blood on it. When they asked Nita what had happened, they said she just laughed and stated, 'I told him I would kill him.'"

Mia sat quietly, no longer crying. Stunned. Overwhelmed by grief. She couldn't comprehend or accept what Xtina told her. How could her own sister, her twin sister, be capable of such hate, such violence?

Xtina responded as if she had heard Mia's thoughts. "Each soul born on Earth possesses the seeds of both good and evil. Then, partly through what they experience when they're young, and partly based on choices each person makes, the good or the evil is nurtured and grows." Xtina paused until Mia met her gaze. "But with identical twins, on rare occasions, the good and evil seeds don't split to each soul. All go to one or the other."

"And Nita got the bad seeds?"

Xtina nodded. "And you got the good. I saw this when I first met you as a child. And I sensed in you the power of good. And that's why I've always nurtured you. And why I told you it is your calling to serve in The Sisterhood."

Mia shook her head. "But I'm no hero. In fact, I'm afraid. And ever since what I did when Kala was in trouble, when…when I killed her husband, I've had doubts that I could ever do anything like that again."

Xtina turned to face Mia directly and placed her hands on both Mia's shoulders. "You alone control your destiny. I can point you to the path, but you must choose to walk it." Then Xtina released her grasp on Mia.

Mia put her head in her hands. *This is all too much. I don't know what to do.*

Mia's thoughts eventually turned back to her sister, and her gaze back to Xtina. "Whatever happened to Nita? Where is she?"

"Nita was sent to a juvenile detention facility where they held her until she was twenty-one. Then they released her on supervised probation, but she disappeared."

Mia asked, "But why are you telling me all this now?"

"I have foreseen that during your attempt to rescue Bella, you will meet Nita. And there will be…trouble. So, I thought you should know. That I should warn you to be ready."

Mia sat dazed by the sudden revelations about her sister. She was distraught by the knowledge of Nita's cruel acts as a child and wondered if she could have done something then. Maybe she could have said something to Nita that would have helped her, or maybe she could have told her parents something, perhaps warned them to be cautious around Nita.

Mia wiped some tears from her face. *And now?* Mia pondered what trouble would there be when she met Nita? *What was it that she would need to be ready for?*

And if what Xtina had divulged to her wasn't enough, if that wasn't *too much* already, Xtina said, "I have something else, a second thing I need to tell you."

Mia shook her head and turned to Xtina. "Might as well go ahead and tell me that too. What's the second thing?"

Xtina put her hand back on Mia's shoulder. She allowed it to linger before speaking. "I have also seen the possibility of…your death. Or that of someone near you."

Mia pulled away from Xtina. "No, no, no." After a pause, Mia said, "Wait. You said the possibility. Only the possibility, right?"

"Death there will be," said Xtina, "and I see that you will be there when it happens. And, Mia, I see that it will be *you* who will have to choose who dies."

Mia's head spun, and dizziness and nausea infused themselves into her being. Unable to focus nor accept what Xtina was saying, that she might die, that someone would die, was too much to wrap her head around. *What? How?* Mia had already begun to doubt her choice to join The Sisterhood. And now…this. Her mind raced. *I'll have to choose who dies? Will I kill someone again? Uggh, I haven't ever recovered from the last time. I don't think I could do it again…. Maybe if I didn't go, I'd be safe, and no one would die.*

Mia found herself rocking back and forth trying to calm down. She didn't know what to do. But after a minute, she took a deep breath and let it out slowly. If Xtina had seen it, then Mia understood, knew in her heart that she needed to accept it as a fact. She searched her soul for strength. *And it's Bella. I have to try.*

Mia looked straight into Xtina's deep green eyes. "I'm afraid…but I have to try. I'll go. But what about Bella? Do we save her?"

Xtina cocked her head to the side and raised an eyebrow. "That remains to be seen." She reached into her pocket and pulled out a chain that had a thin capped cylinder hanging on the end of it. "I want you to have this."

Mia said, "I've seen Victoria and Sally with these."

Zena unbuttoned the top of her shirt and pulled out a similar necklace of her own. "Each of you who do the work of The Sisterhood carries one of these, just in case."

Xtina must have known the question in Mia's mind—in case of what? "Just in case you are facing imminent death. The cylinder is titanium. Inside it is a substance that you can drink that has properties that will keep you alive."

"I don't understand," Mia said, shaking her head. "What is it? How does it work?"

Sally interrupted and said, "I, myself, asked those same questions, Mia. Turning to Xtina, Sally said, "If I could just test a sample of this, maybe I could identify it and perhaps even synthesize it."

"These cylinders contain perhaps the only substance on earth that cannot be synthesized or replicated," Xtina replied, still not giving any explanation about what it was or what she knew about it. Mia couldn't help but wonder *why* Xtina would not explain.

Sally's eyebrows pinched together. "But I have the connections to access the DARPA labs, where they have the latest technology and—"

"Oh, ye of little faith." Xtina spread her arms wide. "Believe and—"

Sally interrupted, "I believe in science. *Facts*, not faith."

Xtina's eyebrows rose. "There is nothing hidden which shall not be revealed. In time, all shall be made known. But not yet."

Sally snapped back, "I have worked for years for The Sisterhood. The things I have done…were not easy to do. And *still*, you don't trust me?"

"Indeed, you have done much. And it has been said of the faithful, by their works shall ye know them. But, the *Book of Sally* has not yet been written."

Sally stood staring silently at Xtina for some time, her forehead furrowed in frustration. Xtina remained as calm as still water, yet immovable as a mountain.

Breaking the silence, Zena spoke. "Whatever it is, it works. I can vouch for that. I got shot in the chest during a firefight with some bad guys. I knew I was done. But I remembered what Xtina said and opened the canister just in time. It works, or I wouldn't be here."

Mia stared open-mouthed at Xtina, astonished by what she heard. But, grateful for an interruption to the contentious conversation between her friends, Mia popped up quickly and craned her neck to peer past Zena back into the storage room. Then she stopped and looked back at Sally. "Can I—"

Sally shook her head and shrugged, then turned her attention to Mia. "I know what you're going to ask. And… the answer is yes. You can take some of the special lipstick canisters that I showed you during your initial training. There's advanced special training to learn how to use the various weapons encased in the canisters. But it seems there is no time now. Go. Get some. This mission is exactly what they are for."

Zena added, "I know what I want. Guns. I'll fill a camo bag."

Xtina looked at Zena and then back at Mia. "Prepare to go. There's not much time."

CHAPTER 11

BELLA'S STOMACH ACHED. The drugs were wearing off, and she was hungry. She sat in the corner by herself, rubbing her bare arms against the chill of the farmhouse basement. Ever since she'd met Felicia, she had been her shadow, but Felicia had gone upstairs to help make sandwiches for lunch, and Bella was alone.

The door at the top of the basement opened, and Bella looked up the stairs hoping to see Felicia with lunch. But it was Nita holding something in the crook of her arm. Fear gripped her chest after what Felicia had said about Nita hurting girls who didn't behave. Did Felicia tell Nita that Bella had been asking questions about how to get out of this place? Was Nita coming to punish her?

Bella saw Nita looking around the big room until her eyes met Bella's and then started approaching her. Bella's body tensed.

"Bella, I have something for you," Nita announced and handed Bella what appeared to be items of clothing. Bella quickly unfolded the items and discovered some sweatpants and a fleece top.

Bella cautiously took the clothing, uncertain why she was receiving it. It was an act of kindness to give her warm clothing for the cold basement. She figured they wouldn't care much about her comfort, seeing as comfy clothes weren't usually considered all that sexy.

Nita eyed her and said, "Your dress is nice. Take it off and give it to me. I'll have someone tumble it and press it for you."

Bella nodded and began to make her way to the bathroom to get changed.

"No, give it to me now."

"Right now? Like here in front of…" Bella looked around at all the other girls in the basement and then back at Nita.

"Yes," said Nita in a vaguely threatening tone, "now don't be shy."

Bella's cheeks burned. It wasn't uncommon for the girls down here to change in front of one another. Bella had already seen some of them do it. They all seemed quite comfortable with nudity. The girls she saw peeled off their clothes as soon as they returned from a job and changed into something more comfortable. But she wasn't accustomed to stripping in front of strangers. She might have been a little more comfortable if Nita wasn't there, but it seemed like this was one of those times when what Nita said went.

Bella reached behind her back, grabbed the top of the zipper, and slowly pulled it down. Then she grabbed the sides of her dress and wiggled out of it as she pulled at the bottom of it. A rush of embarrassment came over her, and she kept her eyes on the floor.

"Come on, we don't have all day," Nita chided.

Bella finished pulling the dress down and stepped out of it. She was relieved to at least still be wearing a bra and underwear. When she was getting ready for the prom she had considered going braless. It was hard to believe how much had happened since then. She handed the dress to Nita, who had a subtle smile on her face. Bella wasn't sure she believed that Nita was going to return it to her, not that she'd ever want to wear it again.

"The auction is tonight. We do it online. With any luck, you'll be gone in a day or two."

Tonight. That didn't give her much time to figure out an escape plan. She hoped her father was using his connections and pushing the police to find her. Or maybe Mia would be looking for her. Either way, she needed to find her own way out of this place before she was sold and sent to who knows where, to do… No, she couldn't even entertain that thought. *I can't let myself be taken.*

Bella was jerked back to reality when she caught Nita staring at her body. Her eyes gazed at seemingly every inch of Bella's flesh. Then she took Bella by the shoulders, giving her a twist. "Turn around," and spent another long moment examining her. "Take off your bra."

A cold shiver went down Bella's spine. She knew she had to watch out for Nita in terms of violence, but before this moment she didn't realize that she would also have to watch out for Nita in the same way that she had to watch out for all the men in this place.

"I–"

"Take off your bra," Nita cut her off before she could say anything to get out of doing it.

Bella realized that her hands were trembling when she hesitantly went to unhook her bra. She fixed her eyes on the floor, unable to face Nita or any of the other girls in the basement. Bella struggled immensely to find the clasp and undo it because her hands were shaking so badly now. Tears pricked in her eyes, and it took all her focus to stop one from spilling over while trying to undo the bra.

When she finally got the clasp undone, she quickly took off the bra and tried to cover her breast with her arms.

"Let me see them," Nita ordered.

Bella was seriously struggling to keep any tears from spilling over and as she went to drop her arms, a few spilled out.

"No need to cry, sweety. Your young tits are something to be proud of; they defy gravity, despite their size. No need for a bra." Nita gave her a smile that made Bella's stomach twist. "Don't worry. You'll do fine in the auction. Then you'll have a man to get you whatever clothes you need or want. We'll need to do something with that curly hair though."

She bent over to pick up Bella's dress and turned to go. Bella quickly folded her arms across her chest and wiped away her tears. Over her shoulder, Nita added, "I'll get this cleaned. We'll dress you up for the auction, but you won't need the dress for long. The buyers will want to see everything."

When Nita finally left, Bella quickly pulled on her sweatpants and top. It was more difficult than it should have been because she hadn't managed to stop her hands from shaking. Before the door had completely closed behind Nita, Bella saw it being pushed back open and her heart stopped momentarily. She realized she'd been holding her breath when she saw Felicia come through it with boxes of sandwiches and she finally exhaled. Bella and Felicia still weren't that close, but she was the only source of comfort Bella had in this place, and she felt the impulse to be near her, so she moved towards the door.

Then Chacho came in right behind Felicia, carrying a plastic tub full of drinks. Bella stopped in her tracks. The fleeting moment of relief was over all too soon.

A pretty, black girl with an impressive figure walked confidently over to Chacho. "What's up, Chacho? Why you down here doing women's work? You in trouble?"

Chacho caught Bella's gaze before she could look away. She held her breath, terrified of what might come next, and fixed her gaze on the floor.

Chacho turned his attention back on the other girl and said, "Nah, I'm just helping out…so I could come see you, Baby."

Bella clenched her fist, trying to stop the shaking. She felt more tears welling in her eyes and she tried to find a place in the basement where she could keep an eye on Chacho in case he changed his mind, but far enough away that she wouldn't feel so on display.

"I've missed you," said the girl. "I ain't been gettin' no attention from you lately."

Bella was confused by this dynamic. She couldn't tell if the girl was being sincere or if it was a survival technique. Maybe something like what Felicia had with Nita, but more sexual.

Chacho grinned. "Don't worry. We can hang out tonight. I'm taking you and a couple of other girls out for a bachelor party for a rich kid and a bunch of his frat brothers. I showed the guy who contacted me some pictures. He picked you and said he wanted you for sure."

The girl smiled broadly, apparently pleased by the compliment as well as the arrangement.

"He paid a lot for you, and you can probably make some extra money in tips too."

"That's all fine and good," said the girl, pouting. "But when can I get with you?"

"Sorry, Baby." Chacho reached into his pocket. "I promise I'll make it up to you. Here, wear this tonight. It was a new addition to the jewelry rack." He slid Bella's pendant necklace over the girl's head.

"Wow. Thanks, Baby."

Bella's stomach dropped. That necklace was her only hope. Her fear of Chacho was quickly turning into a boiling hate. He was the reason she was here and now he could be the reason that Mia wouldn't know where to find her. Mia worried that if this black girl went out on a lot of jobs and took the pendant, that no one could use it to find her and save her from this place. The only times the pendant would lead Mia to Bella would be when the black girl was here, assuming she herself didn't get shipped off soon.

"Be good, and maybe I'll let you keep it."

"What? Did Nita say you could give it to me?" The fear of Nita was obvious in the girl's tone.

Chacho shrugged. "I saw Felicia going to hang it up, and I took it." The girl still seemed nervous.

"It'll be fine, I promise."

He turned and left, shooting Bella one last threatening look before he left. The girl was too distracted by her new necklace to notice.

Felicia walked up to Bella. "Here's your sandwich. Grab yourself a bottle of water or soda from the bin over there. We can sit at that table by the wall after I hand out the rest."

It wasn't much, but the small act of kindness almost brought Bella to tears, as if she'd just been given a hug. She nodded and went to the bin.

She thought for a minute about questioning Felicia about giving Chacho her necklace, but she was worried it would create a wedge between them, and she couldn't risk her only friendship here.

"I see you got some more comfortable clothes," Felicia said as she sat down across from her at the little table.

Bella was in the middle of taking a long drink of water. She hadn't realized how thirsty she'd been. Felicia looked at her like she watched girls guzzle down entire water bottles all the time. Bella came up for air.

"Yeah, Nita brought them for me."

It occurred to her to ask Felicia about getting clean underwear. She wasn't comfortable with Nita and didn't even want to ask. Self-consciously, she leaned forward to ask Felicia. "What do the girls do when they need clean underwear?" she whispered.

"Most of us usually get to have a few pairs. We just wash them in the sink in the bathroom. You just have to go without while they dry."

"Thanks," Bella said, less embarrassed after how casually Felicia had responded. They were quiet after that for a little bit while they ate.

Bella went to the bathroom and saw underwear in several places. She had noticed it before. Some were hanging on the shower curtain rod, others laid over toilet paper on top of the toilet tank. Some were still soaking in the sink. It seemed everyone had decided to wash their underwear around the same time.

Bella took hers off and stood in front of the sink. She caught a glimpse of herself in the mirror. She could hardly believe the girl looking back at her was her. Bella burst into tears, sobbing with her whole body but keeping a hand over her mouth so that she wouldn't attract any attention. It was the kind of cry that felt like it would keep going until her body ran completely out of water.

Someone knocked on the door and Bella quickly gathered herself. "Just a second!" She cleaned herself up the best she could and then went back to the table with Felicia.

Felicia looked at her and Bella knew she could tell she'd been crying. Felicia didn't say anything. Bella figured it was a common occurrence here.

Bella took a deep breath and asked in a low voice, "So, what's the deal with Chacho and that girl?"

"That's LaToya," Felicia said. "She tries to act like his girlfriend, and I've heard him tell her that he loves her. But I don't think it's real, not on his end. But anyway, she *acts* like she loves him and is happy to do whatever he asks. Wouldn't be surprised if he's getting her drugs or something."

Bella nodded. Everything in this place was transactional. That would be important to keep in mind if she ended up stuck here longer than she planned. *No, don't think like that. I'm getting out of here. I'm getting out of here.*

"I heard him tell her that he was taking her to work a bachelor party with some rich college kids," Bella said. "I didn't realize there were jobs like that."

"Bachelor parties are usually some of the better gigs. Parties in general usually aren't as bad. Those are the types I usually opt for. Especially when it's college boys. There's a lot more virgins than you'd think, and they're usually clean. They tip well and some of them aren't bad to look at. Of course, there's always a few guys who are super rough or disgusting and the downside is that you have to do them too. Even on the 'good' jobs you still don't have a lot of options." She took another bite of her sandwich.

Bella was afraid to ask her next question, but she wanted to be prepared in case...

"So, what are the alternatives to the 'good' gigs?"

Felicia gave her a look as if to ask if she really wanted to know, Bella didn't waver.

"Well, there are the streetwalkers and the escorts. Those gigs are rougher because you're forced to fuck and suck off as many guys as possible. It's…well obviously it's tiring, and you get really sore and by the end of it you're just…" She trailed off and then went back to eating her sandwich.

Bella thought back momentarily to the girls she'd seen on State Street right before she'd been taken. Everything in her told her not to ask for more, but she felt like she had to know.

"What else?"

Felicia gave her a look like she was debating continuing. She finished her sandwich and then said, "Well, this probably won't happen to you. But some of the girls are sold right off, especially the illegals. Like I told you before, they're promised jobs as housekeepers or at some restaurant. But I've seen the gangsters who come to pick them up, and I can promise you those are not the jobs they are doing. No one knows where they take them, but they're never seen again. That's one of the worst-case scenarios here, because I'm fairly certain that a lot of them don't survive those jobs."

Bella had felt her body go cold.

She was surprised by Felicia's hand on her forearm and realized that she'd begun trembling again. "Hey, that probably won't happen to you. If you're in the auction, you'll probably get a 'good' gig."

Felicia did a half-chuckle at her attempt to lighten the mood but realized that it didn't help at all. She squeezed Bella's forearm.

Bella let out a slow breath. *I can't stay here.*

CHAPTER 12

FRANK STOPPED PACING back and forth in his apartment when his phone buzzed in his front pocket. He had covered a court hearing first thing in the morning but then had gone home early to be available for any call from the police. He glanced down at his cellular watch, hoping it was some news about Bella. Instead, it was Janelle texting him again asking if he had any news about Bella, so he ignored it again along with all her other latest texts and calls. It hadn't even been twenty-four hours since Bella had been taken, and Janelle had been calling him crying once an hour to see if the police knew anything more and demanding that he make them do something to find Bella.

He looked at yet another text that buzzed on his watch. Again, Janelle. "Why are you ignoring me?"

She was right; he was ignoring her. He hadn't slept, and on top of his own emotional pain, hers was becoming too much to bear. *But I get it. Bella is her daughter too. Of course she's suffering.* Frank's thoughts flashed back to memories of Janelle with Bella—feeding her as an infant, teaching her to walk, proudly telling friends about Bella's great grades in school. *I shouldn't be ignoring her.*

Bzzzz. "Don't you care about me?" she texted.

A sharp ache seized Frank's chest and faded slowly. *Yes, Honey. I do care about you.* Although they were now divorced, they had been together for thirteen years. They were mostly good years. Janelle always had a warm kiss for him every morning and a warm dinner every evening when he got back from court. And the divorce…he didn't want to think about it. *All my fault.* He had given in to the temptations of another woman. *Not my best moment.* Her name was Katrina, and she had the temperament of the hurricane by the same name. The relationship was short-lived and he left it with nothing but his Jeep, his clothes and his regret. *I've got to get my shit together.* Finally, he took a deep breath and called Janelle.

"It's about time," she barked. "What's wrong with you? I've been crying all night. I've been calling you for an hour, and you haven't answered me. Don't you care about me? What's going on with the investigation? What are the police doing? It's like you don't even care—"

"Sorry," Frank said over Janelle's voice. "I'm sorry. There just wasn't anything new to report. But I have been calling, and the detective wasn't calling me back, that is until just a few minutes ago. I have an appointment with him at the police station over the lunch hour."

"What? Why does he want to meet with you? Have they found out anything?"

"No. I called him and had to twist his arm to get an appointment. When I was talking to him on the phone, it didn't sound to me like they had made any progress in the investigation. But I'm hoping that if I get in his face, maybe he'll try harder."

"When *we* get in his face you mean," Janelle added.

"You want to come?"

"Hell, yes."

Frank checked to see if his keys were in his pocket. "Great. On my way."

Frank honked the horn of his red Jeep Cherokee once as he pulled up and stopped in front of his old house to pick up Janelle. It was a two-level built some thirty years earlier as part of a large complex surrounding a small wildlife preserve. A duck nesting in the bushes by the house reminded him how he used to enjoy sitting on the back deck with a beer and watching families of ducks waddle by the chain-link fence next to the stream. *I miss this place.*

The gray-haired widow from across the street, whom Frank had avoided speaking to ever since he and Janelle divorced almost three years earlier, stopped digging in her flower garden just long enough to crane her neck toward him and glare at him disapprovingly. *But I don't miss her.* He turned away and ignored her again as Janelle hurried out the front door with a jacket over her arm.

"What've you been doing to find Bella?" Janelle blurted out as soon as she opened the passenger door.

Frank shrugged. "I called Bella's phone number several times, but there was no answer."

"I did that too," Janelle said.

Frank pulled away from the curb and started down the road. "Then I called the police a couple of times. They told me the detective would call me when they had new information."

Janelle shook her head. "Is that all? If you had been down there pushing them, they might have found her by now."

Frank tensed up. "And if you had listened to me..." Frank stopped himself as blood rushed to his face. He was just about to tell Janelle that she should have listened to him when he objected to Bella going out with a boy he didn't know. But he knew in his heart that it wasn't Janelle's fault that Johnny had taken Bella to a bar or that Bella had refused to go inside and decided to stand out in front of the bar or any of the rest of it. He decided to change the subject. There was something else that he had done to help. He took a deep breath to calm himself first.

"Look, when the police didn't have any leads, I asked my friend Mia to help. She's a private investigator. And she knows some people who—"

Janelle interrupted him. "Oh, you mean your new *girlfriend*, the one who picked out the little red dress for Bella?"

Frank glanced at Janelle and shrugged. Mia was just a friend. Or had just been a friend until last night when... In any case, although he wasn't sure where his relationship with Mia might go, he was sure he didn't want to discuss it with Janelle. He cleared his throat. "She's just a friend. Besides, you're the one who told me to get Bella a new dress."

Janelle wasn't listening to him. "As if *she* could find Bella better than the police. She should leave it to the police. *You* should leave it to the police."

Frank knew he didn't want to argue with Janelle, but he believed they should use every possible resource they could to find their daughter. *And Mia doesn't deserve this criticism.* "It's not just Mia alone. She knows people. She has friends who..."

Frank glanced sideways and saw Janelle glaring at him. *There's that look.* He knew it wouldn't make any difference what he said now. Plus, he had promised Mia not to tell anyone about her connection to The Sisterhood.

Frank nodded forward. "Look. We're almost at the police station," he said gratefully. "We can talk to Detective Gooden. You can ask him whatever you want. Tell him whatever you want to."

After passing through the two big sets of double doors and checking in with the receptionist, Janelle sat down in a nearby chair. Frank started to sit next to her but then bounced back up and started pacing.

Janelle stared at him. "Just sit down, Frank."

He turned to face her so that he could make a retort but stopped himself when he saw her eyes held true concern for him. He stared into those deep-set, dark brown eyes. He always loved looking into them. He glanced away quickly, not wanting to get distracted.

"Thank you, Honey," he replied automatically with his usual term of endearment for her. "I'm sorry I was cross with you. We're both under a lot of stress. I don't want to argue."

Janelle's shoulders relaxed noticeably. She gave him a little smile and looked like she was going to say something.

"Mr. Bravo."

Frank turned to see Detective Gooden.

"And Mrs. Bravo, I assume," he added, nodding at Janelle, who shot an appreciative smile at Frank. "Please follow me."

As they entered Detective Gooden's office, Frank noticed what appeared to be several letters of commendation hanging on the walls and a row of three trophies on top of a bookshelf with figures of men holding weapons in a shooting position.

"Marksmanship?" asked Frank.

"Yeah." Gooden gestured toward the trophies. "Once I stop a suspect, they don't get away. They lie down or they go down."

Gooden smiled proudly at Frank but then saw Janelle glaring at him open-mouthed. He looked down and cleared his throat. Frank was shocked at Gooden's admission, considering that he should have realized that Frank defended those suspects who didn't get away, and because he was in the presence of a woman who was noticeably mixed race. Gooden's police pals probably cheered him for such brazen braggadocio, but what might play well behind closed doors was obviously offensive when spoken publicly.

Frank didn't want to start an argument with Gooden and fought back the pressing urge to give his Black Lives Matter speech. Instead, he decided to focus on their reason for being there that day, and he wanted, he *needed*, the detective's attentive cooperation.

Frank glanced sideways and could tell that Janelle was about to say something to Gooden as well. He caught her eye, shook his head slightly, and shrugged.

Turning back to the desk, he noticed a family photograph—Gooden with his wife and the two daughters he mentioned to Frank when they met.

Frank gestured toward the photograph. "Your two daughters look happy in that photo." He then turned and waited until Gooden met his eyes. "Now, what can you tell us about ours?"

Gooden pulled a file labeled Bella Bravo from the side of his desk to the middle. As he flipped it open, Frank could see the file was almost empty.

"Honestly, not much yet," he admitted. "Of course, it's only been one day."

"I know," said Frank. He nodded toward Janelle. "But it would be helpful for us both to know what you have done or maybe at least what you are planning to do."

"Well, as I told you last night, we have an ATL out on the white van. Unfortunately, it doesn't appear to have a license plate."

"ATL?"

Gooden looked at Janelle and responded. "Sorry, police lingo for attempt to locate." Janelle nodded and Gooden added, "We are also checking known associates of this Chacho kid and his last known addresses. When we find him, we find her."

After an uncomfortable pause, Janelle raised her hand. "What if your Chacho has taken Bella out of the state? I've been reading online about sex trafficking and how they move the victims away from where people know them. They say it makes it harder for the police to find them."

Gooden shrugged but didn't answer right away.

"And some are never found," Janelle added.

Gooden nodded. "That might be true if Chacho were part of a big trafficking ring. But from what we know, his only record is here in Utah. He's just a kid. Not likely to be part of a big trafficking organization."

Frank leaned forward. "But if it's even a possibility that Chacho is part of a bigger organization, shouldn't you widen the search? Maybe get the FBI involved?"

Janelle nodded vigorously at Frank's suggestion, her eyebrows raised high in concern.

Gooden shook his head. "The FBI won't give us the time of day with the information we have so far. They won't put manpower on anything unless there's hard evidence to follow up on. I'm sorry, but unless we get a new lead, I don't think there's much more we can do right now."

Janelle's normally smooth forehead furrowed deeply. "That's it? That's all you're going to say? That's all you're going to do?" Janelle raised both arms and shook them at Detective Gooden. "They've got my baby!"

Gooden just shrugged. "I'm sorry. We can expand the ATL maybe, but other than that…" Gooden fell silent.

Janelle's broad lips pinched tightly together, and a tear started down her cheek. More quietly now she murmured, mostly to herself, "She's just a baby."

Frank stood and took Janelle by the arm. "Come on, Honey. Let's go."

Frank led Janelle out of Gooden's office. She held tightly to his arm and let him lead her as tears streamed down her face.

Frank opened the passenger door for Janelle. She slumped heavily into the seat.

"Don't give up," he said. "I have another call to make."

CHAPTER 13

"BELLA DIDN'T GO WEST," Sally yelled into The Sisterhood's warehouse desk phone to be heard over the noise of the helicopter Zena was flying east to Nebraska. "Her phone was on an 18-wheeler. Our sister agent Li stopped the truck and found the phone. The driver didn't know anything about Bella."

Zena rotated the microphone attached to her flight helmet so that it was directly in front of her mouth. "Are you sure? Could he have been hiding her? Could he have been lying about knowing something?"

"We vetted Li carefully," Sally replied. "She is a master of Chinese acupuncture. She knows how to cure diseases and how to relieve pain. And if necessary, she knows how to use needles to cause pain, especially when she adds electric currents. Suffice it to say that if the truck driver knew anything, Li was confident he would have told her. In any case, she reported that he was concerned and cooperative. But you were right. It must have been a misdirection ploy."

Hearing no other questions from Zena, Sally continued, "How are you and Mia doing up there? Are you able to track the pendant's GPS signal?"

"Yes," Zena said, "we found the pendant's signal in South Central Nebraska."

Sally asked, "How close are you? Where will you catch up?"

Zena looked at Mia tracking the signal on a computer screen and tilted her head at her to answer the question. Mia did a quick calculation and said, "At our current speed, we should arrive around 10:00 p.m."

Zena nodded her approval at Mia's quick answer.

"Okay," Sally said. "Keep me posted on your progress. Sally out."

Despite their audio-connected headphones, the noise of the helicopter kept Mia and Zena from chit-chatting as they followed the signal east. With nothing else to do, Mia refreshed her screen every few minutes. It paid off. She did a double take to make sure her eyes weren't deceiving her. "It's moving. The pendant is moving!"

Zena turned to Mia and glanced at the screen. Too much to process in a split-second time. "Where? Which way? How fast?"

Mia leaned in to take a closer look. "North. I can't tell how fast. Not as fast as us. Bella's probably in a vehicle."

The signal was moving at a 90-degree angle to the helicopter's heading. Zena changed direction by five degrees, estimating an intercept point.

Mia and Zena's tracking of the signal became constant. After heading north for about twenty minutes, the signal changed direction again.

"It's heading east now," Mia exclaimed.

"Can you tell where it's heading? Maybe a nearby town?" Zena asked with a bit of urgency.

Mia zoomed in on her map. "It's headed toward Grand Island."

Zena modulated her heading again, back to due east.

Watching the screen intently, Mia tracked the signal for another twenty minutes before there was another change. She waited a minute to be sure before turning to Zena. "It's stopped near Grand Island."

Zena got the coordinates from Mia, locked the location into her flight computer, and pushed the handle on her right forward to speed their arrival. She slowed as they approached the signal to assess the situation. The signal led them to a huge house on a large property with several high-end cars parked outside on a long, circular driveway.

"Let's land away from the house so as to not announce our arrival, just in case there's security," Zena said as she banked the helicopter and zoomed away from the house. About two hundred yards away, she landed the helicopter behind a small hill. After landing, she pulled off her helmet and asked Mia to wait in the helicopter while she climbed the hill with nightscope binoculars to scan for security guards.

When she returned, Mia asked, "What did you see?"

"I didn't see anyone inside any of the cars nor anyone patrolling the grounds. So, whoever is holding Bella must be inside."

Then Zena reached inside the helicopter and pulled out the duffel bag that she had stuffed behind the seats. Zena was far too tall to try to dress inside the cramped cockpit. She unzipped the duffel and started to gear up like she was preparing for war, starting with a bulletproof vest and a dark camouflage uniform. She selected some knives and handguns. After sliding them into holsters on her belt, she pulled out an assault rifle and an extra magazine.

Mia gave her a thumbs up. "What do you want me to do?"

"Stay here and monitor me," Zena instructed as she slid a small two-way communication device into her ear. "I'll bring Bella back as soon as I find her."

"Maybe I should come too. I can help."

"I like your spirit, but I need you to watch the heli while I'm gone. I may be coming fast if there's security. We can't have any local kids trying to get inside it or anything. We'll need it to get the hell out of here."

Mia thought for a moment that Zena was just trying to make her stay back, just to keep her safe. Zena had been present when Xtina warned her about the danger that would ensue when she met her sister, and when Xtina foresaw the possibility of Mia's death. Mia was a little ashamed that she felt relief about Zena going to the house by herself.

"Okay. That sounds fine," Mia said.

But as she watched Zena strap on her gear, Mia also thought about young Bella and felt a twinge of guilt. And not just guilt, a true desire to help Bella, no matter what. She couldn't just sit here and do nothing. And Mia remembered that Xtina declared that she had a calling to help others, and she had heard Xtina urge Sally to have faith. After all, Xtina had set her on this quest, even knowing the danger, and so must believe that she could do it. Maybe she should have faith now too. Mia drew a deep breath.

"Zena, wait a minute."

Zena slid the rifle over her shoulder and met Mia's eyes.

Committed to helping Zena any way she could, Mia considered the situation. "When we were strategizing with Sally, I know that Plan A was for you to carry out a direct assault. But that was because we were expecting to find a fortified building or some security force. But you just said that you didn't see any security at all. I know I'm new at this, and I could easily be wrong, but…maybe we should go with Plan B, the low-impact stealth rescue."

Zena glanced over at Mia and then back towards the house. After a moment, she said, "You may be new to this, but I think you may be right. Maybe my Rambo routine isn't the way to go this time. This looks like a normal house. Huge, but normal. That's to say there are no electrified fences around it and no visible security outside."

Zena slid the rifle off her shoulder and leaned it against the wall of the helicopter. "Breaking into a crime syndicate's hideout is one thing, but if I bust into the home of regular folks, there is a danger of them calling 911 and then we'd have to deal with the police—which we want to avoid if we can."

Zena paused for a moment, two fingers on her temple. "How about this? Before we decide on the best approach, let's do a bit more recon. Get the dress and shoes from your pack. Maybe we can send you right up to the door to scout the house. You go up there and say that you're just looking for your friend. Then you smile and ask if she's there and may you come in. If you find her and can bring her out without a fight, you do it and I'll back you up. That's the best way not to draw attention to ourselves. Maybe we can avoid a fight altogether. If we can, that's best for everyone. But if you discover a security force," Zena grabbed Mia by the shoulder to command her full attention, "*any* security force, you retreat and wait for me."

Mia grinned, her eyes sparkling with excitement. "Yeah. Let's do it."

Zena opened the helicopter's door. "I'll set up on top of the hill to observe with a tripod for my M-1 just in case I need to cover you."

Mia opened her backpack and pulled out the little black dress and high heels that she had brought just in case. She unzipped her flight jacket, peeled off her jeans, and stepped into the dress. It clung snuggly, flattering her athletic figure, but was made of Lycra and Spandex to be flexible enough for her to move freely. She grabbed a shoe but before putting it on she scanned the broad expanse of open land between the helicopter and the house and wondered how she could traverse the quarter mile hike in heels before deciding it would be better just to put her sneakers back on and carry the heels in her hand until she got to the house.

She found a compact 9mm pistol and selected a belt with a holster for it. *No way they'll let me inside that house wearing this.* She put it back. She wanted to take a weapon, but her dress left nothing to the imagination. There was no way to hide such a weapon. *The lipstick canisters.* Mia grabbed the mini crossbody pouch she brought with her, filled it with the weaponized lipstick cases she had got from Sally, zipped it closed and pulled it over her head to wear cross shoulder for stability. *Perfect.*

Mia pushed a small communication device in her ear and winked back at Zena. Then she started her brisk journey to the house.

"Zena, can you hear me?"

"Loud and clear, Mia."

As Mia neared the parking area, she checked in again with Zena. "Can you see anyone out there?"

"There are lots of cars out there, but I still don't see anyone in the cars. And there still appears to be no security outside the house."

"How about inside the house?"

"Lots of lights are on in the house, but curtains cover the lower floor. There is a terrace on the second level. The windows are not covered there. I see people. People with drinks. Looks like a party."

"Wait a minute," Zena trailed off and then came back loud and clear. "Let me focus in a bit more. Yes, I can see through a thin curtain in a second-floor room. Two. Make that three people are there. The clothing is coming off one of them… a woman. Plus, two men."

"Is it Bella?" Mia asked, lengthening her stride.

"I can't tell," said Zena. "The lights are low. I can only see silhouettes. The curtain's impeding my view… I don't think so, though. This woman's hair is short. Or maybe her hair is just up." Zena checked the electronic tracker. "But Mia, the signal for the GPS pendant is in that room."

Bella's here. Mia's heart raced in excitement. She made sure the radio was fixed in her ear and then jogged the rest of the way to the house. She stopped behind some cars and switched from the sneakers to her black heels and then pranced to the front door to ring the doorbell. Her heart pounded hard in her chest, not so much from the jogging—Mia was in great shape—but from the adrenaline of uncertainty of what she would find behind the door. Would it be Bella? Or maybe the kidnappers?

CHAPTER 14

AFTER WHAT SEEMED to be a long time, perhaps due to her acute anxiety about what danger lurked behind the door, Mia reached to push the doorbell's button again. But just then the door opened. A nicely dressed young man holding what looked like a large mixed drink stood with a big smile. "Are you with the other girls?"

Mia thought quickly and answered vaguely. "I came separately. I'm looking for my friend Bella. She's mixed race. Long black hair. Very pretty."

"There's a black girl upstairs," the young man responded while gawking at Mia's low-cut dress. "Please come in. Everyone's upstairs partying. You can hear the music. I'll take you up in a minute."

Mia followed the young man into a living room area. He sat his drink on the lampstand and plopped onto the couch. "But first, how about a lap dance?"

"Hmmm." Mia was stalling for time. "What should I do with you?"

She heard Zena in her ear. "What's your play, Mia? Do the lap dance and win his trust? Or knock him the hell out? I support your call either way."

Mia hesitated, then smiled. "Okay, baby. Get comfortable. Let me just freshen up my lipstick."

Seeing a mirror, Mia turned and sashayed toward it, letting her hips sway. As she approached the mirror, she glimpsed the young man's eyes ogling her ass. His attention adequately diverted, she unzipped her purse and took a minute to see if she recognized any of the canisters. *That one.* She pretended to put on a little lipstick and then flipped open the top of the cannister. Palming it in her right hand, she strolled back to the couch. The purse slid off her shoulder, and she tossed it onto a nearby chair.

Mia caught the young man's eyes and hiked her dress up to her waist. She straddled his thighs while continuing to face him and then slid forward onto his lap.

"That's right baby," he muttered. "Just like that." He raised his hands to her sides and caressed her arms, then let his hands slide down her back to her butt.

Mia allowed his gentle touch, not wanting to respond in any way that might startle him into a defensive posture. She started grinding against him and kissed him on the right side of his neck just as she pressed the lipstick case onto the left side of his neck and pushed the button on the bottom of the case. A pressurized swoosh shot a needle forward far enough to pierce the skin and inject a fast-acting knockout drug. He twitched and started to lift his arm up to his neck. *Uh oh. Is this gonna work?* She grabbed him and held his arms and three seconds later, he moaned softly, his arms falling to his side, and his head flopping back against the couch.

The smile vanished from Mia's face as she looked around the room "He's out," she informed Zena. "If anyone sees him, I'll just say he must have drunk too much and passed out."

Mia heard Zena's voice in her ear. "I'm coming. Be there in a minute. I'll wait just outside the house. But I'll be monitoring you in case you need me."

"Sounds good." Mia picked up her little purse and pulled the strap over her head again for better security. "I'm going upstairs to get Bella."

At the top of the stairway were a set of open double doors revealing a large suite where several young men and scantily clad girls were mingling, drinking, and talking, but Bella didn't appear to be among them. No one seemed to take notice of her, so she turned and kept walking toward the bedroom where Zena had tracked the GPS signal.

Mia pushed the door open and saw one guy fucking a black girl doggy style and a second guy standing nearby stroking his own dick, apparently waiting his turn.

Keeping an eye on the men to see if they reacted to her entry, Mia walked around to see the girl. It wasn't Bella, but whoever she was wore the pendant Mia had given Bella around her neck. It was swaying back and forth with the rhythmic movements of the girl.

"Hey, a girl for me too," the other guy announced when he saw Mia.

She ignored him and directed her attention to the girl. "Where's Bella?"

"Who the fuck are you?" the girl retorted as she stared at Mia. "Hey, Nita? What are you doing here?"

"Sorry," said Mia. "I'm not Nita."

"What the hell is going on?" said the guy trying to fuck the black girl. The girl had stopped pushing against him and they lost their rhythm. He pulled out of her and turned to stare at Mia, still holding onto his dick.

The black girl's eyebrows scrunched together as if she hadn't understood Mia.

I'm just looking for my friend Bella." She pointed towards the girl's neck. "That's her necklace."

"If you're mad about the necklace, Chacho gave it to me. Ummm, just for tonight. I promise."

Mia shook her head, realizing the black girl still didn't understand. "No. I'm not Nita. Like I said, I'm just looking for my friend. Her name is Bella. Olive skin. Black hair. Ringlets. Where is she?"

The black girl suddenly freaked out and pointed at Mia. "She's not with us. Grab her."

Both guys turned their attention to Mia. The "stroker" let go of himself and reached toward Mia.

Mia lifted her palm out to stop him, and smiled sweetly, hoping to keep everyone calm. "You can keep that hand to yourself please."

She moved to her right to put the guy closest to her in between her and the second man, so that she would only have to deal with one of them at a time. The stroker reached for Mia's neck with his left hand. She leaned back quickly and deflected his arm to her left with her right palm, then and stepped forward just as she swung her left arm around his throat while hooking her left leg behind his left foot, and twisted to her right, taking him down on his back to the floor. He fell hard. Dazed, he glared at Mia and started to push himself up. She made a quick hip turn to her left and executed a roundhouse kick to the side of the guy's face, knocking him back to the ground. This time he didn't get up.

The second guy put his head down and rushed at Mia's waist. She jumped back to avoid the brunt of the hit, balanced her weight on top of him, and wrapped her right arm around the guy's neck. He struggled, but she kicked her legs back to leverage all her weight on top of him and forced him face first to the floor. With her right arm still squeezing his throat she slammed her left arm down on the back of his neck to reinforce her hold and squeezed as hard as she could. He fought, but she maintained her balance until he quit struggling. Then she pushed herself up to her feet.

After hearing the struggle, three more guys rushed into the room. Two big guys, maybe from the college football team, and one nerdy-looking guy with glasses.

"What the hell happened here?" asked the guy in glasses.

The black girl pointed at Mia. "She did it."

"Um, I could use some help here," said Mia.

The two big guys started moving toward Mia. She had slid her hand into her purse and grabbed another lipstick case. Not sure which weapon was built into this particular case, she just pointed it at the oncoming guys and warned, "I wouldn't do that."

The big guys stopped, seemingly unsure of what to do.

"Why not?" asked the nerdy one. "Tell me why they shouldn't."

Mia could possibly take them all but wasn't sure. So, she decided to try talking her way out. She reflected on her experience as a victim advocate.

"You have some underage girls here. Maybe you didn't know it, but you're screwed if you've had sex with any of them. Sex with a minor is a felony."

The guys all stopped in their tracks.

Mia took advantage. "And what I have here in my hand is a…," she glanced at the lipstick, "a miniature video recorder." She waved it toward the naked black girl. So now I have video evidence that's…being transmitted to federal law enforcement as we speak. So, if you touch me, they are, of course, going to see it, and they're going to add assault and obstruction of justice to your charges."

"I'll lose my football scholarship," one of the big guys whimpered.

The nerdy guy whined, "I'll never get into Harvard Law School."

The third guy said, "Well, I'll take one for the team." He reached forward to grab the lipstick case from Mia. She squeezed it instinctively, and a dart shot out and hit the guy in the neck. He crumpled to the floor.

"Hey, I thought you said that was a video recorder," said the other big guy.

Mia shrugged. "My bad."

The second big guy bent down in a football stance preparing to rush Mia.

Mia raised a hand in front of her and shouted, "Hey! Just wait. I need a minute." She looked past the big guy to the door behind him, just as it opened.

"Pick on someone your own size," a voice from the door snarled.

Zena!

The big guy turned to see who made the remark. His eyebrows raised and nostrils flared when he saw that his new opponent was not only as tall as him, but she was also armed to the nth degree. He immediately put his hands up in surrender.

A tense standoff ensued as everyone looked around at each other wondering what to do.

Finally, the nerdy guy with the glasses asked, "Are you cops?"

Zena winked at Mia. "Not exactly," she conceded. "I guess we could make a citizen's arrest, though. That is, if we wanted to. But we just want this girl here. You guys are free to go. We won't report you."

"But this is my house," contended the nerdy guy.

"Okay then, now we're getting somewhere," Zena said. "Who did you hire these girls from?"

"I didn't do it. My friend, the best man for the wedding, hired them for the party as his gift to me."

"Call him in here right now," Zena insisted.

"I would, but when he didn't come back up to the party after going to answer the door, I went looking for him and found him passed out on the couch downstairs."

Zena glanced at Mia, who just shrugged.

"Take a drive then," Zena ordered, putting her hand on one of the pistols on her belt.

"But when can we come back?" asked the nerd.

"Give us an hour."

The three guys looked at each other, shrugged, and turned to leave.

Just before they opened the door, Zena said, "And take your friends with you." Looking around at the disarray, she added, "And their pants. Take their pants too."

The guys Mia had taken down were coming to their senses. Their friends gave them a hand up and helped them out.

After they left the room, Zena turned to the black girl and asked in a kind, gentle voice, "What's your name, Honey?"

"LaToya," she answered quietly. The earlier fight seemed to have left her.

"Where did you get the necklace, LaToya?" Zena remained calm.

"It's mine. My boyfriend gave it to me." LaToya wrapped her hand around it protectively.

"Well, it belongs to a friend of ours," Mia said. "Her name is Bella. We're looking for her. Do you know where she is?"

LaToya looked back and forth between Mia and Zena, seemingly hesitant to answer.

Zena stepped toward her until she was within arm's length.

"She's not here. She didn't come with us. I don't know where she is," LaToya replied quickly—too quickly.

Mia stepped towards the door. "I'll go check the house. Maybe she is here."

"I searched the house before I came into this room," Zena said. "She's telling the truth. Bella's not here."

Zena cocked her head to the side. "But if your boyfriend gave the necklace to you, he had to get it from Bella. So, who's your boyfriend?"

"I can't tell you. He'd be angry." LaToya's eyes opened wide in fear.

"Where is he?" Zena asked, more loudly this time.

LaToya looked down at the floor and remained silent.

Zena put her hand on the top of the knife on her belt but didn't pull it out. She took a breath before continuing. "Look LaToya, we can help you. If you're being held against your will, or being forced to do this, we can take you somewhere safe."

"Don't need your help," LaToya replied, defiant. Then she raised her eyes to meet Zena's. "Don't *want* your help."

Mia stepped forward. She was distraught that Bella wasn't in the house. What would she tell Frank? She couldn't give up. She had been hopeful at first that LaToya would help them, but now it was clear that she wouldn't help voluntarily. *Poor Bella. What might they be doing to her?* Mia couldn't wait any longer. She reached out and grabbed one of LaToya's arms and twisted it behind her. LaToya yelped and tried to fight back but Bella twisted it harder and lifted it high behind her back. "Where's Bella?

Tell us now!" LaToya cried out but didn't answer the question. "If you don't tell us, I'll—"

"Mia!"

Zena's voice drew Mia's attention, and she watched as Zena slowly approached and put her hand on Mia's arm. "Don't."

Mia released her grip on LaToya's arm. LaToya cradled it in her other arm, whimpering.

"Come over here." Zena indicated the direction to Mia with a nod. Zena put her arm around Mia's shoulder and noted that Mia's face was flushed, and she was breathing heavily. "Relax, my sister."

"But—"

"*Shhhhh.*"

Mia's breathing slowed, and a tear started down her cheek. "We've got to find Bella."

Zena took Mia by the shoulders to face her directly. "I know. But remember that this girl is a victim too. She's fighting us, but it's partly out of fear of what could happen to her if she helps us. I saw it in her eyes."

Mia's eyebrows pinched together. "I'm just so desperate to find Bella. And she's *refusing* to help us. She's helping *them.*"

"I know," Zena said. "I've seen it before. It's sort of a Stockholm Syndrome problem. Sometimes trafficking victims who are given favors start to relate to their captors differently. Eventually, some even grow to trust them, and help them. But LaToya is a victim, nonetheless. We should treat her as such."

Mia sighed. She thought back to the ten years she spent as a victim advocate. She too had seen women who protected their abusers. That didn't mean you abandoned them. She had never abandoned a victim.

"But then how?" Mia asked.

"Not like that. Let's try again."

Zena took Mia gently by the elbow and moved back towards LaToya, who retreated a step as they approached.

"It's okay," Zena said, softly, holding up her palm and stopping short of LaToya. "Don't worry. We won't hurt you. We just want to find Bella. She was kidnapped yesterday on her way to the prom. So, they would have just barely taken her to wherever you all are being held. And we just want to find her. We won't do anything to you. Please, just help us find our friend."

LaToya's face calmed. "But I don't know what I can do."

"Can you tell us where she is at least?"

LaToya was no longer belligerent. "I don't know."

Mia stepped forward and LaToya took a step back. "I'm sorry I hurt you," Mia said. "I just need to find Bella." Mia reached to the floor for LaToya's tube top and handed it to her. LaToya slipped it over her head and adjusted it. After Mia's kindness, although a small thing, LaToya's posture relaxed.

"How about this," said Mia. "Can you tell us at least where you last saw Bella?"

LaToya hesitated just a moment but then nodded. "I saw her at the farm. That's where we live. And I promise I didn't know this was her necklace. I didn't take it. Chacho…" LaToya put her hand to her mouth as if she hadn't meant to say the name. "I mean, my boyfriend gave it to me."

Zena glanced at Mia, who nodded. "Where's the farm?" Zena asked.

"About an hour from here," LaToya replied. "But I don't know the address. And anyway…she may not even be there anymore. I heard they were going to sell her at the auction tonight."

Mia threw a hand to her mouth and looked at Zena. "Sell her?"

Zena's eyes met Mia's. "We'd better hurry."

Zena spoke to LaToya again, more urgently now. "How did you get here tonight?"

"Chacho brought us."

"And is he coming back for you?"

"I guess so."

"When?"

"I'm not sure. At about midnight I think he said."

Zena checked her watch and looked at Mia. "That's only twenty minutes from now. We can just wait for him to come then, and um…ask *him* where Bella is."

Latoya suddenly became more animated. "Please don't tell him I told you anything. You don't know him. He's a bad man. He'd hurt me."

Sensing that LaToya had been victimized by her boyfriend, Mia promised, "My friends and I will protect you from him."

LaToya shook her head. "I don't know. It ain't just him. The big boss has security. There's a lot of them. They'll take you two down in a heartbeat. You should run while you can."

"Thank you for your concern, LaToya," said Zena. "We'll be careful, and we'll never say you cooperated in any way." LaToya nodded, apparently satisfied. "Now, pay attention. Here's how this will go down when Chacho gets here…"

CHAPTER 15

"THEY CAUGHT EUGENIA trying to run tonight," Felicia reported as she burst through the door into the bedroom where Bella and three other girls shared two sets of bunk beds in the basement of the farmhouse.

It was her usual bedtime, but Bella had been unable to sleep. In fact, she hadn't been able to sleep since arriving at the farm, afraid she'd wake up to something awful happening to her. Tonight, she couldn't sleep because it was the night of the auction, and she knew someone would be coming to get her at any minute. The other girls were awake and chatting away.

"This is the second time she has run," added Felicia. "Last time was bad. But this time…" Felicia trailed off and didn't finish her sentence.

One of the other girls asked, "When was the first time?"

Felicia sighed. "About a month ago. She'd gone on a job for a construction crew. One of the other girls who went on that job with her said that most of the crew were drunk and smelly bastards. I guess Eugenia resisted one of them and he punched her out before he raped her. When she came to, she snuck out the back door and ran. But someone saw her, and Big D's guys chased her down and brought her back."

Bella hadn't seen Felicia so upset since she arrived. She planned to run too, so she sat up and paid close attention to what Felicia was saying.

"I remember when she first came to the farm, she was so afraid. She was fifteen years old. She told me her father was a reporter in Mexico and had just published an article about how the drug cartel had paid off the chief of the local police department to let the cartel operate. Then, at her *quinceañera* birthday party, some gang members showed up and shot her father and then started mowing down everyone else with machine guns."

"Fuck," one of the girls commented.

Felicia continued, "Eugenia and her mother ran out the back door with only the clothes they had on them, so they didn't have any money except for some gift money Eugenia got from an envelope and tucked into her bra. They took a bus to Mexico City and then jumped on the top of a freight train with people trying to sneak into the states. She called it *La Bestia* because it was the train of violence. They were robbed and had to fight off rapists. But at the U.S. border, some of Big D's guys snatched Eugenia. She didn't know what happened to her mother."

Bella hated how normal these stories were beginning to sound to her.

Felicia was silent for a few seconds. She then looked around at the other girls and continued the story. "She was super depressed when she got here. After her first job, she told me she would rather die than stay in this place. So, I guess she figured she had nothing to lose by running."

Bella finally spoke up. "What happened to her?"

Another girl piped in. "I was here when they got her. They took us all into the barn to watch. To warn us. To frighten us. They threatened to cut her to pieces and feed her to the pigs. But then they…they…"

The girl couldn't bring herself to continue. The horror on her face was clear.

Then another voice finally said, "They made her try to take a horse."

A heavy silence fell over the room. No one knew what to say. The girls who had seen it all looked ashen.

The first girl cleared her throat and added, "They recorded the whole thing. They were all laughing at her. And Big D kept saying how he was going to make a bunch of money from the video."

Bella shuddered. Every time she thought she'd heard the worst thing that could happen to her, she heard something even worse. All she'd been able to think about was running, and now…

"What happened to her then?" Bella asked.

Felicia spoke again, pain in her voice. "She fell into a deep depression. She became submissive after that. They started trying to hook her on drugs. She fought back at first when they tried to inject her, but they just held her down. After that, when she went on jobs, she would just lay there and let the guys do whatever they wanted to her."

The girl with the lower voice said sadly, "This time she didn't even try to be sneaky. She just kind of wandered away from the farm in a daze."

"What's gonna happen to her this time?" a voice meekly asked.

It was quiet for a moment.

"Who knows?" Felicia said. "Once, they left another girl chained in the cellar for three days with no food or water. She almost died."

Bella felt nauseous.

"Wake up, everyone!"

Everyone flinched.

"It's Nita. It sounds like she's dragging something," Felicia said with audible concern.

Bella heard a loud thumping noise with each step Nita took. Felicia was right—she was pulling something, and it sounded heavy.

All the girls scrambled to the common area. Nita appeared in the large room pulling a chain behind her that was attached to Eugenia's neck. Eugenia's legs trailed as Nita finished dragging her headfirst to the bottom of the stairs. A lot of the girls screamed in horror when they saw her, Bella included.

"Shut up! It's lesson time again ladies," announced Nita. "I try to be nice to you. I feed you. I dress you. I get you your drugs."

Nita looked around to make sure all the girls were paying attention to her. She caught someone looking away, and yelled, "Eyes over here!"

Then she gave them all a terrifying look before continuing. "But occasionally, someone's not grateful for the kindness I bestow upon them.

Like Eugenia here. I gave her chance after chance, and still she disobeyed me. She disrespected me. She betrayed me."

Bella observed Eugenia, her small fingers inserting space between the chain and her neck to keep from choking. Peering through her long, tangled black hair were fixed black eyes staring at nothing. Bella realized her own hands were shaking uncontrollably.

Nita kicked Eugenia in the ribs. "Get up, bitch." Nita pulled the chain until Eugenia rolled over and pulled herself to her knees with a pained groan. Then, Nita walked slowly around the room, tugging on the chain with Eugenia whimpering and crawling along behind her. "So, what to do now? What to do now?"

Nita stopped and glanced around the room at each of the girls. Her face held such anger and contempt. "What the fuck do I have to do to convince you ungrateful bitches to obey me?" she ranted.

The room fell silent; the only thing anyone could hear was Eugenia's ragged breaths. Bella's heart was beating so hard she was afraid Nita would hear it and come after her.

After a few seconds of silence, she resumed her trudge around the room again, dragging Eugenia behind her. "Oh, what should I do? What should I do?" Nita glared into the eyes of each girl as she passed, each of them holding their breaths.

Nita stopped suddenly. "I have an idea." She pulled a knife out of a sheath strapped to her leg and quickly slashed Eugenia's face. All the girls gasped at once. Eugenia cried out in pain and tried to pull away, but Nita grabbed her by the hair and made another slash across her face at an angle, leaving an X with flesh dangling from her cheek. Eugenia put both hands on her face to try to hold it together. Blood gushed between her fingers.

Bella felt tears running down her cheeks as a scream choked in her throat. She noticed that many of the other girls were also crying and clinging onto each other. Some of them were trying to look away or gagging at the sight of Eugenia's hanging flesh. Nita glared at them.

After a moment, Nita let Eugenia collapse onto the floor, then went to the door and shouted up the stairs, "Gordo… Gordo!"

"What the fuck, Nita?" shouted a voice from above. "Stop shouting. What the fuck do you want?"

"Tell Big D I'm sending Eugenia to the warehouse."

It was as if the air had been sucked out of the room.

There was a pause. "Are you sure?"

"Yeah, I'm pretty fucking sure," Nita groused. "What the fuck did I just fucking say? Didn't I just fucking say that?"

"Yeah. Yeah. Okay. I'll set it up."

Nita glanced around the room one last time. "I'm leaving her here for now so you can all see what happens if you cross me." Then she laughed. "Yeah. That's it. Easy to remember. If you cross me, I cross you."

As soon as Nita left the room a lot of the girls let out sobs they'd been keeping in. A few girls ran to Eugenia's side and started gently taking the chain off her. One girl ran to the bathroom, about to throw up. But most of them, like Bella, were paralyzed, unable to move or look away from the horrific sight in front of them.

It looked as if there was nothing behind Eugenia's eyes. Her spirit had been broken. She was the shell of a person. For whatever reason, she briefly made eye contact with Bella and Bella's throat tightened. She committed herself to remember Eugenia, and to help her if she could. And she finally understood why everyone was so afraid of Nita and why so few of them dared to even talk about trying to escape. This was hell.

How is this possible? Nita looks just like Mia. But she's a monster! Oh Mia, sweet Mia, where are you? I wish you were here now to save me. Are you trying? Are you coming?

When Eugenia had been freed from the chain, a couple of the girls gingerly led her to another room.

Bella finally broke out of her trance. She turned to Felicia and asked in a low and terrified voice, "What's the warehouse?"

Felicia couldn't meet her eyes. She just stared straight ahead. "It's a place that no one ever comes back from."

CHAPTER 16

CHACHO RANG THE DOORBELL of the mansion of the frat boy hosting the bachelor party, but no one answered. He twisted the knob, and it squeaked open.

"Hi, Chacho," said LaToya, who stood in the entryway waiting. She raised her hand and waved at him shyly.

"Where the hell is everyone?" asked Chacho as he stepped through the doorway.

"Stop right there," ordered Mia, pointing a gun at him.

Chacho turned left to look at Mia just as Zena jumped out from behind the door and wrapped her strong right arm around his neck. Chacho reached up with both hands to free himself, but Zena just tightened her grip.

"Gun!" Zena shouted. With her left hand, she pulled a handgun out of the back of Chacho's pants.

Mia started to walk toward Zena and Chacho.

"Keep your distance, Mia," Zena cautioned, "so he can't reach your gun."

Mia stopped. Zena dropped Chacho's gun to the floor and kicked it to Mia, who picked it up with her free hand and now pointed both guns at Chacho.

"Get down on the floor," Zena told Chacho in a low, menacing voice.

Chacho resisted and went back to grabbing Zena's arm with both hands to get loose. To protect Zena, Mia aimed her gun at Chacho but realized she couldn't shoot at him with Zena holding him. Besides, she quickly recognized they didn't want to kill Chacho; they wanted to question him, to find Bella. Not to mention that according to LaToya, it was Chacho who knew where Bella was being held.

"I said *get down*," shouted Zena as she jammed a knee into the back of the leg Chacho had his weight on and then easily twisted him down to the floor on his back. "Don't move."

Chacho looked at the guns Mia pointed at him and then saw that Zena was armed with guns and knives too. He raised his hands up.

"What do you want?" he asked.

"We're looking for our friend. Her name is Bella," said Zena.

"She was wearing this necklace," added Mia, holding the necklace by the pendant. "Where is she?"

"I don't know nothin' about that necklace," said Chacho.

Zena pounded her boot into Chacho's gut. The air whooshed out, and he twisted to the side, moaning loudly.

"Wrong answer, asshole," said Zena. "LaToya told us you gave it to her."

Chacho looked at LaToya. "What the fuck?"

"Look at me," Zena demanded. "And talk to me, not her."

LaToya recoiled and cried, "They threatened me, Baby."

"I see that you look just fine," Chacho replied. "They were just bullshitting you, you stupid whore. They wouldn't—"

Zena nodded at Mia, and Mia kicked Chacho in the nuts. He moaned but still wasn't talking. This wasn't going anywhere. Mia was desperate to find Bella, and she had reason to believe that Zena wouldn't stop her this time.

"Give me that big knife," Mia motioned to Zena.

Zena raised an eyebrow but, as Mia had expected, she didn't resist handing over the knife. In fact, she made a show of slowly dragging the knife from its metal sheath, scraping the edge of the knife against the sheath for maximum effect. Then she grabbed it by the blade and handed it handle first to Mia. "Be careful. It's sharp."

"I'm counting on that," Mia said, as she pressed the point of the knife into the crotch of Chacho's pants. "Now, if you don't tell me immediately where our friend is, I won't hesitate to cut your dick off."

Chacho's eyes darted from the knife to Mia's face, but he still didn't speak.

"Hold him down," Mia said to Zena.

Zena put her big boot on Chacho's throat with enough weight that Chacho brought both of his hands up to his neck, struggling to breathe.

Mia grabbed Chacho's zipper and pulled it down hard. She unbuttoned his pants, grabbed both sides and jerked them down. She reached into the front slot of his boxers, grabbed his penis, and pulled it out.

"How about now?" Mia asked Chacho.

She nodded at Zena, and she eased her boot off Chacho's throat. "Blow me," he answered.

Back down went the boot.

Mia shocked herself at what she had threatened to do. She had honestly thought that the threat would be enough. But Chacho was still refusing. LaToya said that they were going to sell Bella at an auction tonight. Time was running out. Desperate times… *I'm coming, Bella*. Mia put the edge of the knife on Chacho's penis and started to push on it. He screamed.

Zena said, "I can't hear you, Chacho." Then she turned to Mia. "I think he's saying, 'Fuck you' or something like that. Better start cutting."

"Noooo," shouted Chacho. Zena finally released her boot. Chacho's hands moved quickly from his throat to cover his penis. "You bitches are crazy."

Zena jammed her boot into Chacho's stomach again. Through his moans he seemed to be saying, "Okay. Okay."

Zena took a step back. After Chacho caught his breath, he said, "Okay. I'll tell you where she is, and then you let us go."

Zena asked, "What? So you can call them and tell them we're coming? Maybe move her to somewhere else and set up an ambush for us? No way. You're coming with us."

Zena and Mia got Chacho's car key from his pocket and pushed him in front of them.

Before they walked out the front door, LaToya asked, "What about us?" She and the other girls had gathered in the living room. "What're we supposed to do now?"

Mia's eyes met LaToya's. "You're free to go. Do what you want. Call your family for help. Go wherever you want."

"I ain't got nobody here," said LaToya, frowning. "And no family worth havin."

"You can come with me 'Toya," one of the girls said. "I have family. My mother kicked me out when I stole her wedding ring so I could get high, but my grandma will take us in." She looked at the other girls. "She has a big house. You can all come."

Most of the girls seemed willing to go to the grandma's house. But then LaToya started shaking her head. "No. No way am I going to no grandma's house. I'm the Queen of the night, baby." Then Latoya started singing and dancing like she was on stage.

LaToya stopped and looked at all the girls who had gathered and said, "Any of y'all who don't wanna go to grandma's house can come with me. Let's get the *hell* out of Nebraska and go somewhere with some damn nightlife. We can start our own escort service. And we won't have to share the money with no Chacho or nobody."

Mia noticed that the girls who didn't want to go to the grandma's house seemed interested in LaToya's plan.

Zena said, "Mia, there's nothing more for us to do here. Let's go."

Mia nodded and followed Zena out the front door, with Chacho in tow.

CHAPTER 17

"IT'S TIME FOR your auction, sweetie," Nita said as she slowly combed out a knot in Bella's natural curls in front of the farmhouse bathroom's large mirror. "Hurry and finish the lemonade I poured for you."

Bella was terrified of Nita ever since she'd seen what she'd done to Eugenia. Some of Big D's men had come and dragged Eugenia away and an hour later Nita had come back downstairs to get Bella. Now Nita smiled and behaved sweetly to Bella as if she were a totally different person, which scared Bella even more somehow; she was too damned unpredictable.

Bella obediently drained the glass of lemonade. It was sweet and she had been thirsty, so it was a pleasant thing she had to do. She wished, however, that her hand hadn't been trembling slightly when she lifted it up.

Nita did some finishing touches on her hair. "There you go. All done," she said beaming with pride as if Bella was her work of art. "Now, pull off those sweats, and put your little red dress on and your heels, and I'll be back to get you as soon as we're ready in the barn."

When Bella heard that the auction was going to be in the barn, she became somehow even more nervous than she had been about the auction before. She shuddered at the memory of the story about Eugenia and the horse. She tried to calm down by reminding herself that the horse had been a punishment, that it probably wasn't something done at the auctions. She prayed that was the case at least. How much sicker could these people get?

A knot of desperation swelled in her chest. All she could think about was escaping. She had scoured the basement, there was no way out. The only other doorway went further down to the cellar, where they chained girls up as punishment. Bella had a flashback to Eugenia's empty eyes and shook her head. She hated the thought of it, but she had no choice but to cooperate in this auction.

Bella stepped into her red dress and pulled it on shakily. It brought her no comfort. It was hard to believe that at one time this dress had been her most prized possession. It was hard to believe that only a day ago she had been putting it on and contemplating how far she wanted to go with Johnny, and now she was putting it on for the men bidding over who would get to rape her.

A few tears ran down her cheeks as she hoped that the police or Mia were close to finding her. But she hadn't seen Latoya since she went to work at the bachelor party, and she didn't have high hopes of being found either. *How would they even know where to find me without the pendant?*

Bella thought of her father. When she'd had nightmares as a small child her dad told her to imagine him as the hero that would come to defeat the monster, and it used to make her feel better. She used to get into arguments with the other kids about whose dad would win in a fight because she wouldn't back down about it being hers. As she got older, she started to realize his limitations more and that he was just a man. But even so, he was always there for her in big and small ways.

A memory played in her mind of him coming to pick her up from kindergarten. Instead of walking down the stairs with him, she had rushed over to the concrete block on the side of the stairs, ran to the end of the block, closed her eyes, and jumped off the edge with her arms wide. Her father rushed to catch her mid-air and gently set her down.

He sighed with relief before laughing and commending her. "Sweetie, you just did a perfect swan dive. I didn't know you knew how to do that." Then his voice got very serious, and he said, "But, Honey, why did you close your eyes and jump like that? What if I hadn't seen you? You could have hurt yourself. That was very dangerous, my love."

He looked at her quizzically as she just smiled and giggled. "Because I knew you would catch me, Daddy."

But her father wasn't here now. There was a very good chance he still had no idea where she was. Bella wished desperately that she would've just been a bad kid for once and gone into the bar with Johnny. Her father would have been able to catch her then. He was a lawyer after all, he could've helped her handle that one. But this…

Maybe he's coming…or…or maybe he sent the police…maybe… maybe…

She sobbed. She had never felt so alone in her life.

A little while later, Nita came for her. On the walk outside to the barn, Bella paid attention to her surroundings, trying to find places to run and hide. But it was so dark she couldn't see much at all, plus she was feeling funny. She was starting to think that Nita had put something in her lemonade.

When they walked into the barn, Bella saw a video camera set up on a tripod in front of a horse stall. Bella barely processed the information as Nita walked her through the instructions of what she was expected to do during the auction. Nita told her that she would have to come out of the horse stall, turn all the way around, and smile. Then, she had to slowly take her dress off and then her panties. They would lead a horse out of the stall behind her, and she'd bend over like they were going to make her take it. Bella felt the blood drain from her face when she heard that, her worst fears coming true.

"Don't worry, honey," said Nita, smiling sweetly. "We won't make you take the horse. We promised the bidders we'd keep your virgin cunt nice and tight for them."

Bella was trembling involuntarily. Fear and panic clawed inside her chest. She felt a lump forming in her throat. She could barely breathe.

Big D strolled in and visually inspected Bella from top to bottom. The look in his eyes made Bella nauseous. "She looks great, Nita. But, if the bidding doesn't go high enough, take her over by the horse."

Nita nodded enthusiastically.

She motioned for Bella to go into the stall. Dizzy and weak, Bella stumbled.

Nita caught her. "Come on now. Stay awake. And smile. The buyers are watching remotely." Then she stepped away to call the buyers on her phone.

Bella overheard her making sure they all had audio and video. Any hope Bella had of a last-minute rescue was slipping like sand through her fingers.

"Action," Nita stated enthusiastically into the microphone.

A spotlight landed on Bella as Nita took her hand and pulled her from the stall. It was so bright that Bella couldn't see in front of her. As if in a nightmare, she heard Nita say, "What can I get for this sexy young calf? Bidding starts at $50,000."

Bella followed the first few steps easily, although uncomfortably. But then she heard Nita say, "Take your dress off."

She froze, paralyzed. Nita's sweet demeanor dropped. She gave Bella the look, from behind the camera, that she'd given the girls right before she cut the X in Eugenia's cheek.

Bella's hands shook violently as she struggled to slide the dress off her shoulders. Slowly, she managed to take it all the way off and step out of it. Goosebumps covered her body, even though it wasn't particularly cold. A few tears slid down her cheeks, but Nita didn't seem to mind those.

"Take your panties off," Nita ordered.

Bella shivered. A few of her warm tears fell onto her feet as she hesitantly hooked her thumbs in the sides of her underwear. Nita gave her a look that said to hurry it up. Bella shook as she reluctantly slid them down and off.

"Do I hear 60?"

The world wobbled in front of Bella. Suddenly she didn't feel like crying anymore. She couldn't feel anything.

"Now bend over, pull your ass cheeks apart, and smile at the camera."

Bella gave Nita a pleading look but got a threatening dart of a stare in response. For a moment, Bella considered how painful it really would be to have Nita cut into her with a knife. But she knew it wouldn't stop there if she refused to do this.

She reluctantly followed Nita's instructions, her body trembling. Her smile was toothless and forced. She didn't bother to wipe away her tears.

"The bidding's at 70, do I hear 80?"

Nita nodded as if things were going well. "Put your fingers in your mouth. All of them."

Bella did, barely able to breathe. Her nose was a little congested from all the crying.

"Reach over and touch the horse's penis."

Her hand was shaking horribly as she held back a sob, but she did as she was told.

"Do I hear 90?"

Bella started to take her hand off the horse, but Nita told her to hold for a photo before instructing her to stroke it.

Then suddenly it was over. The spotlight turned away from her. She had been sold.

Big D laughed and showed her on his iPad how much he had made off her, but Bella couldn't focus her eyes well enough to read it. She gathered that she'd done well and heard him saying something about her being delivered to a yacht. Then he quickly diverted his attention to the next girl in line to be auctioned.

Bella couldn't find her panties but pulled her dress back on then walked slowly out of the stall, stumbling in the dark.

Nita asked, "Where do you think you're going?"

"May I go to the bathroom?" Bella asked submissively.

Nita nodded and then got completely distracted by the auction. It was her job to keep it moving. She put all her attention on the next girl.

Bella turned the corner to the hallway where the bathroom was, stopped for a minute, and then peeked back towards the auction. She was a bit surprised that Nita had let her walk away. But, unlike Eugenia, she had been cooperative. Not to mention she was drugged and now everyone's focus was on the next girl to be auctioned. She pulled the heels off her feet so she could walk quietly and slipped out the door.

Outside, she looked around in the dark and didn't see anyone. She walked quickly away from the barn, a hopeful feeling growing at the mere fact that she'd made it outside successfully. She looked around cautiously one last time, and then she turned to the cornfield and made a break for it, adrenaline bursting through her veins, running harder than she had in her entire life.

CHAPTER 18

MIA STARTED UP Chacho's Ford Expedition. Zena put a flex-cuffed Chacho in the back seat and pushed him over to the passenger side before climbing in next to him. Usually, Zena cuffed detainees behind their back for safety reasons, but she allowed Chacho to keep his hands in front so that he could keep pressure on his bleeding penis.

She caught Chacho twisting to look at the guns in the back of the SUV and backhanded him in the chest. "Try anything, and I'll finish the job."

At Zena's direction, Mia first drove to the helicopter where Zena filled the cargo area of the SUV with the rest of the weapons she had brought from The Sisterhood's warehouse. Then she called Sally to let her know they had commandeered a new vehicle and were abandoning the two-million-dollar helicopter so The Sisterhood should send someone to pick it up.

After speeding westward on Interstate 80 for about half an hour, Chacho directed Mia to exit the freeway and head south.

They drove in silence down a dark two-way road for maybe another half hour before Zena asked, "How far is it?"

Chacho shrugged. "I think you may have passed it."

"What the fuck did I tell you?" shouted Zena.

"I can't see from back here," Chacho shouted defensively. "The turn-off to the farm isn't well marked. It just seems like we should have turned by now. I don't know."

Mia found a spot with a wide shoulder and then turned around and headed back the other way. She gritted her teeth and pushed the pedal down hard.

After a few minutes, Mia saw lights flashing behind her. "It's the police."

"You guys are screwed now," chuckled Chacho. "Gonna be hard to explain kidnapping me and cutting me."

Zena replied calmly. "*You* are the one who doesn't want the cops to investigate. We have you on videotape kidnapping Bella in Salt Lake City. You're the star of that show. The trial will take about five minutes, and you'll get a life sentence. Oh, and by the way, never mind that you also run some underage girls for sex. That makes you a party to the rape of a child. You're looking at another life sentence for that."

Mia slowed and looked for a place to pull over but didn't stop.

Chacho clammed up after Zena's speech, but she had one more thing she wanted to make sure he understood. "And never mind those life sentences. They may mean nothing at all because if you try to fuck us over, your life will end tonight."

Chacho shook his head. "Okay. Okay. But what are you gonna do when he sees you have me tied up?"

The police car activated its siren.

"I have to stop." Mia glanced over her shoulder at Zena. "Let me try to talk my way through this."

Just as the cop got out of his car, Zena glared grimly at Chacho but then used her knife to cut him loose and tossed her guns on the floor at her feet. Hopefully, the cop wouldn't look in the back where the rest of the weapons were stored.

The cop appeared to be a local sheriff's deputy, maybe twenty-something. He approached Mia's door with his hand on his holster.

Mia smiled sweetly as she rolled down the window. "Hi, officer. Is there a problem?"

The officer relaxed his posture a little. "Miss, you were speeding. May I see your license and registration?"

Mia paused for a minute. As part of their preparation for the rescue, she and Zena had decided not to carry identification. She improvised.

"Sorry, officer," Mia put on a dim-witted act and gave the young officer a flirtatious smile. "As you can see, I don't have any pockets right now." She giggled.

The officer pointed his flashlight at Mia and down the front of her little dress. He had to clearly see that, in fact, it didn't have any pockets or anywhere to put anything for that matter.

"How about your little purse there?" he asked as he quickly shone his spotlight on it.

"Sorry," said Mia with another giggle. "All I have in there is lipstick." She opened it just a little bit so he could look inside. She didn't want him to look too closely at those things.

"Well then, how about the vehicle registration at least?" He craned his neck toward the passenger side of the vehicle.

Mia turned to the back seat and saw Chacho nod at the glovebox. "Just a minute," she said and leaned over to open it. As she stretched to get over the center console, she could feel the night breeze on her butt, and her thong didn't cover much back there. She was sure the officer could see just about everything. No matter how much integrity he *thought* he had, no twenty-something red-blooded heterosexual male could pass up looking. *Good thing I waxed.* She took her time to give the cop plenty of time to enjoy the view, hoping it would soften his attitude toward her a bit.

Finally, she found the registration and rolled back into the driver's seat. "Here you go," she said. Her dress had scrunched up to her waist when she was stretching for the glove box. Now, she didn't bother to pull her dress down over her thighs. *Better to let him see.*

The officer took the paperwork and finally moved his flashlight from Mia to the papers. "This vehicle is registered to the Big D Ranch," the officer stated with a frown on his face. "Why do *you* have it?"

"I work for Big D," said Chacho from the back seat.

The officer pointed his flashlight in the direction of the voice. "What's your name?"

"Carlos Martinez. They call me Chacho."

"I know Big D," said the cop. "And some of his boys. I've heard your name too." The cop shined his flashlight again around the SUV. "So, where are you all going tonight?"

"To Big D's farm," Chacho replied.

The officer nodded. "Wait here." He went back to his car. In her rearview mirror, it looked to Mia as if he were making a phone call.

When the officer returned, he said, "I was going to impound the vehicle, but Big D says it's okay for you to have it."

Then he looked at Mia and smiled. "Young lady, next time you should carry your license."

"Yes, sir. I will." Mia returned his smile. "I promise."

"Follow me," said the officer. "Big D's ranch isn't far. I'll show you the turnoff. You can't see it from the road. He should show some pride like the other ranch owners and get himself a decent ranch gate entry sign with those artistic metal designs so everyone can find his place."

Mia heaved a sigh of relief as the officer walked away. Maybe him coming with them would help them get Bella back. Maybe the people at the farm would just hand Bella over with a cop there.

But wait a minute. Wouldn't the officer then wonder why they hadn't told him they were trying to rescue a kidnap victim at the farm right after he pulled them over? As soon as he got to the driver's side window? And then point out that they had the suspected kidnapper in the back seat and didn't say anything? She didn't know what to expect now and looked around her headrest at Zena, who simply shrugged. She put the SUV into gear and followed the officer's car to the Big D Ranch.

Zena said to Chacho, "When we get there, you just be ready to do whatever I tell you. Do you understand?"

Chacho chuckled. "When we get to Big D's ranch, maybe it will be me telling you what to do."

The last thing Mia saw in the rearview mirror before she turned right to follow the officer's car was Zena holding her big knife tightly against Chacho's throat.

CHAPTER 19

BELLA RAN, FEAR PUSHING her forward. The corn stalks were still a little fuzzy from whatever Nita had put in her lemonade, but she was able to keep her footing.

The cornstalks only came up to Bella's waist, so they didn't provide much cover for her from being seen by anyone at the farm. At the same time, some light from the moon filtered through some high clouds but not through the cornstalks. As a result, she couldn't see the ground clearly and continually stepped on rocks and weeds that injured her bare feet.

Bella stopped to put her heels back on and glanced back at the ranch. She had run straight up the row of corn and could see all the way back to the farm. If she could see them, then maybe they could see her. She needed to put a little more distance between them and herself. She turned to her left and started moving through the corn against the rows. The stalks of corn chafed her legs, but at least her feet were no longer being torn up by the rocks on the ground. But eventually the wobbly corn stalks and uneven ground got to her. She twisted an ankle and fell to her knees.

A light from a flashlight swung through the corn near her, so she dropped all the way to the ground, face down. She lay still to make sure not to rustle any of the corn stalks. She heard some shouting. She waited and listened. The shouting began to fade away until all she could hear was her heart thumping in her chest. As soon as the light disappeared, she stood up to start running again. This part of the cornfield was muddy, and mud now caked the front of her dress.

She ran until her feet and twisted ankle hurt too much to continue. Bella pulled her heels off again and held them as she pushed through row after row of corn, picking her path more carefully. Still dizzy from the drugs, she sat down to rest for a minute. *What now?* She stood up and looked around. No way they could see her now. If she could get to the road, maybe she could try to stop a car driving by and get some help.

With a newfound hope, Bella stood up again and started limping forward. Then she stopped and realized that she didn't know where the road was.

She had run without a destination and without knowing where she was going. Then, fearing she might be seen, she had changed direction and zig zagged through the cornfield. *Which way did I go? Where am I now?*

Bella sat back down on the ground, trying to get her bearings. She had no idea what to do. But she'd gotten this far and had to keep going.

Bella heard dogs barking. Those must be Big D's dogs. Nita said they were trained to follow only his orders. He must be coming for her. Her heart started pounding in her chest again.

Think, Bella, think! She stood up and looked in the direction of the barking dogs. She could see the outline of the farmhouse in the distance. And there was the barn. *Okay. Okay. What was the orientation of the road related to the farmhouse and barn?* She tried to remember the layout of the barn and farmhouse from when she had first arrived at the farm and got out of the van.

She looked again at the house and barn and compared it to what she remembered from when she first arrived and then thought she had a sense of where the road had to be. She lifted an arm up, tried to orient herself, and then let her arm down in the direction of her best guess for the road. *That way!*

The dogs were getting closer. They must have picked up her scent. She had to move fast. Bella ran as fast as she could toward the road, crashing through row after row of corn.

The barking of the dogs had receded momentarily. They must have followed her scent down the first row and then maybe kept going a bit further in that direction. But now, it sounded like they were getting closer again. They must have doubled back and picked up her scent again. Maybe she could stay down, keep quiet, and stay hidden from the men until they gave up looking for her. But the dogs? The dogs would find her.

Bella risked standing up slowly to look around. Yes, in the distance, the corn stalks were moving. They were catching up. She had to move. She turned in the other direction. She could see the end of the cornfield. That must be the road. She saw lights. A car. *Yes!* She turned and ran again as fast as she could toward the lights until she burst through the last row of corn and onto the street.

Limping badly from the damage to her feet, Bella walked down the middle of the road waving her arms at the oncoming vehicle. There would be no hitchhiking with a thumb up from the side of the road hoping that someone would see her in the dark and hoping they would stop. She decided that she would force them to stop. She stayed in the middle of the road as the vehicle approached with her arms held high.

Yes. Thank God! They were stopping. It was a King Cab. Just as they stopped, a barking dog broke through the corn thirty yards behind her. She hurried up to the passenger side of the truck, shouting, "Please let me in! Let me in!"

"Sure. Get in the back."

Bella grabbed the handle, opened the door, jumped in and started shouting. "Please get us out of here! Fast!"

But the driver didn't move an inch. Big D and his dogs had caught up to the truck now. Big D looked in the open passenger window of the truck.

"Got her, Boss," said the driver.

Bella looked at him in horror. She couldn't believe how close she had gotten. And now they were probably going to kill her or worse.

Big D yanked Bella's door open. He glared at her as the dogs bared their teeth and growled right behind him. "I should slit your throat right now and let my dogs tear you to pieces," he exploded.

Bella went very still. On the outside anyway. Her heart was racing at a hundred miles per hour and nightmare scenes of her being surrounded by vicious, bloodthirsty dogs flashed through her mind.

Big D said, "No. Not here. Not now. I should take your ass back to the farm so the other girls can see it. That'll put the fear of God into 'em."

She had a flashback of Eugenia with the chain around her neck, holding her flapping flesh onto her own face, blood gushing through her fingers. Her eyes dead. *Oh god, is this my end? Not like this. Please not like this!*

Big D was quiet for a minute. Then he tilted his hat back. "But I reckon I cain't do that neither cuz I just took a hunderd K from Mr. E., and I ain't gonna mess that up by killin' you."

Bella silently waited for him to reveal how he would punish her instead.

Big D gestured towards the driver. "Take her back. Lock her up until Nita can clean her up. We gotta fly her to the Gulf tomorrow to deliver her."

Bella was finally able to take a breath, amazed with how easy she'd gotten off. But that was tonight, tomorrow new horrors were waiting for her.

She had tried. Now all she could do was go back to hoping for a rescue before anything else could happen to her.

CHAPTER 20

MIA FOLLOWED CLOSE BEHIND the police car until it turned off the two-lane highway onto a hard-packed dirt road with corn growing on either side. About a half mile in were two large buildings with a well-lit area in between them. As they approached, she identified one of the buildings as a large farmhouse and the other as a huge barn.

Zena stuck the point of her big knife in Chacho's crotch. "You better be right that Bella's here," she threatened.

"Yeah, yeah. She's here. She's here."

The police car pulled up right in front of the big house and parked. The officer got out of his car but then just leaned back against the side of the car with his arms folded.

Zena said, "Mia, pull around by the side of the house and then park facing forward in case we need to leave fast."

"Got it. I'm learning a lot of tactical stuff from you on the fly."

"Stop here with the back of the SUV blocked from view by the house," Zena said. "I'm going to need to get in the back to get some of my gear."

Mia said, "I'll get out and see what's up. You watch Caca here and get your stuff."

"That's Chacho, you bitch." If looks could kill…

Zena backhanded Chacho in the face and left him dazed.

Mia got out of the SUV and walked towards the front door of the house where the officer was waiting. A tall man with a cowboy hat and boots walked out the front door and down the steps cautiously. Two other rough-looking young men followed him out of the house but stayed at the bottom of the steps.

The officer nodded at Mia. The tall man looked at Mia and said, "Shit, Nita, what the hell are you doing out here in the dark? And dressed like that?"

Mia didn't answer but continued walking up to the man.

"Nita's my sister," said Mia, offering one of her sweet smiles. "My twin sister."

"Well, I'll be a monkey's uncle. By the way, they call me Big D. Damn if you don't look just like her. I'm pleased to meet ya."

Mia pointed at her forehead. "Well, you can tell me from her by the scar on my forehead. My ex-husband tried to kill me." She paused and wondered if she should add what she was thinking, but then went ahead and said it anyway; she couldn't help herself. "But he's the one who's dead now."

Big D shook his head and squinted at Mia in the dim light. "Not so fast, missy. You sure you ain't Nita cause Nita has a scar on her forehead too. Said she got it in a car accident."

The officer interrupted them. "Hey, Big D, do you need me for anything? Want me to arrest them maybe?"

Mia shot a look at the cop. She thought he was on their side. Apparently not. *Dammit.* Being arrested was not an option right now. But neither was assaulting a cop.

"Thanks, Junior," said Big D. "Me and the boys'll take it from here. You should probably go. Best you not be here for this next part. By the way, thanks for calling ahead. I'll give you a little somethin' extra for your good work at the end of the month."

After watching the officer drive away, Big D turned to Mia. "So, little girl, what're you doin' way the fuck out here in the middle of the night?"

She had been nervous already. Now that the officer had left, her heart started to pound. She glanced back toward Zena who was standing by the passenger side of the SUV near the front. The vehicle blocked her from the waist down.

Mia steadied herself and thought about what she was there to do—find Bella. Besides, Zena had her back. Feeling a bit more confident, Mia turned back to Big D. "We came to get our friend, Bella."

Big D tipped his cowboy hat back with his index finger. "Well, you two girls wandered onto the wrong farm tonight." Then he looked over his shoulder and yelled, "Get 'em boys. Take 'em down. And then feed 'em to the hogs."

Mia understood they meant to kill her. She knew she must fight back or die. But her mind flashed back to her first kill. She had killed a man she didn't have to kill. She choked him to death and then crushed his nose into his skull. That was a total violation of the moral code she had held up to that point. Trust the law. Trust the system. Now, the burden of remorse from that first kill froze her feet to the ground.

Xtina had warned her she would face life and death. *Was this the moment?* Xtina had also promised her that she had the power to fight evil. *But where is that power now?*

As one of the men approached her, darkness in his eyes, adrenaline and necessity pushed doubt out of the way. Zena started to take a step forward around the front of the SUV, but Mia looked back at her and held a hand up. She knew she may not look like she was ready to fight in her little black dress, and she expected they would underestimate her. That would give her an advantage. Plus, she was wearing tactical heels that she had brought with her on the helicopter, and she still had a couple of Sally's special lipstick canisters. *They have no idea.*

Luckily, one man hung back, so she wouldn't have to contend with both at once. As the first man reached out to grab Mia by the neck with his right arm, she quickly side-stepped to her left, grabbed his wrist with both hands then quickly moved forward and twisted his arm upwards behind him, locked his elbow, and pushed it upwards from behind sending the man forward. She also stuck her left leg in front of his right foot removing any leverage he might otherwise have had to keep his balance. He fell hard to the ground moaning as she forced his arm upward behind him and twisted it with all her strength until she heard something pop.

From his knees, he looked up at her with anger flaming from his eyes. She hated those eyes and so did a hard side kick straight into his face. Her four-inch stiletto heel struck through his eye until her heel hit his face. She had to shake her leg hard to get him off her foot. His hands went to his eye as he fell backwards. He screamed in agony for a moment and then moaned and went limp.

Mia turned just as the second man was coming at her. He was bigger than the other one and coming fast. He was bent over getting ready to tackle her. Mia decided she did not want to wrestle with this one, so she clicked her heels together and released a serrated knife blade out the back of her right stiletto. As he approached, Mia ran towards him and jumped high. As he rushed forward beneath her, she pushed her stiletto through the right side of the man's neck. It tore a gaping hole in his carotid artery. He fell to the ground. Still alive, he stood up, turned, and lifted his arm as if to throw a punch at Mia. Suddenly, he dropped to his knees, clutching helplessly at the side of his throat as blood spurted between his fingers.

Big D had stopped at the front door of the farmhouse. Seeing his men down, he pulled out a pistol from the back of his pants and aimed it at Mia. "Let's see if you can kick this."

"Wait!" Zena shouted.

Big D turned to look at her as she pushed Chacho on his knees around the front of the SUV. Zena held him in front of her with one arm and the other pointing a gun at his head. "How about a trade? she shouted. "Chacho here for our friend Bella. Then we go. No more trouble."

Big D let his gun drop to his side for a minute and squinted into the dark. "Is that you, Chacho?"

A spark of hope. *Maybe we'll get out of this after all.*

"Yeah, Boss. I—"

"Shut up," shouted Big D. He pushed the top of his cowboy hat back with the tip of his pistol. "Ya know, you've done a lot of good work for me over the last cupla years." He paused and then added, "But damn, boy. You are dumb as a bag of rocks. You're the idiot that took that girl from Salt Lake. Sure, she is damn pretty, I'll give you that. But now look what's happened. They've come to look for her. That's why I told you not to just grab girls off the street. And now I got two good men down."

Big D walked down the stairs and took a couple of steps toward Chacho and Zena. Mia started to back away slowly and reached into the small cross shoulder purse. She wished she had finished her training so she could tell which of Sally's special lipstick cases was which in the dark.

Then Big D said to Chacho, "But I got no more use for you," and he quickly raised his pistol and shot Chacho right in the chest. Chacho fell to the ground in front of Zena, leaving her exposed. She raised her gun and pointed it at Big D.

But Big D lowered his pistol again. "Now, you two girls are pretty. I'd like to offer you a job. Stay here, and I'll put you to work with Bella."

Mia grabbed one of the lipstick cases and pulled it out of her purse. Her actions didn't go unnoticed. *Offer us a job here, huh? Murderous bastard son of a bitch!* Whatever doubts Mia had were fading fast.

"What're you doing?" Big D raised his pistol halfway.

Mia smiled. "Just putting on some lipstick."

Big D relaxed, and Mia opened the top of the lipstick. Then she said, "Look, Big D, we're going to give *you* one chance to give us Bella, or you and all your men are dead."

"I like your spirit," said Big D to Mia with a chuckle. "And you are a dead ringer for Nita, right down to her manner of talkin. But you're gonna lose this fight."

Mia quickly aimed the lipstick at Big D and fired, hitting him in the chest, releasing a bright flash of light and puff of gas. He raised his left arm over his eyes and stumbled backwards, coughing.

That must be the flash-bang mace spray.

Big D put two fingers up to his teeth and let out a loud whistle and then started firing his gun wildly as he staggered backwards toward the house.

Mia turned and ran back to Zena, who had taken cover behind the SUV.

Suddenly, the barn door flew open, and more men rushed outside just as Mia got to the SUV. They looked at Big D.

"Kill em," Big D shouted, coughing, as he stumbled through the front door of the house and slammed it behind him.

Mia and Zena ducked as the men raised weapons. Bullets peppered the SUV.

Zena turned to Mia. "I love the lipsticks, honey, but here, take a gun."

Mia picked up a large semiautomatic pistol. She was afraid it would be too hard for her to control and sorted through the other guns until she found a smaller one.

Zena said, "Stay down. I'm going to check to see how many there are." She flicked the switch on her AR-15 to full auto, reached the gun over the top of the SUV, and fired a short burst at the barn. Then she immediately stood up and sprayed bullets across the whole yard between the house and the barn and quickly ducked back down again.

"Six," said Zena, as she jammed a new magazine into the gun. "Well, now five. I got one of them. But one was headed around the back of the house. He'll be trying to flank us. Go and wait for him at the corner of the house."

"Got it, Sis," Mia said and scrambled away in the other direction.

Zena smiled at the term of endearment and bent down to peek under the car. She saw boots running toward the vehicle, swung her rifle under the car, and fired. The feet tripped, and a body fell. When she saw the guy's head hit the ground, she took aim and fired a bullet into his forehead.

"Make that four," shouted Zena.

Mia turned to Zena and held a finger to her lips. She was supposed to be hiding and waiting for the guy to come around the back of the house. She turned back just in time to see the guy two feet away with a raised handgun pointed at her face. *Oh shit, I should've been watching!*

Mia let her gun slip to the ground as she quickly crossed her arms in front of her. She used her left hand to strike the back of the man's right wrist just as her right hand grabbed the barrel of the gun and twisted it out of his hand.

A shot went off but flew wide to her left. The man moved toward Mia to grab her, but she leapt back to avoid him. His pistol was upside down in her hands, but somehow, she managed to point and fire it several times just as she landed on her back.

The man fell backward from the force of the bullets hitting his chest. "It's three now," Mia shouted back at Zena.

"Good job, Mia," Zena yelled back.

Mia and Zena exchanged gunfire with Big D's men for several minutes.

During a lull when everyone was reloading, Mia heard a loud motor start. She stuck her head out around the back of the house and saw a small airplane starting down what must be a runaway leading away from the back of the house.

She shouted, "Big D must be making a run for it. How do we stop him?"

Zena replied, "We can't chase him right now. We're pinned down. But once we get Bella, we'll figure out how to track him."

Zena peeked over the top of the SUV but had to duck quickly as a spray of bullets hit the side of the vehicle.

"Fuck this," she said. "Let's go get Bella."

Zena stood up and emptied another clip at Big D's men and then hustled to the back of the SUV and grabbed a grenade. Now that she had gained a clear idea of where Big D's men were barricaded, she pulled the pin and tossed it to where they were holed up.

Then she turned to Mia and yelled, "Stay down!"

The explosion rocked the yard. Zena shoved a new clip into her AR-15 and went charging into the smoke.

Mia steadied her pistol on her arm on the front of the SUV to back up Zena and waited for a chance to shoot.

Mia heard a bang. Then, *bang bang*. After a moment Zena came walking through the smoke back to the SUV.

"Are you okay?" asked Mia.

"Yes, sister," said Zena smiling. "Now let's reload and bust down the door to the house."

CHAPTER 21

NITA SAT NEXT TO BELLA at the kitchen table. She used a washcloth to wipe the mud off Bella's face, trying once again to make her ready for delivery to the billionaire who'd bought her at the auction. She was surprisingly calm; it frightened Bella. When they heard a gunshot outside, Nita stopped and tilted her chin up, eyes searching around as if she seemed to be listening. But then she resumed her task at hand—cleaning their asset for delivery. Bella noticed that apparently one gunshot didn't seem to bother Nita at all and assumed that this kind of thing must be normal.

"I'm going to have to put you in the shower," Nita said.

But suddenly, there were many gunshots, and Big D came bursting through the front door into the farmhouse. He slammed and bolted it behind him before stumbling toward the kitchen, rubbing his eyes with one hand while reaching out in front of him with the other.

"What the fuck is going on out there?" Nita yelled as she stood up from the table.

"Some people came for the new chick. For her." He pointed at Bella.

Bella's heart jumped with hope. Someone had come for her! But Big D's men were armed, and all those gunshots… Her heart sank again, afraid that whoever had come had already been killed.

"Sounds like a war zone out there," said Nita, putting down the comb. "How many guys are there?"

"Zero. Just two women, but damn, they can fight. Nita, get me some water and a clean towel." Big D wiped his eyes with his sleeve. "I can't see shit."

Nita ran to the kitchen and filled a bowl with water. She grabbed a kitchen towel and hurried back towards Big D.

"Two women?" Nita furrowed her eyebrows. "I saw Joe and Billie go out with you. Your guys couldn't handle them?"

"Well, baby, one of them is big, dressed in fatigues, and armed to the teeth. Geared up for war." Big D cupped water from the bowl in his hand and splashed water into his eyes before he continued. "But it was the other one, a small gal wearing a little black dress and high heels. *She's* the one who took down Joe and Billie."

"You're fucking kidding me." Nita stared at him with her mouth open.

"No. And she did it without a weapon."

Maybe my rescuers are okay.

"Fortunately, I had six other armed guys in the barn," Big D said. "They should finish 'em off."

Or maybe they're not.

"By the way, Nita," Big D added, "the little lady in the black dress looks like you. Said she's your twin sister."

Nita froze. "Mia? Mia's here? Why?"

Bella was shocked to hear Nita say Mia's name. *They're really sisters? Twins?* She could think of no two people more different. One all good. One despicably, horrifically evil.

"I told you. They said they came for the girl."

Nita asked, "But how did she find us?"

"Chacho brought 'em." Big D shook his head and rolled his eyes.

Nita went to the window to peek through the drapes to see if she could see Mia just as a hail of bullets careened off the front of the house.

"Motherfuckers," Big D yelled. "I'll grab my shotgun. You bring the girl and whatever else you need. We gotta git."

Nita ignored Big D and continued cleaning and fixing Bella like a visual merchandiser does for a display mannequin to showcase in the store's window. Bella was now her work of art. So, while Big D raved and ranted, Nita was determined to finish her masterpiece.

"She's not ready," she retorted in a distracted voice. "I have a clean set of clothes for her, but she's not cleaned up yet. Plus, I haven't finished her hair and makeup. I also need to pack a bag and—"

Big D interrupted Nita. "I gotta deliver her, or I lose that 100K, and maybe worse, I piss off Mr. E."

At the mention of Mr. E., Nita finally quit arguing and stuffed some clothes she had already gathered for Bella into a shopping bag.

Big D grabbed some keys out of a drawer. "I'm gonna start the plane."

"I'm not finished packing yet," Nita argued.

"Well, just grab her now and the clothes and come with me. You can clean her up on the way, or after we get there. Make sure you keep an eye on her for me, though. Gotta get her down to the Gulf tomorrow. And don't worry. We'll be arriving early. I'll buy you some clothes for her or whatever else you need. Come on! Let's go."

Bella was determined not to let that happen. But before she even started fighting, something occurred to Nita.

"Wait. What about the other girls here? There's no one watching them."

"Hell, I don't know when we'll be back. Just put your key on the counter. I've got six trained security guys out there. They'll watch the other girls once they take care of business."

More gunfire exploded like a string of firecrackers out front. "Gonna need to go out the back," said Big D.

With the shopping bag hanging on her right shoulder, Nita grabbed a pistol from inside a cabinet and took a hold of Bella's arm with her left hand.

Bella jerked away. She had to stay. Mia and someone else had come for her. She knew there was a good chance that they had already been killed, but she was choosing to believe that they were still alive. There was no way she was going to leave with Nita and Big D, especially not now.

Nita screamed at her and gave her one of her terrifying stares. "We're gonna go now! I've been going easy on you since your little escape attempt but that's only for the buyer. I'm sure he'll understand if I have to use some force to get you to him."

Bella still wouldn't budge. They were right outside. This was her last chance.

Nita put down her gun and undid the sheath on her leg. Then she pulled out her serrated hunting knife. She grabbed Bella by the throat and pressed the tip of the blade into Bella's cheek.

"So, you want to join Eugenia?"

Bella shuddered. "No! I'll go with you."

Nita relaxed a bit and warily drew her knife slowly away from Bella's face. Seeing her chance, Bella quickly crossed her hands in front of her and knocked the knife out of Nita's grasp.

Bella then jumped toward the gun Nita had placed on the table. She saw Nita lunging as well, but Bella got to the gun first. She grabbed it and turned it toward Nita, trying to make sure she was holding it right to fire it, but Nita also grabbed at the gun before Bella could fire it and tried to wrestle it away. Just as the two women crashed to the floor together, the gun came loose, and Big D picked it up.

"Get up," he shouted at Bella. As she got to her knees, he hooked his left arm around her throat and lifted her off the floor until her feet dangled. She could barely breathe. "You don't get it, you dumb little bitch. I'll kill you right now."

Bella remained silent. Not only was she fighting to breathe, but she knew that Big D didn't want to kill her. He needed to deliver her to the man who bought her so he could collect his $100,000. She tried to kick at Big D while he held her.

Nita dragged herself to her feet. "She doesn't seem to be worried about her own safety. But what about her friends? Her family? Can you get to them?"

"Hell yeah. Good idea." Big D lowered Bella to the floor but kept his arm around her neck.

Finally, she could breathe.

"Listen, you little cunt! We know where you live. I've got cops on the payroll, and we can find your family. And I've got some of the meanest motherfuckers you ever seen working for me who won't blink at cutting your father's head off and gang-raping your mother and then torturing her to death. I'll do it too if you don't stop fighting me."

Bella stopped kicking. Hearing the threats against her family stopped her heart for a minute. She went limp and started crying. Big D loosened his grip on her and let her slide down until her feet hit the floor. Bella whimpered.

"C'mon Nita. Grab her and let's go. Now!"

Nita grabbed Bella by the arm and started dragging her towards the back door. Bella stumbled along behind her listlessly until they got to the door, her heart shattered.

Bella suddenly remembered her father talking about how these kinds of guys would say anything to get their victims to cooperate. She wasn't one of the illegal immigrant girls, they had no hold on her family. He was probably lying to her, and she knew her parents would want her to at least try.

She dug her heels in and ripped her arm free from Nita and turned to run to the front door.

"Fuck it," shouted Big D. He took a quick step toward Bella and hooked his arm around her throat again. Bella pulled at his arm, but he was too strong. She tried to gasp in a breath, but he tightened his grip. She fought until her face prickled and everything got foggy. Finally, she lost consciousness.

Big D threw her small frame over his shoulder and picked up a bag with his free hand. "Let's get to the plane!"

Big D yanked open the door to the plane and heaved Bella through it. Her knee scraped against the metal floor, and then she hit her ribs against one of the two back seats. That woke her up, but she lay dazed bent over the seat.

"Listen, your friends are dead now," Big D shouted as he scrambled into the pilot's seat. "Get into that seat and buckle up," he shouted over his shoulder.

The plane's engine fired up just as Bella sat up and got her arms around the passenger's seat. Big D pulled out a knob from the dashboard, and the plane started moving. The plane jerked forward, and Bella struggled to get into her seat. The plane slowly gained speed, and they moved down the bumpy runway faster and faster.

An explosion reverberated on the other side of the house as the plane continued to speed down the runway. The loud noise roused Bella from her stupor.

Mia, she thought, devastated.

Nita pulled the seat belt over her shoulders and clicked them into the buckle. "Hold on," she shouted at Bella over the roar of the engine.

Nervous, Bella dragged herself onto her own seat and felt around her in the dark until she got hold of the seat belt and figured out how to connect it. She looked back up front and saw Big D pull back on the handles of the steering column until the plane lifted off and roared up into the dark night sky.

Once in the air, Big D yelled over the noise to tell Nita to dial Mr. E.'s private number. "Call it now while we're still low enough to get cellular service."

Bella couldn't believe that this was really it. Mia had failed. This was her new reality. She felt herself go numb.

As soon as someone answered, Nita enunciated, "It's Big D calling for Mr. E."

"He's not available at the moment," stated the person on the other end of the call.

Big D held the phone away from his face and made a growling sound. Then he said, "Tell him we have the item he requested, and that we're on our way."

As the plane sped upwards into the night, leaving behind Mia and any chance of rescue, Bella couldn't help but think that now, after all her fighting, she was also finally leaving behind her old life—her friends, family, and all her hopes and dreams. She didn't dare imagine what her new life would require her to do to stay alive. And she didn't try to wipe the tears that started running down her face.

CHAPTER 22

ZENA HAMMERED HER BOOT into the front door of the farm-house. Two times. Three times. "Shit. This door's solid, and it must have a big dead bolt too."

"I can help." Mia reached into her little purse and pulled out some more lipstick canisters. How about this one?"

"No, that's a spider web. Very sticky. But won't open the door." She gave Mia a half-smile.

"Oops," Mia said. "I hope one of these has that, what did Sally call it, X4?"

"It's C4," Zena corrected. "Let me see." She examined the three canisters. "Yes, it's this one." She pulled it out from the other two.

"Great. Show me what to do, and I'll—"

"I don't have time to explain right now. Just watch." Zena grabbed a tab and pulled it, unraveling a layer of tape from the case. "This is adhesive to keep it in place." Then she popped open the top of the lipstick case. "Here's the explosive."

"Hey," Mia said. "I've been carrying that around while I've been fighting and flipping around. I could have blown us up."

Zena chuckled. "No, you have to twist it to push the explosive up into the fuse. Then you push down on the top of the cap and count to ten. Only then does it explode. Watch this."

She twisted the lipstick case to insert the C4 into the fuse and pressed the case into the crack a couple of inches above the door handle. Then she looked at Mia. "Ready, set, go!" she exclaimed and pushed the button on the top of the case.

They ran all the way to the SUV and hid behind it.

Blam!

Mia peeked out and saw that the front door had swung open.

"Grab a gun," Zena said, "and follow me." She ran to the door with Mia right behind her. When she reached the threshold, she held her hand up to signal for Mia to stop. "Let's clear the upstairs first," Zena suggested.

"But Chacho said Bella was being held in the basement," Mia reminded her.

"We need to clear the main floor before we check the basement. There might be security guys just waiting to ambush us," answered Zena. "If we don't take care of them, then we'll be putting Bella and whoever else is in the basement in danger. Be careful. I'll go first." She glanced at Mia and then straight up the stairs. "Ready?"

Mia nodded.

"Let's go," whispered Zena as she ran through the front door moving quickly through the living room and then checking behind the kitchen counter.

"Clear," noted Zena. "Now let's check the other rooms. You watch our backs. Make sure no one sneaks up on us from behind."

Zena pointed her AR-15 in front of her and slowly started down the hallway. At the first door, she checked the knob, and Mia saw it twist in her hand. She glanced at Mia and nodded. Zena then pushed the door open, took a quick look inside, and then turned back against the wall to the side of the door. After a second, Zena turned and went back into the room.

Mia caught herself peering into the room to watch Zena and totally forgot that she was supposed to be keeping a lookout behind them too. She spun around quickly, saw that it was clear, and let out a big sigh of relief.

In a minute, Zena came back out. "Clear," she whispered.

Zena and Mia continued that way until they got to a bedroom at the far end of the house. There, they found a girl cowering in a corner on the far side of a dresser.

"It's okay," Zena said, lowering her rifle. "We're here to help."

"I heard the explosions and the bullets," said the girl. "So, I hid." But she didn't budge from where she was crouched.

Mia approached her slowly. "What's your name, honey?"

"They call me Missy," the girl said softly. "My name's Elizabeth."

Mia asked, "Where is everyone? Why are you up here all alone?"

"Billie and Joe brought me up from downstairs to fuck me. I did them both good, so they let me stay up here."

Zena stared intently at the girl. "Who are Billy and Joe? And where are they now?" She stepped out of the room to check the hallway.

"They're two of Big D's security guys. I guess someone came to the house. Big D called them to go outside with him. I don't know where they're at now."

"We know," said Zena. "They tried to fuck with my friend Mia here. They won't be coming back. But where is everyone else? Where's Big D?"

"I don't know," Missy answered. "It's a big house. I heard Big D yelling at Nita that they had to go. After that, I didn't hear anyone in the house. But I think I heard the plane take off."

Mia asked, "Where're all the girls? Chacho said the girls are being held downstairs."

"Yeah," said Missy. "But it's locked."

"Show us," Mia prodded.

Missy buttoned her shirt and led Mia and Zena to the kitchen. She pointed to a door with a metal frame and sensor to the side. "There," she pointed. "That's the door."

Zena walked over to the sensor and inspected it. "Electronic lock. It uses a key card, which we don't have."

She stepped back. Then she ran at the door and kicked it. It only shuddered but held. "Damn metal frame," she cursed under her breath.

Mia added, "And I'm fresh out of exploding lipstick."

"Maybe there's an axe in the barn," Zena offered. "We can use it to cut right through the middle of the door."

"I'll go and see," Mia offered.

But before she could leave, a voice on the other side of the locked door yelled, "Help!"

Zena pressed her ear against the door. "Who's there? What's your name?"

"Felicia."

"Felicia, we've come to help," Zena shouted at the door. "We're looking for a young girl named Bella."

"Oh my god," Felicia responded. "They took Bella."

Mia pushed her face close to the door. "Took her where? Where did they go?"

"I don't know," said Felicia. "All I know is that they sold her to a rich guy and said they had to fly her to the Gulf."

Mia's heart sank. *Sold her? Sold Bella?* "Where on the Gulf?"

"I'm sorry," Felicia shouted. "That's all I know."

After a pause, Felicia asked, "Hey, can you open the door? Help us get out of here?"

"I don't know," Zena responded. "We're gonna try."

Mia put her hand on Zena's shoulder. "But we've got to go get Bella."

"Go where? We don't know where they went."

"I know, but…" Mia's voice trailed off, realizing Zena was right. In the meantime, they could help these girls. And one of them may know something more about where Bella was taken.

"Felicia," Mia said, "the door looks like it needs an electronic key to open it. Do you know where we can find it?"

"Nita keeps a fob on a chain around her neck," Felicia responded.

Mia briefly closed her eyes at the sound of her sister's name. "Okay. Where's Nita?"

"I think she left with Big D and Bella."

Zena had been focused on trying to open the lock. "Mia, I'm calling Sally. Go look for an axe in the barn."

Missy had retreated quietly into a corner of the kitchen but now spoke. "There are girls in the barn too."

"What are they doing in the barn?" asked Mia.

"Lot of things," said Missy. "Some are there for video shoots. Big D sells movies. Animal lovers. Farm girls. Titles like that. Big D sells them online."

"How do you know all this?" Mia asked.

"I got in trouble for hiding tips. And there's a shed out back too. I've never been in there though."

Zena said, "Hold off a sec, Mia. If some girls are out there, more security might be out there too. Let's call Sally and then go sweep the barn together."

As soon as the line connected, Zena put her phone on speaker.

Sally asked, "What's your sitrep?"

Zena answered, "Bella's gone. We tracked the pendant. Someone had taken it from Bella, but we…persuaded him to assist us, and he led us to a farm where Bella was being held until a few minutes ago. We repelled an ambush. Witnesses reported that a plane left our location and Bella was on it. Heading unknown except to somewhere on the Gulf Coast."

"*On the Gulf Coast* could mean anywhere from Texas to Florida," Sally said, "and that's not even counting the coast of Mexico itself."

Zena looked at Mia and sighed heavily. After a pause, Sally continued, "Zena, I'll lock onto your phone signal to establish a starting point and try to track the plane via satellite. I should be able to find it because it will probably be one of the only planes not flying from an airport. I'll try to determine its heading and estimate its destination. Plus, a small plane doesn't have the range to make it to Mexico. That narrows the search considerably. I'll let you know as soon as I have a destination."

"Roger that," said Zena.

Sally said, "If a plane took off from where you are, a plane can land there too. I'll send you a fast ride. Sit tight for now." She then hung up.

Zena looked at Mia. "We have some time. Let's take advantage of it and go sweep the barn and see if we can find the other girls and an axe or something."

"What's this?" asked Missy. She held up a chain with a round blue fob on the end.

Mia grabbed it and touched the box on the side of the locked door. It clicked.

Felicia pushed it open and burst through the door with a look of relief and a huge grin. "Thank you! Thank you," she gushed at Zena. Then she turned to Mia and her eyes popped open wide. "No!" She jumped back and hit the wall behind her awkwardly. "Nita!"

Mia held both hands up in front of her. "No, no. I'm not Nita. I'm her sister. Her twin sister."

Felicia regained her balance, and her face started to relax, but she still looked doubtful and fearful.

"My name's Mia."

Felicia seemed to calm down.

Some other girls started coming up the stairs behind Felicia. All were young. Some seemed frightened while some looked relieved.

"Do you have somewhere you can go?" Mia asked.

"Can't I stay here?" asked one of the girls.

Mia answered, "This is not a good place to be right now. Don't you have family somewhere?"

"Yes," said the girl. "I have family, but I ran away from there because—"

Mia interjected, "Well, we know somewhere you can stay if you don't have anywhere else to go."

Felicia, still somewhat skeptical, asked, "What about Big D's men? We can't just go. They'll stop us."

"We've taken down eight of them," Zena responded.

"There are sometimes more than that here at the farm," Felicia stated. "None of the girls will dare leave if they think they'll be caught. Some girls have been killed for running. Others, after they were punished, wished they had been."

Zena glanced at the girls. "We'll go check the barn and the shed. Wait here."

Mia and Zena jogged over to the barn. After inspecting the open areas, they started checking some enclosed pens that ran the length of the wall.

The first one just had a horse. He whinnied and started to raise up when Zena entered his pen.

"Calm down, big boy," said Zena softly, patting the horse on the shoulder until he started to relax. "Good boy."

In the next stall, they found a girl on a dirty mattress chained to the wall. After explaining what she and Zena were doing there, Mia asked, "Do you have any idea where the key is to these chains so we can get you out of here?"

The girl replied, "There's more than one. Some of Big D's guys carry one. There may be some in the office."

"I've got this," said Zena. "I carry a cuff key on my gear. These keys are usually universal, so it should work."

The key slid right into the keyhole and quickly unlocked the girl's handcuff. "You can go now," said Zena. "Maybe back to the house."

"Not yet," said the girl. "They brought a friend of mine to the barn at the same time they brought me. Please see if you can find her. But be careful. I think I heard some guys talking after the shooting started. They may still be around here somewhere."

Zena nodded. "Okay, wait here for a minute. We'll be back."

Mia and Zena crept forward, carefully checking all the hidden areas they could find. They heard a dog bark ahead. In the last stall at the back of the barn, they opened the door and saw a girl bent over a barrel naked and tied with rope. Two big dogs were in there with her. One of them was sniffing her.

The other dog bared its teeth, growled, and crouched to jump at Zena. A quick burst of bullets knocked him backwards onto the floor. He rolled over and took a few deep breaths before going quiet.

The second dog whined and backed into a corner. Zena walked up to the side of the dog and said, "Bad doggie" and then shooed it out the door. Zena used her big knife to cut the girl loose.

"Oh my god! Thank you," exclaimed the girl.

"You're free to go," said Zena. "There's another girl that was chained up in a stall at the other end of the barn. We got her loose, but she wouldn't leave without you. We told her to wait there so that we could check to see if any of Big D's guys were out here. I think we've cleared the barn now. It seems safe for you two to go."

"No, wait," said the girl. "The two who tied me up may still be here. When they saw Big D's plane leave, one of them said, 'Let's have some fun before we go." After tying me up with the dogs, they took another girl to the shed. I think they meant to hurt her. She refused to fuck one of them." She looked back and forth at Zena and Mia; neither reacted to her comment. "That's the worst sin you can commit here," she explained.

Zena said to Mia, "Okay. Let's go check out the shed."

"Please hurry," said the girl. "I think I heard her screaming. I'll wait here. I need to know if she's okay."

Mia and Zena walked the short distance to the barn door and looked toward the shed about thirty yards away. They slipped out the door and quietly jogged to the shed.

"Look. The door's ajar," Mia whispered to Zena. "Finally, an open door."

Then they heard a scream.

"Let's go," said Zena as she quickly moved through the door and ran straight into one guy who was just inside the door. He was about to warn the other one, but Zena gave him a hard pop on the cheek with the butt of her rifle, knocking him out.

Mia saw a naked girl with her hands high over her head and bleeding in several places. She looked up and saw that the rope holding her was looped over the ceiling truss. The second man had his arm cocked and ready to release a whip.

Mia leapt just in time to grab the whip. She gave the guy a short side kick to the knee, knocking him off balance. Mia jumped onto his back and rode him to the ground and then grabbed the whip and wrapped it around his ankles and made a knot. When he tried to roll over, she scooted her weight up toward his shoulders and pressed her fingers against the carotid arteries on each side of his neck until he passed out. Then she pulled his feet up behind him and used part of the whip to tie his hands behind his back and wrapped the rest of it around the ankles and knotted it.

Zena said, "Where did you learn that? That's not part of The Sisterhood's training."

Mia smiled. "It's my version of the hog tie technique. I saw it in a rodeo once."

"Well, Yippee Ki Yay, sister." Zena grinned and then reached up to cut the rope holding the girl. She came down, whimpering. Zena pulled a small med kit from a deep pocket on the side of her tactical pants. "These medicated towelettes will help a little bit until we can get you back to the house."

"Thank you so much," said the girl, wincing as Zena wiped the wounds on her back.

Zena added, "After that, you can call the police."

The girl hesitated before asking, "Do we have to call the police?"

Mia and Zena looked at each other. Mia had a guess as to why the girl may not want to call the police but decided to make sure. "Why would you not want to call the police?" she asked.

The girl looked at the two guys lying on the ground, temporarily disabled. "Because I want some payback." She spat in their direction.

Mia pulled Zena aside. "The officer who led us here seemed to be on Big D's payroll. So going to the police may be a bad idea anyway. What do you think we should do?"

Zena replied, "You know what I would do."

Mia looked around the toolshed that held, well, tools—hammers, saws, even an axe.

The bleeding girl followed Mia's gaze and then locked eyes with her. Mia saw the pain on her face and sensed her anger.

Mia turned to Zena. "I think we should probably go." She opened the door just in time to see the other two girls approaching.

"She's okay," Mia told them. She looked back at the bloody naked girl shuddering from the cold or from shock or both. "Well, she's not okay, but she is alive."

As soon as the other two girls entered, the bloody girl nodded at Mia and Zena. "They agreed not to call the police. I want some revenge. Do you two want to help?"

She met Mia's eyes once more. Undoubtedly, her intentions were bad.

Mia turned to Zena and nodded her head toward the door. Zena glanced at the girl and exited the shed with Mia right behind her.

CHAPTER 23

WHATEVER HOPE BELLA had been holding onto had been ripped from her fingers when the aircraft lifted off from the farm. She had no idea if Mia had survived the standoff with Big D's men, and even if she did, Bella was nowhere near the pendant now. She wasn't even sure what her destination was, but either way she didn't know how Mia or the cops, for that matter, would be able to track her now. The idea of escape seemed so far out of reach that she didn't even entertain it anymore. All she could do now was learn to survive Big D, Nita, and whoever this Mr. E was.

She was glad, at least, to have been able to change from her little red dress into a sweat suit, but cold air swirled around her as Big D pulled the little plane further and further up into the dark night and it didn't do much to keep her warm.

Luckily Nita was bothered by it too. "Isn't there any heater on this thing?"

"Yeah, yeah, of course. Give me a fuckin' minute," Big D shouted. "I'm trying to fly the goddamn plane. The controls are more sophisticated on this new Cessna than my old crop duster. I'll fire up the heating system in a minute."

Big D glanced to his right and could see Nita pouting. For all his gruffness and evil, it seemed to Bella that he cared for Nita. His voice softened. "There's some Mylar blankets in the emergency kit if you want."

The plane banked and climbed. Bella tried to orient herself. She was hoping to figure out which direction the plane was headed. But in the dark, she had no idea. She craned her neck around and thought she spotted a parachute, not that she would know how to use it. She had seen movies, though. If she could get to the parachute, she figured she could put it on and there would be a cord to pull to get the chute open. But if she didn't figure out how to use the parachute in the dark on the way down—*no way. Forget it.*

She closed her eyes, feeling hopeless. She thought about her mother and father, missing them in a way she hadn't since she was just a little kid. She remembered one of the phrases her dad always used to repeat before her karate tournaments. "You can't beat someone who never gives up." She felt another tear slip down her cheek. *But how do I keep going, Daddy?*

After a while climbing, the plane settled in and leveled out.

Big D said to Nita, "There's a little storage cabinet aft. See if any beer's been left in it."

"What do you mean aft?" asked Nita.

"In the back, dammit," Big D snapped.

"Jesus. Calm the fuck down." Nita shot him a scowl.

"Sorry, Baby."

Nita got up to find the storage cabinet. After she returned with two beers and handed him one, she asked, "So where are we going?" She pulled off the tab from her can.

Bella listened intently but stayed extremely still and quiet.

"We're going to the beach, baby. To the Gulf of Mexico."

Nita asked, "But don't we have to file a flight plan or get permission to land or something?"

Big D looked at Nita for a moment. "No, Baby. We're not going to the fucking airport." He tilted his head at Bella. "I don't want to take this girl through fucking TSA security, goddammit."

"Then where?" asked Nita, taking a sip of her beer.

"Don't you worry your sweet little head about that, Baby. Mr. E. and I have it worked out. He has a house on the coast. There's a private landing strip nearby outside of where Air Traffic Control monitors. We can land there and deliver whatsername to Mr. E."

Bella wrapped the mylar blanket that Nita had given her around herself and closed her eyes. She was so tired. She couldn't remember ever being so completely exhausted. She didn't have a watch, but she thought it must be well past midnight. She hadn't slept at all since she'd arrived at the farm. The heat had come on, and the steady drone of the plane lulled her to sleep.

• • •

Bella woke up to a dark sky that was giving way to a golden light that glowed from the horizon. They were flying much lower than any planes she had ever flown in.

Big D was holding the plane's steering column with one hand and his phone with the other.

"I know I'm early," Big D shouted into his phone over the roar of the engines. "Did you ask why?"

He paused. Bella didn't know who he was speaking to because she could only hear Big D's side of the conversation.

Big D then announced, "I just need to find a nice place on the beach. I need a vacation."

He glanced over at Nita, who was giving him a thumbs up.

He nodded back, and said, "I'm headed to the usual place. Can you send a car?"

Big D's face was scrunched into a big frown. Bella wasn't sure if he was just struggling to hear over the noise or he was upset by bad news. She focused her attention on listening for any clues as to where they were going.

"Got it. A boat. Roger that. Then we wait at your Smith Point place until you arrive?"

Bella committed the name Smith Point to memory. More to tell someone just in case she could find a phone or someone who would help her.

After Big D disconnected his call and put his cell back in his shirt pocket, he put his headphones back on. After a minute, he put his hand to one side of his headphones and held it close to his ear. Next, he appeared to check his instruments. Suddenly, he banked left.

"Where are we going now?" asked Nita.

Bella hoped that Nita would keep asking questions so that Bella could keep gathering information on where she was headed.

"Don't worry, Baby, we're still going to the same place," replied Big D. "We're going to get a beautiful suite in a luxury hotel on the beach and have pretty girls bring us drinks with umbrellas."

Nita smiled and put her fingertips on her left hand to her lips and then touched Big D's lips with them. Bella marveled at Nita's demonstration of affection. It was such a shocking contrast to the violence she knew Nita to be capable of.

Big D said, "But we're not going to the beach just yet. We're approaching an airport where there's lots of plane traffic and I'm just flying around it."

After about five minutes, Big D banked and started a long wide turn to the right. Soon after, he headed downward. Bella noted everything she saw—water ahead, which must be the ocean, and an inland bay connecting to the ocean. But this was no airport, not even so much as a runway. She sat straight up in her seat and checked her seatbelt.

After a long curving turn, Big D straightened the plane and headed down to a grassy area. Bella looked out the front window. A strip of land that looked like a road laid ahead. *It must be a runway,* she thought.

Big D landed and taxied the plane to the far edge of the landing strip. "Look," he said, pointing, "There's a boat over there."

Bella followed Big D's pointing finger to a sleek motorboat. But Big D had steered away from the bay. Bella craned her neck and saw a canal of some sort that snaked inland from the bay.

"Let's go," said Big D after he brought the plane to a stop.

Nita grabbed the bag she had brought with her and grabbed Bella's arm roughly. They walked over to the waiting boat.

Bella observed the boat as they approached it. Two men were on the boat. A short and stocky one seemed preoccupied with keeping the boat tethered to a tall wooden post at the edge of the grassy landing strip. The other man was tall and dark with a short beard and long, dark hair. His attention was focused entirely on Bella. She looked away from him as they neared the boat.

Once they were all aboard, the stocky man started the engine and motored slowly down the canal until it entered the bay. The boat picked up speed and raced down the coast until they slowed again and puttered up slowly to a dock near a large house. Again, Bella was grateful to be in the sweat suit because of the wind that enveloped her on the ride.

Nita took Bella by the arm. "Come with me," as the three of them climbed out of the boat and walked down a long sidewalk to the house.

Once inside, a woman dressed as a housekeeper greeted them. "Welcome," she said. She motioned to an oversized office with French doors to the side of the foyer. "You can wait in there. Mr. E's representatives will arrive soon. In the meantime, can I get you something? Food? A drink?"

Big D answered, "Both."

The woman gave a short nod and backed away quickly before leaving them alone.

Bella said to Nita, "I need to use the restroom."

"Me too," Nita said. She gave Bella a look before saying, "You're also gonna need a shower before we turn you over to him."

Bella had not bathed since she was taken about a day and a half ago. She had fought, she had run, and she had sweated from sheer fear. She had avoided taking her clothes off at the farm when she could out of fear of what might happen to her if she did.

When she got in the bathroom, Bella peeled off her fleece top and dropped her sweatpants to the bathroom floor and stepped out of them. She now realized that she never had found her underwear after she'd run.

She turned the shower on and reached her hand out into the water until it was warm enough. She stepped into the large, tiled enclosure covered with small stones and stood directly under the showerhead. The warm water started to rinse the cornfield's dirt out of her hair as well as the farm scent from her body. Bella closed her eyes and enjoyed the warm water on her skin. She was grateful to finally have a moment to herself.

It was short lived. She suddenly felt like she wasn't alone. She looked over her shoulder and saw Nita standing at the shower door. Naked. She opened the door and stepped into the shower, then softly touched Bella's back before Bella could even turn around. Bella pulled away instinctively. Nita paused for a moment, then touched her again.

Bella was in absolute shock, of all the things she'd feared Nita doing to her, this was not one of the things she had been actively worried about. She had no idea what to do. Her options were slim. She could probably get away from Nita despite her being cornered in the shower due to the slipperiness of the shower and the ground. But after that, she didn't have anywhere to go. She couldn't just run naked into the house full of guards and other men. No matter what she did, someone would rape her. And if she resisted Nita, she was sure she'd get worse than that later. She wondered if Nita did this to a lot of the girls.

She was so tired. Nita ran her hands up and down Bella's back.

Fighting wasn't an option. But the side of Nita that Bella had seen on the plane with Big D led her to believe that there was some shred of humanity in her.

Her voice shaky, Bella mustered up the courage to say, "Please, Nita, I don't want—"

Nita reached around and caressed Bella's breasts before she could even get a full sentence out. Bella trembled, a lump forming in her throat. Nita pinched one of Bella's nipples.

Bella went numb. All she could do was disassociate as Nita continued to touch her body.

Finally, Nita reached between Bella's legs. Bella squeezed her thighs together tightly.

Nita paused for a moment. Then she grabbed Bella by the hair and twisted Bella's head to face her. Nita's grim glare reminded Bella of Nita's harsh treatment of the girls when she was angry. Eugenia's face flashed in her memory. Then Nita's mouth curled into a twisted smile. "You may be going to Mr. E, but you'll be mine before you're his."

Bella was completely paralyzed, numb. Tears started flowing down her cheeks, mixing in with the shower water. She closed her eyes and prayed that it would be over soon.

CHAPTER 24

BELLA SAT AT THE CORNER of a long, shiny wooden table in the main dining room that was perfectly centered under an elaborate crystal chandelier. Nita was at the table too. Bella avoided her gaze and tried to push the memory of the shower out of her mind. But she couldn't. She wished she could get farther away from Nita. *And far away from here.*

A silver centerpiece overflowed with a variety of fresh fruit. Bella's intricately painted plate sat on an embroidered cloth placemat and was surrounded by a variety of forks, knives and spoons lined up on either side of her plate—more than Bella had ever seen. *Is this my new normal?*

While they waited for lunch to be served, Big D walked over to the table and asked Nita if Bella was cleaned up enough to send to Mr. E., Nita smiled and replied, "Yes, I made sure she's clean." Then she winked at Bella and added, "Everywhere."

Then Big D said he had already eaten and was tired from flying all night and was going to lie down in the bedroom to rest until Mr. E's men arrived. Bella noted that another man, an athletic Hispanic man with a short beard who didn't seem to speak to anyone, stood inside the front door. He had a bulge under his sport coat. Bella thought it odd that he was wearing a jacket at all, given how warm it was in the house, and speculated that the bulge was probably a gun, and that the man probably worked security for the house, and that if she made any move to escape, that he would stop her. As she stared at him, he turned and met her gaze. His icy glare confirmed her assumption, again without him uttering a sound.

Nita attempted to engage in small talk with Bella, as if what she'd just done had somehow made them friends. "I can't wait to eat something, how about you?" "Nice house, right?" "I wonder how big the boat is." "Wish I could go with you. Wouldn't that be fun?" Bella stared at her plate blankly, barely processing Nita's words.

Soon, the housekeeper brought serving dishes loaded with hot baked chicken, mixed vegetables and steamed mashed potatoes with gravy. The food was simple, but delicious, perhaps in part because Bella was starving. She cleaned her plate without speaking a word, except to quietly express thanks to the housekeeper when she had finished. Afterward, Nita directed Bella to sit in a big chair facing the patio and wait.

Bella sat in the chair and pulled her legs up against her chest. With nothing to do but wait, she took in her surroundings. The house was two stories tall. Chandeliers hung from the first-floor high ceilings. Once she memorized the inside, she turned to stare through the large French doors that led to a patio filled with exotic tropical plants.

As Bella waited, she wondered what was going to happen to her. She had been sold to the man on the yacht. Nita told her she was lucky, that she would have the finest things and she would see beautiful places. But all Bella could think about was what he and his friends were going to do to her.

Just two days earlier, Bella's thoughts of her future had been focused on her senior year in high school. Maybe she would be president of her class. Subsequently, she would go to college. She wanted to become a doctor and maybe meet a man who would treat her like the queen her father had always insisted she was. *My parents were so proud of me,* she thought. *But now what? Will they only suffer in silent sadness every time they think of me, not knowing what happened to me?* Part of her was glad that they wouldn't have to know all the horrid details.

Bella wiped a tear from her eye and looked out past the patio. She noticed that the elegant French doors before her were stained dark brown and closed in the middle. She counted ten glass panes on each side. Out in the distance was the bay. And boats. And maybe…the possibility of escape. The possibility of freedom. But from this chair, surrounded by the people in this house, the dark frames crisscrossing the two doors looked like the bars on a jail cell.

CHAPTER 25

HAVING RETURNED to the farmhouse after clearing the barn of Big D's remaining security team, Mia and Zena huddled in the kitchen, assessing their situation. Bella was gone. In an airplane they couldn't follow. To a place unknown.

"You want my assessment?" Mia asked Zena. "Hopeless. We'd need a miracle now."

"I haven't seen you call Frank," said Zena. "When are you going to give him an update?"

Mia paused, unsure of how to answer. "How can I tell him we failed? I, I… I don't think I can form those words with my mouth. How could I ever look him in the eye again, knowing that I lost her?"

Sighing, Zena said, "Let's call Sally. She might have an idea."

Zena hit the one-touch communication button and waited. Sally must have never stopped monitoring the phone. She picked it up right away. Zena put it on speaker.

"Sally, as we reported before, we lost Bella. They took her in the plane that took off from the farm. So, do you think you can track that plane? If not, I don't know what else we can do."

"I think so," said Sally. "I've borrowed a satellite."

Zena's eyes widened in surprise. "A satellite? From whom? How?"

"It's a military satellite, so all I can tell you is 'Don't ask, don't tell.'"

Zena and Sally shared a chuckle before Sally finished giving her the information she had discovered. "The plane left some twenty minutes before I was able to start my search, so I've had to make some assumptions.

For example, I'm assuming the plane has traveled in a straight line away from the farm. It's a small plane, so it's probably flying at around 150 miles per hour. In twenty minutes, it would have traveled about fifty miles from the farm, so I'm looking for small planes on a flight path straight from the farm at about that distance. That has helped me distinguish other planes that are on standard flight paths between one airport and another."

Zena exhaled loudly. "Still, that's a lot of area to cover."

"Yes, it's far too much area," agreed Sally in a somber voice. "Especially because if any of my assumptions are in error, then my flight path tracking analysis would be useless. Rather, it would all be useless except for the clue you said you got from one of the other girls at the farm, that Bella had been sold to a guy on a boat on the Gulf. So given the limited range of a small airplane, I'm trying to track planes en route to airports on the nearest coast, probably small air strips."

"Good thinking," commented Zena.

Sally said, "Let me get to the point. I have found a likely target heading south at 169 degrees from your location."

Zena leaned closer to the speaker. "What? Why didn't you just say so? Where's it heading? Can we intercept it? Let's get going!"

"Slow down," answered Sally. "I didn't lead with that because I wanted you to understand the prerequisite assumptions I made to get there. Just so you wouldn't be over-eager to jump on that one lead—like you are doing now."

"Okay, okay. Just tell us what you know."

"That's better. So here it is. The target plane is heading toward the Gulf, somewhere to the east of Houston."

"What type of plane is it?" asked Mia.

"I can't tell in the dark," Sally replied. "But given that the coast is some 740 miles from your location, that narrows down types of planes that could make it that far."

Zena said, "The girl here told us she has seen Big D's plane, and it's not a jet. It has one engine with a propeller and the wings are high."

Sally didn't reply as Zena and Mia heard her typing on her keyboard. "It could be a Cessna," she finally announced.

Zena asked, "How long do we have before it lands?"

"At about 700 miles, at the optimal cruising speed for the Cessna of about 140 miles per hour, that's five hours."

Mia said, "They left an hour ago. How are we going to catch up?"

"I'll send a Harrier," said Sally. "The trainer has two seats and can fly at up to 700 miles per hour. Sit tight. I'll let you know when it's been arranged. Sally out."

Mia turned to Zena. "There's still hope. Thanks to Sally."

Zena replied, "But we have some time, maybe we can help the girls. Perhaps send them to The Refuge."

Mia nodded. "Great idea. I'm on it."

Mia gathered the girls together. They were a motley group of misfits. She said, "We want to offer you some help."

One girl seemed suspicious of the offer and sat back and crossed her arms. Others seemed eager, even desperate for an opportunity to escape.

"Some of you may have family," Mia started. "We can arrange transportation for you if you want to go home." She glanced around the room. "How many of you would like help getting home?"

A few girls raised their hands.

"I'll connect you with my friend Victoria. She'll arrange it for you."

"What about you two?" asked one of the girls gesturing toward Mia and Zena. "You can't just leave us here alone. What do we do if they come back?"

Mia replied, "We have to go. Big D took our friend Bella. We need to go get her." She tilted her head toward the door. "Besides, if you want to go outside and look around, you'll see that the rest of Big D's guys are, well, you don't need to worry about them. They're not going to bother you ever again."

Zena gazed at Mia and smiled.

"If the rest of you have nowhere to go," Mia said, "there's a place in Utah called The Refuge. A friend of ours runs it. You can stay there if you need to. You can go to school, or our friend will help you get a job. Whatever you need. If you want to go, I'll call my friend, and she'll send a van."

Felicia raised her hand. "I thought I wanted to go. But I've been here so long that I don't have anywhere else to go. And it's not so bad for me here. I'm thinking I might stay. That is, if they let me."

Mia replied, "That may not be possible. If we're successful, Big D won't be back."

"What do you mean?"

"Either the police will arrest him, or…" Mia glanced at Zena, who shook her head slightly. Mia understood that she shouldn't say too much about The Sisterhood, or its practices. "Or, as I was saying, now that he knows that everyone knows what he was doing here at the farm, it wouldn't be safe for him to operate here. So, he won't be coming back. Ummm, ever."

Mia glanced at Zena who nodded.

"So, you see, you might want to think about coming to The Refuge and getting a new start."

"I don't know. It's so far away," Felicia stammered.

Mia reached out and put her hand on Felicia's arm. "You'll love it there. I lived there myself for quite a while at two different times, once when I was a child after my parents died in a car accident and again later when I was an adult and needed help. In fact, just meeting the woman who runs it, Xtina, will change your life."

"Okay," said Felicia. "I'll think about it."

"Just come, my friend," Mia smiled with encouragement. "I promise you won't regret it. Unlike this place, you can leave whenever you want to."

Felicia asked, "Will you be there?"

Mia nodded. "Yes. I'll come to see you."

Felicia rushed forward and hugged Mia. "Okay. Then I'll go."

Mia turned. Zena collapsed into a big stuffed chair and had her arms and legs stretched out.

"Rough night?" Mia asked.

"You know it, sister," replied Zena.

"Rest. I'll call Sally or maybe Victoria to have her arrange transportation for these girls to wherever they want to go."

Zena dragged herself out of the chair. "No. I'll do that. I think you should call Bella's father and give him an update."

Mia hesitated. "But what can I tell him? That we were too late? That Big D escaped with his baby girl? You should have seen him when he found out she was taken. He was devastated, heartbroken."

"I don't know. Just tell him the truth, I guess."

Mia nodded. "Okay. Thank you, sister." She reached into her little purse and pulled a sleek flip phone out of a sleeve. Before calling, she turned back to Zena. "One more thing. We should try to find poor Eugenia. Felicia said that Big D's men took her to a place they call the warehouse. Felicia said it used to be a meatpacking plant that went out of business. When you talk to Sally, see if she can find it. Tell her the girls here say that anyone who goes to the warehouse never comes back. I'm concerned. Send someone to look for Eugenia please and see if there is anyone else there."

"Got it," said Zena. "Go. Call him."

CHAPTER 26

FRANK DIDN'T ANSWER his phone. Mia wondered if he had fallen asleep or something. Knowing that Frank would be desperate to hear from her, she tried again. Still no answer. She needed to get through to him.

Suddenly, she realized she was calling him on a burner that would show on Frank's phone as an unknown number. She quickly sent a text. "Frank, it's Mia. Pick up." And then she called again.

This time Frank picked up on the first ring as if he had in fact just been sitting and waiting for the call. "Mia, I didn't know that was you. I didn't want to pick up any other call so I'd be available when you called. I've been trying to reach you. Has The Sisterhood found Bella?"

Mia hesitated just a moment, realizing that she had not told Frank that she herself was looking for Bella. *Zena said just to tell the truth. So here goes…* "Yes, or at least we found where they were holding her—on a farm in Nebraska. But Frank, while Zena and I were fighting off the security here, an airplane took off. We're pretty sure she was on the plane."

Frank didn't answer right away. "What do you mean, fighting off security? Where are you? What're you doing?"

"I came with Zena on the mission to find Bella."

"Oh my god, Mia. That sounds dangerous. I didn't know."

She didn't know how much to tell Frank, certainly not the details of the circumstances of the girls' captivity. And probably not that she had been shot at about a hundred times and was lucky to be alive. Finally, she decided to keep it simple.

"I'm safe with Zena. We're being careful. I promise."

"Jesus, Mia." After a long moment, Frank asked, "Where is the plane? Can you track it?"

"Our friend Sally is looking for it now."

Frank said, "The police here aren't doing shit. They say they don't have any leads. I'm afraid if I have to rely on them to find those bastards, I'll never see Bella again. They seem to have given up altogether while it seems that you and your people are making progress. Are getting close at least…. Mia, I have a question to ask… or maybe it's more like a favor to ask. A request."

"Yes, Frank. What is it?"

"You said that The Sisterhood gets justice for abused women when the legal system fails, right?"

Mia remembered her conversation with Frank at her house right after they had learned of Bella's kidnapping. Then, Frank asked her only if The Sisterhood could help the police find his daughter. Now, again, she thought she knew what Frank was about to ask, but she needed to hear him say it.

"Go ahead, Frank. Ask me your favor…. Ask me *anything*."

He spoke quickly. "The system is failing…failing my baby girl. I've spent the last twenty years of my life making sure that people who are accused of committing crimes get due process, making sure they get all their constitutional rights, making sure that they get their day in court." He paused as if searching for words. When he spoke, she could hear rage building in his voice as he spoke louder and louder. "But, if you find them first, …then fuck the cops. Fuck the system. You tell The Sisterhood to take them down. To take them out. Do you understand me?"

Frank's emotion overwhelmed Mia. Tears streamed down her face. "Yes, Frank. Trust me. I know what you mean. I know exactly what you mean."

Frank paused again, "Will you be able to find Bella and bring her back?"

"I told Zena I didn't know what to tell you when I called. She just said to tell you the truth." Her throat tightened with emotion. She couldn't bring herself to tell Frank that Bella had been sold at auction and that the odds of finding her at all were slim to none. Finally, she got some words out. "The truth is…I won't come back without her."

Zena called out to Mia. "It's Sally. Come."

"Gotta go, Frank."

"Be careful," cautioned Frank. "I don't want to lose you both."

CHAPTER 27

AT DAWN, AFTER A FITFUL ATTEMPT to rest while awaiting an update from Sally, Mia rushed to Zena's side at the dining room table where Zena had relocated because the rescued girls were all in the kitchen.

"It's about the plane," Zena whispered to Mia, not wanting to interrupt Sally.

"…. So when the sun came up, I borrowed another satellite and got a better look at the plane that I told you I had picked as a possible target, probably the most likely target. The one flying due South from the farm. It does appear to be a Cessna. When it was approaching Houston airport, the plane swerved east. Based on the extreme change in flight path it looked like an intentional move to avoid any communication with the tower."

Zena said, "So what's your take? Is this Bella's plane?"

Sally replied without pausing. "The pilot's change in direction may be evidence that this pilot doesn't want to be found. That together with its direction heading south from Nebraska and that it is approaching the Gulf makes it likely, in my opinion, that this is our plane."

Zena stood. "Where's our jump jet?"

"The Harrier should be there any minute," said Sally. "The pilot will hand the jet over to you, Zena. She'll stay at the farm to make sure the girls stay safe until Victoria arranges the transportation for each of them."

"Roger that," said Zena.

Mia said, "I hope you sent a flight suit for me. My little black dress is pretty dirty. I've got lots of blood on it."

"I hope none of it is yours," Sally teased.

"Not so far," replied Mia, chuckling. "But the day is young."

Sally laughed. "Yes to the flight suit. I made sure there was one in your size."

"Thank you, sister."

"I also sent another assortment of my special lipsticks. Zena said you like them."

"Excellent!" Mia shook her fist in victory.

"One more thing," Sally's tone turned to serious. "I tracked the plane to a grass airstrip called Hawkeye Air. It's forty-one miles east of Houston TC at a heading of 97.36 degrees. It is on the east side of Trinity Bay. The plane just landed. Now I've lost the satellite. I'll have the pilot program the exact coordinates into the Harrier's flight computer."

Zena said, "Thank you, Sally."

"You are welcome of course. But hurry, ladies, or you'll lose them."

CHAPTER 28

"THEY'RE HERE."

From the lounge chair on which Bella was resting in the living room, she turned to see the housekeeper looking out the front window of the house. She held a watering can in one hand and gestured toward the window with the other. The man with the bulge in his jacket, who had been walking around the perimeter of the house every fifteen minutes, moved quickly into the living room from the kitchen.

A minute later, two tanned men walked through the front door. The thin one wore short pants, a colorful shirt, spotless white sneakers, and sunglasses. The other man was larger both in height and weight and wore fatigues and boots. Both had handguns tucked into holsters attached to their belts.

The large man asked, "Where is she?"

The housekeeper now pointed her other arm in the direction of Bella.

Bella went cold.

Both men walked to Bella just as Nita and Big D entered the living room from the bedroom just down the hall.

When Bella didn't move, the large man grabbed her by the arm and jerked her up.

"Hey, easy," Nita said. Bella didn't know why. She had never seemed to mind violence before.

Big D walked over and stood between the men and the front door. "Did you bring my money?"

The large man turned to Big D. "As soon as we get her to the boat, we'll call you and then wire it to wherever you want it deposited."

"That wasn't the deal," Big D retorted, moving his hand toward his holster. "Mr. E. and I had a COD deal—cash on delivery. Now that you're taking delivery, you owe me the cash."

The large man turned to face Big D. Growing tension filled the room. Somehow, she hoped they might shoot it out and kill each other. Then she could—

"Hold on," the thin man interjected, raising his palm in the air, signaling for everyone to stop. He pushed his sunglasses up and on top of his head and said to his partner, "It's okay. This guy's regular deal with the boss is always cash on delivery. We're taking her now, so go ahead and give him the money."

That answer appeared to be good enough for the large man. He slid his small backpack off his shoulders and pulled out four fat envelopes.

Big D finally moved his hand away from his gun and reached for the envelopes. "Done deal." He opened one of the envelopes.

Bella could see tightly wrapped stacks of what looked like hundred-dollar bills in Big D's hand. He licked his dirty fingers and started thumbing through the edge of one of the stacks. Then he gave a low whistle. "Yesiree, Bob."

"So Big D," said the thin man, "I suppose you'll be headed back to the farm now?"

"Not right away," Big D answered, trying to stuff an envelope in each pocket. "The farm's a little hot right now. Besides, me and my lady are due for a vacation." He gazed at Nita. "Maybe the Keys."

The thin man nodded. "Sounds good. Until next time then."

The large man pulled Bella toward the door.

As they started through the front door, Bella looked over her shoulder at Big D and Nita. They were completely focused on the money. That was all she'd ever been to them, a product.

The men walked Bella to a long, sleek speedboat tied to a dock extending into the bay in front of the big house. They took her to a small area below the deck and told her to take a seat on a bench. Once the thin man steered the boat out into the bay, Bella walked out of the hold to the deck with her hands holding her stomach. She yelled, "I'm seasick and need to be on the deck." She just wanted to see the horizon to try to figure out where she was.

The driver shrugged. Bella grabbed onto a handrail on the side of the boat that would give her a good view of her surroundings. *How will I get away at sea?*

When the speedboat approached the yacht, Bella was stunned at its size. While she was on the farm, several people had talked about her going to a boat. This wasn't a boat; it was a ship almost big enough for a cruise line but with a super-sleek design.

The speedboat pulled up to the landward side of the ship and waited while a motorized stairway unfolded down from the first deck. The men on the ship gave Bella a hand up to the stairway, and she climbed to the top. Then the speedboat took off.

A friendly looking young man wearing a crew uniform greeted Bella with a smile. "Welcome aboard, young lady." She wasn't sure what role he played in her new hell. "Follow me," he said. "I'll take you to your quarters. Your host, whom we affectionately call Mr. E., is on a business call and will send for you when he is free."

Bella was relieved to hear that she wasn't being taken straight to Mr. E. Maybe she could find a way to escape before then.

The polite crewman showed her to an elegant stateroom with an extra-large porthole facing the sea. As he turned to walk away, he took a radio off his belt and spoke into its mic. "Captain. She's on board. Mr. E. said to pull the anchor and get underway as soon as she arrived."

After waiting a few minutes, Bella carefully twisted the knob on the door of her room. It wasn't locked. She thought that if she could get back to where she had come from, back down to the water, then maybe she could escape before they started out to sea.

She slowly pushed her door open and stepped into the hallway. Her mind raced as she remembered seeing some life preservers. If she grabbed one maybe she could—

"Sorry, Miss," said a large, gruff-looking man with a short beard standing in front of her door, "You are to stay in your quarters until the boss calls for you."

Bella's heart sank. "Sorry, I was hungry. Do you think I could go get some food before–"

The man shook his head. "I'll call someone to bring you whatever you want. The boss said to bring you anything you needed."

Bella nodded and stepped back into her room. What she needed was to get off this boat.

Despondent, Bella stared out her window. A seagull stood on the railing just outside. It looked at her, and Bella imagined forging some kind of connection with it. She imagined that it cared for her, it was probably the only thing anywhere near her that did.

Bella heard a motor engage and a grinding sound. She wondered if it was the anchor coming up. She looked back at the seagull just in time to see it fly away. Her heart ached as she watched it take off so freely, wishing she could do the same.

Bella crumbled onto the cabin's bed. How could anyone know where she was? She had been moved so many times. No one was coming to save her.

She started sobbing uncontrollably. She closed her eyes and covered them with her forearm.

I'm lost.

CHAPTER 29

AFTER A FAST FLIGHT to the coast, Zena circled the Harrier slowly around the coordinates Sally had given the prior pilot to program into the jet until she saw the grassy airfield they were looking for.

Mia pointed through the window. "Look, Zena. Over there. A plane on the ground. Maybe that's it."

"I'll take her down." Zena slowly maneuvered the jet's engines from behind the plane to underneath it and then sat the Harrier down as if it were a helicopter.

"Wow," said Mia. "Where did you learn how to do that? Were you in the military?"

"Advanced training with The Sisterhood," said Zena, smiling. "If you live long enough, you too will learn to fly and see the world."

Zena and Mia gathered their gear. Mia stuffed some of Sally's super-spy lipstick cases into her pockets. Zena shoved a huge pistol into the holster strapped to her leg and filled her camo duffle bag with weapons. She said, "First, let's go check that plane."

Zena and Mia scoured the inside of the plane. Mia was sure that Bella would leave a clue if she could, but she didn't find any. After all, Sally said it might not even be the right plane. But she did say it was the most likely candidate.

Outside the plane, though, they found some footprints in the soft wet ground and followed them to a nearby canal.

Zena said, "Three sets of footprints. One large and two smaller sets. That's consistent with our intel, that Big D and Nita left the farm with Bella."

A small boat with an outboard motor was attached to a tall pole cemented into the side of the canal.

Mia smiled at Zena. "Well, they said they were taking Bella to a boat."

Zena laughed. "Let's see. Maybe fourteen feet long. Paint peeling off. Outboard motor. Yeah, looks like a billionaire's boat. Case closed. We can go home now."

Mia suggested, "Maybe we should call Sally."

Zena pulled her phone out of her pocket and dialed Sally. "Hi, Sally, we think we found the plane. But they're gone already. Now what?"

Sally replied, "Your contact at the farm, the girl Felicia, said that she heard Big D and Nita talking about taking her to some billionaire's boat. So, I sent out a drone to look at the yachts in Houston harbor. As it turns out, Houston harbor extends for about forty miles. There are lots of big boats, including several yachts of various sizes. But there is only one yacht near you, just outside Galveston Bay. And it is huge."

Mia asked, "But is it the one we're looking for?"

Sally replied, "I think it may be. I discovered that it's owned by a private corporation based in the Cayman Islands. I found almost nothing on the corporation. Private offshore companies are notoriously secretive. But with a little more digging, I found that the primary member of that corporation is a rich dude named Jason Edgarton."

Zena asked, "Could he be our billionaire?"

Sally said, "His holdings are varied and hard to value, but even his *reported* assets are described in at least the hundreds of millions. And he could be hiding other funds in these offshore accounts."

"How do we get to that ship?" asked Mia. "How big is it? Can we land the Harrier on it?"

"Slow down Mia," said Sally. "Even Zena couldn't land the Harrier on a moving yacht. And it wouldn't be a good idea even if she could land it. It would be almost impossible to take off again and would draw a ton of unwanted attention. But hear me out. The yacht is anchored. If it's there only to pick up Bella, it would probably have left by now. So, she's probably not on board yet.

"Wait a minute, everyone," Zena cautioned in a loud voice. "We don't know if that is even our ship at all. And we don't know if that Edgarton fellow is the billionaire we're looking for." Zena's voice continued to rise in volume." We don't even know where Bella is right now." Shouting now, Zena said, "The only thing that we know for sure is that we don't have time to waste trying to board the wrong ship."

"All true, my sisters," acknowledged Sally, in a calm, professional tone born of years of high-stakes, life and death work in the field. "What do you suggest?"

Zena shook her head. "I don't know what to do. All I know is that I want to kick some ass!"

After a moment of silence, Sally spoke again. "Look, I agree that we don't know anything for sure. But we have a working theory, with some information to back it up. Lacking any other options, I think we must assume, for the moment at least, that this Edgarton is the guy we're looking for."

Zena nodded. "Yeah, yeah. I agree. I'm sorry, I'm just frustrated."

Mia put a hand on Zena's arm, to provide moral support, and was temporarily startled by the strength in Zena's bicep. Being the new girl on the team she had been deferring to the experience of the others, just trying her best to keep up with them.

Zena stopped and reached her opposite hand over and put it on top of Mia's and managed to squeeze a half smile out of her lips.

"Sally, I agree with you also," Mia interjected. "We go with what we have. So, what's our next move?"

"Okay, so I searched to see if there were properties in the vicinity in the name of either the Cayman corporation or in Edgarton's name. And guess what?"

"Aaaggh," growled Mia, "Don't make us beg."

Sally chuckled. "Edgarton owns a residential property on Smith's Point, which just happens to be located a few miles south from where you are right now. If he is the billionaire we're looking for, then Bella might have been taken to that residence."

Zena shook her head and pursed her lips. "That's a helluva lot of ifs, Sally."

"I know," admitted Sally. "And I have one more *if* for you. *If* you have a better idea, now is the time to share it."

Mia and Zena looked at each other. Zena said, "We're on our way, Sally. We'll let you know what we find."

Mia and Zena loaded their gear into the motorboat, which, thankfully, had some gas in the tank, and cruised down the coast of the bay until they arrived at Edgarton's house. Zena drove the boat toward a small rocky beach under the cover of a hill and some bushes, cut the motor as they approached and let the boat run aground.

"Wait here. My boots are made for this." Keeping a firm hold of the bow of the motorboat with both hands, Zena reached her long leg over the edge and stepped into the water. Once she found a firm foothold, she pulled the boat further up onto the beach.

"Give me your hand and come straight up over the bow." Mia grabbed Zena's strong hand and Zena pulled her forward and then grabbed her around the waist with both hands and easily swung her over the bow to a gentle landing on the beach.

They scrambled up to the top of the hill and found a grassy spot behind some bushes. "Look, that must be the house," Zena said, handing a pocket telescope she had in her gear belt to Mia.

Mia looked through it but after a few seconds, said, "I can't see inside the house from here." She continued to scan the area. "But wait. There's someone outside sweeping the front porch."

"Okay, let's wait until she goes inside so she doesn't see us coming,"

Zena said. "Then we can coordinate by radio and bust in at the same time, me through the front and you from the back and—"

"No. Wait," interrupted Mia. "What if it's the wrong house? We don't want to bust in shooting the place up. That would not be bueno."

"You're right, we should have a plan before we just barge into someone's house." Zena replied. "Like you said, it could be the wrong house, which would likely lead to a 911 call to police. And we don't have time for that. Or, if it *is* the right house, we *definitely* should have a plan. What do you suggest?"

"How about this: I'll just go knock on the front door with the just-looking-for-my-friend story. That worked before. But you cover the back just in case they *are* there and they run."

Zena nodded. "I think you're getting the hang of our Sisterhood thing. Good call. Let's do it."

As Zena used the cover of trees on the large property to sneak around to the back of the house, Mia walked up to the front of the house as if nothing was wrong. Nothing at all.

The housekeeper appeared to be startled to see Mia approaching the front door from the bay. She said, "What? How did you get here? *No entiendo—*"

Mia interrupted to try to put the woman at ease. *"Por favor, no se preocupe, señora."*

The woman relaxed a little bit, and Mia climbed up the stairs to the porch. "I guess you don't get many visitors out here. My name is Mia. I got separated from a friend of mine who may also be visiting this area, and I'm wondering if she happens to be here. Her name is Bella. She's sixteen years old. Long black curly hair.

"Who the hell are you talking to?"

Mia heard a man's voice inside, and it was coming closer to the front door. It sounded familiar.

Mia's heart jumped. Her hand flew to the radio in her ear. "Zena, It's Big D! This is the place!"

Big D came thundering through the front door. Startled, Mia stepped backwards quickly but missed the step behind her and tumbled down the stairs to the ground. Big D clambered down them and jumped on top of Mia, pinning her to the ground.

"I don't know how y'all found me, or how you're still alive, missy, but I'm gonna fix that right now." He reached behind his back and pulled a pistol out of a belt holster. He brought it slowly around, pointed it at her forehead, and said in his unique accent, "Adeos muchacha."

"Hey, pick on someone your own size you fat sack of shit."

Zena got Big D's attention for sure, and he brought his gun around and pointed it at her. She took a quick step forward and kicked the gun out of his hands. Then she spun around and planted her back heel into his face, knocking him sprawling to the ground.

Mia rolled over and slowly got to one knee. Big D had knocked the wind out of her when he landed on her.

Zena said, "Mia, leave this one to me. Go look for Bella."

At Bella's name, a shot of adrenaline pumped into Mia's bloodstream. She jumped up and flew up the steps two at a time and in through the front door. She rushed from one room to the next, calling out, "Bella! Bella!"

"What the fuck?" said a thin Hispanic man with a scruffy beard. He approached Mia from the kitchen with a befuddled look on his face. I just saw you on the back patio. How did you—"

"You saw *me* on the patio, idiot, not her," announced another voice.

Both Mia and the man turned to see who made that remark. Nita!

Mia felt her face flush and her skin crinkle into goosebumps. She instinctively took a quick step towards her sister but stopped short when she saw Nita take a step backwards. Mia felt both the pull of her desire to find the twin she thought was dead and the repulsion from knowing that Nita had helped kidnap Bella. Mia searched Nita's eyes for a sign of recognition, or acceptance, or maybe happiness to see her, but found only what felt like aversion. She decided to proceed with caution. And to try to gauge Nita's intent.

The Hispanic man pushed back the edge of his sport coat and put his hand on the gun at his side, but Nita held up a hand to stop him from pulling it out of its holster. He obviously understood but kept his hand on the handle of the gun, nonetheless.

"Hi, Nita," said Mia. "Long time no see. In fact, I didn't think I would ever see you again. I thought you were dead. They told me you were dead."

"I am dead. Or should I say the little girl you knew is dead and gone. I buried her a long time ago."

Mia and Nita spent a long moment staring at each other. Scanning each other's faces and bodies. Mia had tried to picture this moment ever since Xtina told her she would meet her sister. Even though Xtina said there would be "trouble" when they met, Mia had nevertheless written a script in her mind where they would run and pull each other into a tight embrace, like they did after every separation when they were kids. Would they sit down together while each took turns sharing the traumatic histories they had each endured and at least feel compassion for the suffering of the other?

But the warm sunlight flowing through the French doors only served to illuminate the icy glare in Nita's dark eyes.

Mia leaned to move closer to Nita but glanced at the man with the gun and caught her weight on her front foot, deciding to stay where she stood.

"What happened to you? I was told that you killed our parents. How could you—?"

"Nice to see you too, dear sister," said Nita, interrupting. "Not a great way to start a family reunion." She shook her head at Mia. "And don't try that holier-than-thou bullshit with me. From what I heard, I think you killed more people just yesterday than I ever did. So maybe we are more alike than you seem to think."

Mia shook her head. "Nita, if you are like me or care anything for me, you will help me now. Please help me."

"And how exactly do you think I could help you."

"I'm here to get Bella. Tell me where she is. Take me to her."

"Sorry, Mia. I can't do that. Even if I wanted to, I couldn't do that now. Big D sold her. She's gone."

Mia's heart ached as she looked at her sister. All of Mia's dreams about the happy moment of when she would meet her sister again disappeared like the shadows when the sun rises on a cloudless day.

Mia asked, "Sold her? Sold my friend? No, Nita, other than how we look, we are most definitely not alike. Not at all. I do what I do to help people. You seem to hurt people for your own benefit. I heard about what you did to Eugenia. No, we are *not* the same."

Nita's face, which had displayed not so much a smile as a wry grin, now changed into a surly scowl. "I always thought we would meet some day. I wondered how it would be to meet you. I loved you." She paused for a moment, as if in thought, and then her face started to turn red. "But now I see that you are just such a self-righteous bitch, and you are fucking up my shit!"

Nita stopped and put her smile, or what passed as a smile, back on her face. "But because you are my sister, I'll give you one chance to leave. Go, now, or you'll see what I'm capable of. I promise, you don't want to see that."

Mia replied, "I can't do that, Nita. And because you're my sister, I am going to give *you* one chance now too. Help me. Tell me where Bella is."

"Or what?"

"Or you will see what I'm capable of. And I promise, you don't want to see that either."

"I can't let you take Bella back. We got paid a lot of money for her. That deal is done." Nita looked at the Hispanic man with the gun and nodded toward Mia. "Would you mind tying her up or something, at least until Mr. E's security guys get back here?"

Mia nonchalantly put her hands into the large front pockets of her flight suit, reaching for one of her lipstick cases.

"Stop! Hands out of your pockets," shouted the man as he pulled his gun from his holster and held it at a low ready position.

"Okay, okay," said Mia quickly. "It's just a lipstick." With her hand still in her pocket, she wasn't sure which one she had picked. She flipped the top and waited.

When the man took a step in Mia's direction she yanked the lipstick out of her pocket, pointed it at the man's hand, and activated the trigger. A web of something stringy shot out and enveloped the man's hand and gun. He jerked at his hand but couldn't pull it loose.

Ha! Spider web. That'll work.

But then the man came charging at Mia with his free arm. She ducked under his arm and side kicked his knee, sending him to the floor, then quickly spun around and kicked him hard in the temple with the toe of her boot, knocking him out.

She turned back just in time to see Nita coming at her holding a knife up in the air poised and ready to stab. With a surge of adrenaline, Mia pivoted away from Nita just as she heard a shot ring out from behind her. She jerked her head around to see Nita falling backwards.

Zena charged forward with her pistol pointed at Nita lying on the ground. She kicked the knife away.

Mia rushed forward and fell to the floor by Nita. "No! Nita!"

Then Zena dropped to one knee, her eyebrows raised in the middle with deep concern. She placed her hand gently on Mia's back. "I'm sorry. I had to stop her."

Mia carefully pushed Nita's long dark hair out of her eyes and then caressed her cheek with her right hand. When Xtina had told her that she would meet Nita, she had dared to imagine the possibility a happy ending, even after Xtina told her that there would be death. Despite the evil that Nita had done, Mia's heart ached.

Mia scanned Nita's chest but found the bullet entry wound in her right shoulder. Then Nita moved, shaking her head, and reaching her left hand over to put pressure on the wound. "Fucking bitches," she cursed in between moans.

Mia glanced at Zena. "You missed?"

"I never miss." Zena cocked her head to the side. "I just didn't want to kill your sister."

Nita tried to roll over as if she were going to try to get up.

Mia quickly reached out a hand and put it on Nita's chest. "No, rest here. I'll call an ambulance," she instructed.

"Don't be stupid," Nita hissed. She lifted her head and glanced around the room. "Cops will respond with the ambulance, and under the circumstances, I don't think any of us want cops here right now."

Zena turned to Mia and shrugged. "She's probably right."

"Big D will get me some help," Nita said.

"Umm, about Big D…," Zena said.

Mia and Nita both stared at Zena, waiting for her to finish her sentence.

"Yeah, what about Big D? Mia asked. "Maybe we can make him talk and tell us where they took Bella."

Zena shook her head. "Nope. Sorry. I accidentally crushed his windpipe and broke his neck."

Mia cocked her head to the side. "Accidentally?"

"Well, after seeing the farm, I was pretty pissed off, so, you know how it goes."

"Shit, he was my ride," Nita said.

Mia looked at Zena and then back at Nita. "We can help you if you—"

"Mia." Zena shook her head slowly. "There's no time. We either help Nita, or we try to find Bella."

Mia looked back at Nita. "I…, I'm sorry. I'll come back for you, or you can call me. You can find me in Salt Lake, or—"

"Jesus." Nita grumbled. "Please just fuck off. Leave me alone."

Zena took Mia by the elbow and gently lifted her to her feet and guided her away from Nita.

Mia looked back at Nita and then turned to face Zena. "Let's go get Bella."

"Easier said than done," Zena replied. "We don't know where she is."

Mia nodded. "But Sally said that since this house belonged to the billionaire, then maybe that yacht in the harbor belongs to him too. If so, we just need to get out there."

"Agreed. Let's call Sally and see if she can help."

CHAPTER 30

BELLA SAT AND JUST STARED out the window of her stateroom. The crewman who met her when she arrived had brought stiletto shoes and even a diamond necklace.

"My boss wants me to let you know not to wear any underwear. He said he wants to see how the dress drapes your figure."

As the crewman handed Bella the dress, she watched his eyes try to penetrate the sweatsuit she was wearing. Bella hated how used to this she had become since getting picked up by Chacho. Men were the scum of the earth. She knew she would never trust one again. The thought of falling in love seemed impossible.

She knew all men couldn't be this awful, men like her father. But it was getting harder and harder to believe that they weren't the majority.

"Be ready for dinner in an hour," said the crewman.

Bella begrudgingly took the dress by the shoulders and let it fall onto the bed in front of her. Normally, it would have elicited great excitement to be given such a beautiful dress. But it was just gift wrapping for her next rapist. The gray-green fabric shimmered in the light as gravity slowly unfolded it. She had never seen anything like it.

She looked at the label. Armani. No wonder. Curious now, Bella laid the dress out on the bed and looked at the shoebox. Manolo Blahnik. She had heard of these shoes but that's all–heard. The bright colors and style were extraordinary, unlike anything she had ever seen.

She slid them onto her feet. Somehow, they knew her shoe size because they fit perfectly. She loved the cushioned lining and space for the toes. For a stiletto, they were amazingly comfortable.

Bella removed her shoes and peeled off her sweat suit. The direction she was given was no underwear. She didn't have any anyway.

She took a deep breath. She held the dress over her head and let it fall through her arms onto her shoulders. The sheer fabric was so lightweight that she barely noticed as it settled softly onto her shoulders. The mirror didn't lie. It did indeed drape well on her.

But when she saw her own face, the look fell apart. She looked miserable, sleep deprived, and broken.

She picked up the heavy diamond necklace that the crewman brought. This necklace must have cost at least as much as what he paid for her, if not more. It appeared that this Mr. E. was trying to make a good impression. Or maybe he just wanted his new purchase dressed in a very particular way.

She turned back to the porthole and looked out at the ocean. The ship was moving fast now. They had left the coastline far behind them. It felt like she had left her old life far behind as well.

Bella gazed through the portal at the high white clouds that dotted the blue sky. Cloud-gazing calmed her and filled her with a quiet joy for life–usually. But not today. Still, she leaned listlessly against the window and tried to find recognizable shapes in the sky. One long cloud had wings, well, if she used her imagination a bit, it reminded her of the seagull that visited her earlier. Another one could be Italy perhaps. She had always done well in geography. Yes, it looked very much like Italy.

Tears started brimming in Bella's eyes. *Daddy, I should have listened to you.*

Sighing, and turning back to the sky, Bella tried to decide what the next cloud passing could remind her of to distract herself from her hellish situation. The cloud was moving faster than the others. It didn't look like a cloud at all. *A parachute maybe?* Bella shook her head and balled both fists to wipe her wet eyes, hoping to get a better look.

She pressed her cheek to the window to get a better angle. *Yes!* She wasn't imagining it; someone in a wing-shaped parachute had zoomed past her window. Bella's heart started pumping hard. Could it be someone coming for her? Had they found her?

CHAPTER 31

"FOLLOW ME," SAID ZENA. Then she grabbed the sides of the open door, flexed her legs and leapt out of the airplane.

"You gotta go, gotta go," the pilot shouted at Mia over the roar of the engine.

Mia took a deep breath and flung herself out the open door. While they waited at the airfield for the plane Sally had hired to chase Mr. E's ship, Zena had just given Mia a crash course in skydiving. As she hurtled through space toward the back of the moving yacht, she found herself wishing that Zena hadn't called it a *crash* course. But she remembered to point her head down and to spread her arms and legs to take advantage of the aerodynamic wings built into the squirrel suit.

Mia adjusted her arms to bank to her left to match Zena's trajectory. Coming up fast on the yacht, Mia focused her attention on being ready to pull the tab on the front of her suit to release the small parachute on her back.

Zena had told her to watch her to know exactly when to pull it. When Zena was almost at the ship, she released her parachute. Mia had calculated that she was about three seconds behind Zena, so she counted to three and pulled hers too.

The wind caught Mia's parachute and pulled her backwards hard. The pressure slammed the air out of her chest, and she was momentarily stunned.

Then she remembered that she needed to steer herself toward the boat. She tried to grab the handles of her chute. She got the right one but missed with her left hand on the first try, which pulled her off course to the right. She found herself heading fast toward the ocean.

Mia grasped for the other handle, determined to take hold of it. *Got it!* She pulled the left handle hard and steered toward the boat. Zena pulled up short onto the second level, but the front of the boat was the most open, and Mia was still going too fast to land where Zena did. So, she steered toward that open area. She was still coming in fast, too fast.

What was she supposed to do? Oh yeah, pull the handles back hard to tilt the wing on the chute to slow her down. Still going in fast, Mia crashed to the deck. She absorbed the shock with her legs but then the wind pulled her off balance and her momentum carried her to the bow of the ship.

No! she screamed in her head. *I'm going to go over. Wait. Release the chute!* Mia grabbed the front clip of her parachute and jerked it as hard as she could. It released off her shoulders and the wind carried it over the front of the ship. Mia fell hard into the front railing but had made it safely to the deck. Her back and legs were aching as she unzipped the squirrel suit and pulled it off.

She dragged herself across the deck and hid behind a helicopter. Then she looked for Zena and found her waving from the second deck. When she caught Mia's eye, Zena held up a fist. Mia understood that Zena meant for her to stay put and wait where she was. Then Zena ducked away.

Moments later, Zena moved around the edge of the helicopter, slung her AR-15 over her shoulder, and crouched next to Mia.

"Mia, that was an awesome jump. You can check off your skydiving training. It usually takes two weeks. You did it all in one jump."

"Thanks," Mia said, grimacing.

Zena asked, "Hey, you okay?"

"Everything hurts right now, but nothing's broken. I'm good to go."

"You are one tough cookie, sister. Let's go find Bella."

"Where should we look?" Mia asked.

"Probably the nicest quarters are on the third deck. Let's start up there."

"Or how about this?" teased Mia. "I'll just find a crew member and do my little lost-girl routine. *Hi, I'm just in the area looking for my friend Bella. Is she here?*"

"Love it," said Zena with a chuckle. "Except that it's much harder to explain how we came to be on this ship at sea than how we arrived at a house." She stood and reached down and grabbed Mia's hand and pulled her to her feet. Then she turned and headed around the edge of the helicopter.

Blam, blam, blam!

Zena got hit in the chest with two rounds. Another tore through her shoulder. She fell hard backwards onto the deck.

Mia grabbed Zena by the arm with both hands and dragged her back behind the helicopter. Zena's eyes were closed. Mia scanned her body for bullet wounds. *"Zena!"*

"Ugh! I'll make it." Zena moaned and slowly opened her eyes. She patted her chest. "Thankfully, the vest stopped the first two shots. The other one just grazed my shoulder. Fortunately for us, it was my left shoulder, and I'm a righty, so that won't slow me down."

"We need better cover," Mia stated as she glanced around their area.

"Wait," said Zena, as she rolled over and pushed herself up onto her knees. "The one who shot me is on an upper deck. We're sitting ducks." Zena winked at Mia. "But we're ducks that know where the hunter is. Still, we can't move until we take him out. Let me set up for a shot, then you distract him, and I'll shoot him."

"Distract him?"

Zena pulled out the shoulder stock on her AR-15, flipped off the safety, and said, "Now."

Mia unzipped the top of her flight suit, ran out to the side of helicopter, and pulled her top open wide.

A half-second later, Zena fired one shot. The shooter's head jerked backwards. Mia glanced at Zena. "You *got* him."

Zena frowned. "That wasn't what I meant, Mia. I wanted you to shoot at him to get him to take cover, not strip in front of him. Then when he comes back up, I'd be ready to shoot."

"Guess I still need some more training," Mia frowned and then smiled mischievously. "But it worked, didn't it?"

"Yes, my sister," responded Zena, grinning. "It worked great. Follow me."

Zena took off running toward the staterooms on the ship to look for a guard. "Someone would likely be watching Bella, especially now that shots have been fired."

As they got to the corner, Zena said, "Get low, and peek. I've got your back."

Mia squatted and glanced around the corner.

"Yes," she said. "A guy's standing in the hallway in front of a door. Looks like he must be a guard. Maybe Bella's down there. I'll check."

"Wait," said Zena.

But Mia jumped up anyway and walked down the hallway with her hands up. As expected, the guard spun around to her. Mia gave him her best smile and sashayed to him, swinging her hips. Her zipper was still down halfway to her waist. The guard noticed and gawked at her chest.

"Hi, the boss wants to see the girl who just came onboard. Can you bring her upstairs?"

The guard frowned. While reaching for his handgun, he asked, "Who the hell are you?"

Mia sighed and then remarked, "So it's the hard way, huh?"

She ran towards the guard and leapt into the air. Trying out a take-down move she had been practicing with her martial arts instructor, she hooked his neck with her left leg and clamped her right leg around her left foot. She torqued her body and used her weight to spin him to the ground. With her legs still around his neck, she squeezed hard. He had a hand up by his throat to protect his airway. So, Mia reached into a pocket and pulled out the first lipstick case she could grab, hoping to quickly disable him.

Zena arrived to see Mia staring at the case. "You still don't recognize them all, do you?"

"Okay, okay," she confessed and continued squeezing the guard's neck. "Just tell me, what's in this case? We could use a knockout dart right now."

Zena studied the lipstick case in Mia's hand. "What you have there is truth serum."

"Damn, that would have come in handy when we were interrogating Chacho."

"Actually, Mia, I liked your technique just fine. Once you put your knife on him, the truth came right out."

"If it's truth serum, we could use it to see what he knows."

Zena shook her head. "Takes too long. Other security is probably on the way now."

"Well, let me get another lipstick."

Zena said, "I've got this. Let him loose for a second."

Mia released her legs, and the guard started to sit up. Then Zena slammed him hard across the bridge of his nose with the butt of her rifle.

"Looks like he's out now," Mia said. "I'll check the room." She tried the doorknob and found that it was locked. She banged on it and shouted, "Bella, are you in there? It's Mia."

"Mia?" came a voice from inside the room. "Mia, you came!"

Mia's heart hammered. *I can't believe we found her. Gotta git her outta here right now.* Of course I did. Can you open the door?"

"Duck, Mia," shouted Zena as she fired her rifle down the hallway where Mia had been standing. "Fall back around the corner. Go. I'll cover you."

Mia glanced over her shoulder. Several armed men tried to hide in doorways as Zena sprayed bullets at them. "Wait, Bella. We'll be right back." Mia stayed low and ran past Zena, back around the corner to take cover. As she ran, she heard Bella shouting, "No. Please don't leave me!"

Zena followed Mia around the corner just as a hail of bullets tore through the wall behind them. "I counted six men. I'm pretty sure I got two of them, so make that four left. But this is my last clip." She shoved the clip into her rifle. "I couldn't carry more and still operate the squirrel suit. We've got to grab Bella and get the hell out of here."

Zena peeked around the corner. Several men were advancing in their direction. They had almost arrived at Bella's stateroom. Zena ducked back just in time to avoid a bullet to the head.

Mia checked her pockets. "Look, here are some of Sally's lipstick cases. Isn't this fat one a grenade or something?"

"Good try, but that one is a smoke screen." Zena picked through the cases in Mia's hand. "But *this* one is in fact a grenade. We can use them both. First, toss the grenade. When it explodes, I'll charge down the hallway blasting anyone who's still alive. Then we grab Bella, and you toss the smoke bomb to cover our escape."

"But then how do we get off the boat?"

"I saw a launch with an access stairway just thirty feet around the corner from here that we can release into the water and use as a getaway craft."

"Got it," said Mia, flipping the cap on the grenade to arm it.

Zena readied her gun. "Ready, set, go!"

Mia drew her arm back just as she stepped into the corridor and...

"No! I can't do it. They've got Bella with them."

Zena waved her hand frantically and shouted. "It's live. Get rid of it!"

Mia took a quick step back and launched the grenade in the direction of the sea.

Zena grabbed Mia by the back of her flight suit and tossed her to the ground just as the bomb exploded in the air over the sea.

"Dammit," yelled Mia, slapping her hands on the deck. "Wasted it. And they still got Bella! Now we've got nothing to fight them with."

"Come on, sister," said Zena. "I think maybe you've forgotten the last part of The Keeper's Creed."

Mia thought for just a second. "No, I haven't forgotten it." She dragged herself to her feet. "I will never give up. I will be my sister's keeper."

Zena said, "Good. Now let's follow them and look for a chance to take her back."

Bella and the men were gone, so Zena jogged down the hallway checking the two men she had taken down. She picked up two clips and a handgun. She returned with a huge grin. "Now I'm good to go."

"What's that sound?" asked Mia. "Is it the helicopter?'

Mia and Zena ran around from the back of the ship to see the helicopter's rotor spinning. Two men were dragging Bella towards it, with two others close behind them. A tall man wearing an elegant jacket was just climbing into the front passenger seat.

Zena and Mia crouched at the last edge of where they still had cover. Zena said, "We've got to make our move now. It's live-or-die time."

"I am my sister's keeper," Mia responded. "Let's go."

Zena steadied her rifle on her left arm, took careful aim, and fired at the trailing member of the four men who had taken Bella. He went down immediately, which sent the other three men scrambling. One of them continued to pull Bella the remaining twenty feet to the helicopter, and the other two turned and charged at Zena and Mia.

Zena switched her AR-15 to automatic and began to fire at the oncoming two men, and they quickly split up. One quickly ducked and took cover, so Zena focused on the other man and emptied her clip at him. The last several shots hit him high in the chest and knocked him back to the ground. The sole remaining guard on the ground ran and took cover again. Zena packed the last clip into her gun.

Bella struggled to keep from being dragged onto the helicopter. She turned and caught Mia's eyes. The desperation radiating from Bella's eyes tore at Mia's heart and stoked her fury.

"I'm coming, Bella!" she vowed.

Mia put her head down and sprinted off to the helicopter. Zena raised her gun to cover her. The guard at the helicopter also saw Mia coming and ignored Bella, letting her drop to the floor of the helicopter. Instead, he focused his attention on Mia and lifted his gun at her.

Bella got up on all fours and jabbed her foot into the guard's knee, bending it sideways and making his shot go wide of Mia. But the remaining guard on the ground now had a clear shot at Mia. From his protected position, he fired three bullets. One hit her in the back, knocking her to the ground.

Zena stormed forward trying to get a line-of-sight view of the guard who shot Mia while the guard in the helicopter steadied himself and pointed his gun at Bella.

As soon as Zena came into the view of the guard lying in wait for her, he fired several shots at her.

Mia watched helplessly as Zena fell, powerless to help her.

"Nooooo!" Mia's eyes followed the sounds of the loud outcry to the helicopter. Ignoring the pistol pressed against her temple, Bella reached out an arm as if she wished nothing more than to help Mia and Zena.

The guard who shot Zena pointed his gun at Mia. *Give me strength.* It was a good thing he hesitated, probably believing she was already done, because she needed a moment to feel Sally's lipstick cases in her pocket and pick one she recognized, the one she had wanted to test-fire the first time Sally showed it to her, but Sally wouldn't let her because she didn't want Mia damaging her storage room.

As the guard approached and started to raise his gun, Mia asked, "Do you want a kiss first? I just need to put on some lipstick."

Puzzled, the guard hesitated. Mia pulled the lipstick case out of her pocket, flipped open the cap, extended her arm at the guard's face, and fired it. A .22 caliber C4 hollowpoint bullet penetrated his eye and exploded in his head, sending brains gushing out his eyes and ears.

Mia wiped some of the guard's brains off her face and glanced toward the helicopter. Now that the last guard on the ground was down, the helicopter started to lift off. Mia shouted *"No!"* and with all her remaining strength, dragged herself to her feet and limped toward the helicopter. But was she too late?

The helicopter had started to lift off the deck. The stony stare of the rich man morphed into an amused grin as he watched her stumble toward them.

Bella's desperate eyes stared at Mia, helpless and hopeless. Mia yelled, "Jump, Bella!"

Bella scanned the distance from the helicopter to the deck. "It's too far."

Mia's felt sick as the helicopter rose further from the deck. With all her remaining strength, she shouted, "Trust me."

As Bella reached for the sides of the open helicopter door, the guard there struggled to get up to stop her. Bella braced herself and launched the fiercest sidekick Mia had ever seen into the guard's neck. As the guard crumpled and flopped limply forward, he fell out the helicopter's door and into the ocean. Bella stood at the open door, eyes wide.

"Jump, Bella!" Mia shouted.

Bella scanned the distance from the helicopter to the ship. The helicopter had been hovering, but now began to tilt as the pilot prepared to veer up and away.

"I'm afraid!"

Mia's heart ached as she imagined Bella being dragged away from her, maybe never to be seen again. She had come too far to let that happen.

"Trust me, Bella! I'll catch you. Trust me. And jump!"

Bella squeezed her eyes shut and launched herself from the edge of the helicopter, arms wide.

Mia tried to get her feet set under her to catch Bella, but she was too weak to hold her, and they both crashed to the ground.

Bella squeezed Mia hard and started sobbing on contact. "Thank you, Mia. Thank you! Bella pressed her face against Mia's chest while Mia wrapped her arms around her. Whimpering, Bella said, "It was horrible. I was living a nightmare. I'd given up. I thought I'd lost everything." Bella pulled back and met Mia's gaze. "But you came for me. You *came* for me!"

Bella started to get up off Mia when a shot rang out from the helicopter. Bella fell hard. Mia glimpsed the pitiless glare of the rich man holding a pistol as the helicopter banked and soared away.

She reached into her pocket and found one more lipstick case. The truth serum. *Dammit.* She threw it helplessly at the disappearing helicopter and started to cry. "Bella, I failed you," she wailed as she reached towards Bella's still body.

Then Mia realized that she herself was bleeding badly. Feeling faint, she lay quietly on her back. *At least I tried*, she thought as the world grew dark around her.

• • •

"Mia." She woke up to someone calling her name. It was Xtina's voice. She knew it well. It had always brought her warmth and peace.

Mia, remember the platinum vial I gave you. It's hanging around your neck. The liquid in it can save your life. Now is the time I told you about. Now is the time I warned you of. Now is the time for you to use this gift.

Mia shook herself awake, but she worried she was about to die. Xtina's words about the vial reverberated through her mind.

She dragged herself to a sitting position and took the vial in her trembling left hand. She cautiously tried to remove the cap with her right hand, but she didn't have the strength to twist it open. Taking a deep breath, she focused her remaining strength on opening the cap and finally twisted it open. She put it to her lips.

But then she paused. What else was it that Xtina had said about the vial? That someone would die but that she would have to choose *who*. Was this that time? *But what did you mean, Xtina?*

Mia fought to retain consciousness. Her thoughts wandered back in time. She remembered many happy times growing up and playing with her constant companion, her twin sister Nita, only to end up losing both Nita and her parents. Mia remembered how suffering as a victim of abuse herself led her to become a victim advocate and spend several years feeling that she was doing good work and helping abused women. Later, she found The Sisterhood and learned how they worked to balance the scales of justice.

Now that she was dying, she asked herself, *has my life been worthwhile?*

She shifted her gaze to Bella. Yes, much of her own life was full of satisfaction. She had helped so many women. And Bella, Bella had become her fast friend. Mia had risked everything to try to find her. To try to save her. But she was too late after all. Bella lay beside her, bleeding, not moving.

Mia wiped a tear, focusing her fading sight on Bella, wishing she—

Wait! She's still breathing! Light filled Mia's mind and illuminated her thoughts. Mia suddenly understood what it meant to be a member of The Sisterhood, to be her sister's keeper. She took the vial from her lips and moved over to where Bella lay, pursed Bella's lips with her fingers, and poured the contents of the vial into Bella's mouth.

Mia forced a few final words out of her mouth, *"Be well, my sister"* and then collapsed on her back.

CHAPTER 32

BELLA WOKE TO THE FEELING of the sun on her face. She opened her eyes, blinking at the light that surrounded her. She realized that she was still on the boat, lying on her back. She had been shot. She was alive but weak.

A warm rush within her made her chest burn. Electricity sparked out to her fingers and toes. Energized, she sat up.

Mia lay by her side in a pool of blood. Bella gasped and knelt quickly at Mia's side. Remembering her Advanced Placement anatomy class, Bella pressed her fingers against the artery in Mia's neck. She waited. She moved her hand a bit and tried again but found no pulse. "Mia!"

Bella heard a groan nearby. She turned and watched as Zena dragged herself slowly to her feet and then limped to Bella's side and knelt on one knee by her side.

"I think she's dead," Bella cried out.

Zena checked for herself. Several moments passed as Zena's fingers tried several pulse points. Finally, Zena grimaced. Tears welled up in her eyes before her head dropped. Zena nodded slowly.

As Zena turned slowly away, Bella threw herself on top of Mia. "No, no, no...," she whimpered quietly. Then she looked up at the sky and screamed, "NO, NO, NOOOOOO," and started wailing uncontrollably. Eventually, she choked out, more quietly now, helplessly..."No, no! *Please* no!"

Zena looked at Bella sadly and then noticed a bullet hole in her dress in the center of Bella's back.

"Are *you* alright?" Zena asked. "You've been shot."

"Yes," said Bella as she sat up and patted herself with both hands. "Look, here's a hole in the front of my dress," she said, sticking a finger through it. Then she touched her chest.

Zena peered towards the back of Bella's dress. "And here's where the bullet came out," she said, poking her finger through a hole in the middle of Bella's dress. But how? What happened?"

"I don't know," said Bella. "I got shot, and I fell to the ground. I saw my family in my mind, but then I lost consciousness. I don't know what happened after that."

Zena reached toward Mia's neck. The platinum vial that hung around Mia's neck had been opened and was empty. "She must have used her vial for you," said Zena, glancing at Bella. "Instead of for herself. And saved your life."

Bella felt like she couldn't breathe. She broke into sobs. It was like one nightmare after another. Finally, she gathered herself enough to look at Zena and noticed that she was also wounded.

"You're bleeding too," Bella said. "Are you okay? I don't understand how, but if what you're saying is right. If somehow what's in the vial can save your life, then maybe you should use it, like *right now.*"

Zena replied, "I just have a few flesh wounds. I'll bandage them up, and then we can go."

"Go where?"

"Back to headquarters," Zena said. "I'll call for help now."

Bella shook her head. But…then…*your* vial. Can we use it for Mia? Please, can we use it for Mia?"

Zena's lips twisted slowly into a deep frown. "I'm so sorry, Bella. It only works while you're still alive. Xtina says once you're dead and your soul leaves your body, it's too late." Zena shook her head. "I'm afraid it's too late for Mia. She's gone."

CHAPTER 33

THE BODY OF THE SISTER known as Mia lay on a mobile hospital bed in a sitting room at the headquarters of The Sisterhood. She wore a long white gown and was being prepared for burial by a nurse's aide. The doctor who had declared her dead was packing her medical kit and getting ready to go. Xtina, Sally, Victoria, and Bella stood around the table.

Victoria asked, "Xtina, is there anything you can do?"

Xtina moved to the top of the table and put her hand on Mia's forehead. She answered, "I sense that Mia's soul has left her body. Modern medicine has no way to bring her back."

After a long moment, Xtina said, "Mia grew up here in The Refuge. She was like a daughter to me. Please let me sit with her awhile."

The other women nodded and left the room and stood together in the hallway mourning Mia's death and reminiscing about her brave exploits during her short time as an agent of The Sisterhood.

After several minutes, Xtina came out of the room and approached the nurse's aide. "You may go back in now." Then she turned to the other women present. "Let's all join hands and have a moment of silent prayer for Mia."

The nurse came running into the hallway. "I don't know how, but she's breathing! Where's the doctor?"

"She went that way," said Victoria and pointed behind her.

The nurse and the doctor came running back into the room. "Please wait out here, and give us room to work," said the doctor as she rushed back into the room with Mia.

Everyone waited impatiently in the hallway for about twenty minutes until the doctor finally came out. She said, "Either I am totally incompetent and didn't realize that the young lady was just in a deep coma, or, and I've never uttered these words before but…it was a miracle."

Everyone gathered closely around the doctor. "Regardless, Mia is alive, but she's dehydrated and has lost a lot of blood. She's conscious and asking to speak to all of you. Please be brief though. I'm going to need to set up some IVs with blood, fluids, antibiotics, and vitamins."

Sally said, "We get the idea, Doc."

The ladies walked into the room. Xtina's face was the first Mia saw. Her sparkling green eyes penetrated Mia's soul and filled her with joy and warmth and love. Mia burst into tears. Tears of joy. Tears of gratitude.

She looked around her to try to get her bearings. Her last memory had been dying on a ship after a fierce battle to rescue Bella. Now she was in a bright room filled with flowering plants and intricate mosaic wall designs.

Xtina's face appeared to be glowing. In fact, there was a glow around her whole body. Mia tried to center herself, tried to take in her surroundings, tried to focus her consciousness. Disconcerted, she asked, "Am I in heaven?"

Xtina smiled. "The spirit does continue after death, my dear Mia, but your spirit has come back to us. You are still here with me." Then she lifted her arm and waved her hand slowly around the room. "Here with us."

"How long was I gone? I thought I was dead."

"It's been a full day since you were on the boat. You've been here at your old home, The Refuge, since late last night."

Mia turned her head and saw that Zena was there. And Sally. Her heart filled with joy at seeing them. Then she searched the room but couldn't see Bella. Grief started to fill her heart.

"Where is Bella? Was I too late?"

Xtina said, "No, Mia. You saved Bella. In fact, Zena told me that you sacrificed your own life to save her." Xtina paused and closed her eyes and wept silently. Mia had known Xtina for many years and had never seen her cry. Eventually, Xtina opened those sparkling deep green eyes and gave Mia a look that seemed to penetrate to her core. "It is a rare thing for a human to do that. To sacrifice one's life for another."

Mia looked at Zena. "Are you alright? I saw you get shot."

"I'm hard to kill," replied Zena. "Many have tried, and I have the scars to show for it. But all have failed."

Xtina said, "Mia, Bella is here. She's been waiting for you. Her father came to take her home last night, but she refused to leave. They've both been here all night." She put her hand on Mia's shoulder and added, "By the way, when Frank was here at your side, I sensed that he has deep feelings for you too."

Mia met Xtina's eyes. "Yes, I know."

"He asked to be called when the doctor was finished. And look, here comes Bella now."

"Mia, I'm here," said Bella hurrying to her side. "I was just calling my father to tell him the good news about you. He's in the other building. He's on his way."

"Bella!" Mia exclaimed. She tried to get up but realized she didn't have the strength. So, she just reached out her hand to Bella, who grabbed it with both of her hands, bent over, and kissed it.

While she continued to squeeze Mia's hand, Bella said, "Zena said you saved my life. I don't understand what happened. But I'm so grateful. I don't know what to say. I'm so very grateful to you. I love you. I owe you everything. Thank you, my friend."

Mia replied, "I consider you more than a friend, Bella. You're my sister now. There is no higher compliment than that here at The Sisterhood."

Xtina led everyone out of the sitting room to let Mia rest. Bella was so relieved that Mia was okay. It was all she'd been able to focus on since she'd been rescued. Now that she knew Mia would pull through it felt like the nightmare was finally over. She was safe, but then something else occurred to her.

Bella turned to Zena. "What about the other girls from the farm? Were you able to save any of them?"

"Yes, all of them. Several of them came back with us. Victoria is just getting them settled now at The Refuge. Volunteers from the Utah Coalition against Sexual Assault should be here by now also."

"Are they all okay?"

Zena smiled at Bella. "They'll be safe there. The Refuge is a safe haven for girls and women who have suffered abuse. Now we'll give them medical assistance, help them search for family, and connect them with other services in the community. They'll even get them immigration lawyers if they don't have papers."

Bella felt like she might burst into tears. "Good, good. Can we go see them? I want to see if my friend, Felicia, is here. She helped me while I was at the farm."

"I'll take her," Sally offered and approached Bella. "I'll show her the grounds and take her to see the other girls."

Xtina caught Sally's eyes, and raised an eyebrow, but then nodded at Sally.

Sally said, "Come with me, Bella."

As they approached the entry of the building, Bella said, "Zena told me that you were helping her and Mia find me. They said they would never have been able to locate me if it weren't for your help. I'd given up hope, I was moved around so much. So, I just wanted to say thank you. You as much as anyone saved my life."

Sally replied, "well, we worked as a team, and we all did our part. But when it comes right down to who to thank for saving your life, I think it must have been Mia. Zena told me that Mia used the titanium vial that Xtina gave her to save you."

Bella said, "I still don't fully understand those. What is in the vial? How could that save me?"

Sally shook her head. "I don't know. I wanted to examine the contents. Run some tests. But Xtina asked me to just take it on faith. I don't believe in faith, though; I believe in facts. When I asked her to just tell me the truth, she said that the world is not ready for the truth. All I do know is what I've seen. And there have been a few cases I know of where the sisters' injuries were so bad that the only explanation that made sense was that the contents of the vial saved their lives. And more than that, they were better, stronger than before. And one even seemed to have Xtina's ability to see the future."

Bella was stunned by how casually Sally talked about all these things, like they were just normal everyday things. But she was simply too emotional and wired to really think about how crazy all of this sounded, so she just took it all at face value.

Sally stopped and took Bella by the shoulders and turned her until they were face to face. "You, for example. After what you've just been through you must be extremely traumatized. You may never be the same as you were before you were taken. Any child would be in shock. But here you are, full of energy, almost euphoric. But I need to warn you. That feeling will fade in a few days."

Sally's serious stare penetrated deep into Bella's mind. Maybe she looked well to Sally, and she did feel unusually energized, but the constant fear and despair of the last few days still haunted her mind. "I don't know how to describe my feelings at the moment," she finally said. "It's like I have lots of feelings, good and bad, all at the same time." Bella noticed deep kindness and concern in Sally's eyes. "But I do feel so grateful that I was rescued. I'm excited about that. And I'm happy to be meeting you and Xtina and the others."

Sally nodded. "That all makes sense. Hopefully, I'm wrong."

"I think I'll be okay," Bella said. "But what about Mia? Zena said she was dead. When we were on the ship, I checked her too. She had no pulse.

And Zena said the contents of the vial only work to save you while you're still alive. So…how is Mia…? I mean, I don't really understand any of this that well, but…how is she alive?"

"I wish I knew. But apparently Xtina doesn't trust me with the answer." Sally sighed.

Bella wasn't sure what to make of that, but again, she didn't have the energy to give it much thought. She was now focused on seeing if Felicia was okay.

Sally led Bella out of the building. They walked quietly, not speaking again until they were outside in the courtyard.

Sally pointed back at the building they had just left. "This building is the headquarters of The Sisterhood's primary business unit. It's called The Sower's Paradise."

Bella saw the Sower's Paradise sign high on the building and an engraved statement underneath it.

"As Ye Sow, So Shall Ye Reap," she read out loud. She turned back to Sally and asked, "Isn't that from the Bible?"

"Yes, it is, and it totally applies to the food-growing business. But Xtina teaches that it also applies to our actions in life. Those who do good to others tend to have good things happen to them."

Bella felt a tinge of anger burning in her chest, "I like that idea. That means that bad things tend to happen to those who do bad things."

Sally gave Bella a knowing look and nodded, "Yes, little sister. You catch on quick."

Bella didn't want to linger on thoughts about those people, so she asked, "Why is it called the Sower's Paradise?"

"It is mainly because of the extensive gardens housed in giant greenhouses, some of which you can see out there beyond the other buildings. Lots of the girls who stay at The Refuge work there, and some also study botany and horticulture. There are also residences for other workers and a general store out there too. Some of the food is sold fresh, but much of it is packaged and sent to homeless shelters and food banks around the world. The rest is sold to pay the bills. And Xtina sells antiquities at auction when necessary, as well."

"But it's so dry out here. Where does the water come from to support so many plants?"

Sally chuckled. "All that Xtina will say is that it was prophesied that this desert would blossom like a rose. She can be so mysterious sometimes. Personally, I think there must be a deep well to an underground aquifer." She tilted her head away from the building. "Follow me."

As they crossed the large courtyard Sally pointed and said, "We are on our way to The Refuge, which is straight ahead. On your right is the gym where the girls can work out and get martial arts training. On the left is the schoolhouse. Well, it was a schoolhouse the first time I saw it. But now it's a high-tech building with video feeds to classes at major universities around the world."

As they approached the center of the courtyard, Bella pointed at the larger-than-life statue in the center of a complex mosaic design on the pavement. It looked like a warrior to Bella, with her shield, lance, armor, and helmet. She asked, "Who's this?"

Sally replied, "It's the Greek goddess, Athena. She's the goddess of war. But in what seems to some to be an odd contradiction, she is also the goddess of wisdom. That is what the owl on her shoulder represents. If I were to summarize what it means to me, it would be that it means that it's important to pick your fights wisely. That's what we try to do at The Sisterhood."

Bella asked, "The Sisterhood? What's that?"

Sally hesitated long enough to consider what else she could say. Bella got the impression that it wasn't something she was really supposed to talk about. She gave Bella a serious look. "Can I tell you something in confidence? It's a secret you can't repeat."

"Of course," answered Bella, furrowing her brow.

"There's a secret group of women called The Sisterhood. Their mission is to get justice for abused women when the legal system fails to protect them."

Bella stared into Sally's eyes, giving her complete attention. "When you were taken, it was The Sisterhood that Mia called for help to get you back. Zena and Mia, you saw in action."

"Yeah. I saw Zena fighting on the ship, she is like Athena but human."

Sally smiled at Bella's characterization of Zena. "Zena is indeed a warrior. That's why we call her Zena now." Sally put a finger to her lips. "Don't say anything, but it's not her real name."

Bella smiled. She was pleased with the friendship blooming between Sally and herself, but they hadn't known each other for very long and she wasn't sure what made her privileged to receive this information about The Sisterhood.

"Why are you telling me all this?"

Sally pondered her question and then responded, "I don't know. I guess I just thought you should know who it was that saved you. Can I ask you one question, Bella?"

Bella wrinkled her brow and said, "Sure. Go ahead."

"Who was it that saved you?"

Bella was confused for a moment. She went to answer and then realized that she was being tested. "Who saved me? Well, I don't know."

Sally laughed and said, "Like I said, you catch on quick."

They kept walking until they arrived at The Refuge. Bella hurried down the hallway ahead of Sally, hoping to find Felicia. She vowed never to forget Felicia's kindness to her at the ranch. Bella saw a big cafeteria and long hallways that appeared to lead to bedrooms. A group of girls were meeting in a common area. She circled the room but didn't see Felicia. Despair started filling her stomach. Finally, she found one of the girls she shared her room with at the farm. "Hey, is Felicia here?"

The other girl replied, "No. She didn't come with us."

"No," said Bella, her voice breaking, "She stayed there? At the farm?"

The girl gave her an apologetic look. "No, God, I'm sorry. I meant that she didn't come with us because she was able to find her grandmother in Texas."

"Her grandmother?"

"Yeah. She got out."

A tear ran down Bella's cheek. The girl gave her a look of understanding and comradery.

"Thank god."

Bella looked around at the other girls from the farm. Among them were several women wearing name tags on their lapels who she didn't know. They held clipboards. *They must be the victim advocate volunteers,* thought Bella. She overheard them asking the girls questions like, "Could you leave? Were you made to work excessive hours with little or no pay? Did you have any untreated illness or injury?"

Bella heard another woman with a clipboard speaking in Spanish to a girl from the farm that Bella had been told was taken by Big D's men at the border. Bella had studied Spanish for two years in high school and understood some of the conversation. *We can help you claim asylum and get you a T-Visa.*

Bella hurried forward to speak to the volunteer. "Sorry for interrupting. There was another Spanish speaking girl. Eugenia. Have you seen her?"

The woman flipped to a list of names and scanned it. "No. Sorry. Her name isn't on the list." Then she turned back to the girl she had been speaking to, but Bella felt another tear sliding down her face. She didn't think that Eugenia would be there, but she'd hoped. She knew she would never forget Eugenia, nor Felicia. And she would keep their memory alive.

Sally caught up with Bella and asked, "Pretty amazing, right?"

Bella nodded and quickly wiped away her tears.

Sally added, "It's not just what you see here either. Xtina is committed to helping them all transition into a new life. The Refuge will pay for their education, help them find jobs, and help them transition to a new life. But it will be harder for some than others, and unfortunately, we can't save them all."

"Yeah," Bella said, holding back more tears.

"Your father will be here soon, right?"

The mention of her father only made Bella more emotional. Soon her nightmare would really be over.

CHAPTER 34

FRANK BRAVO HURRIED BACK through the hallways at The Refuge after he was told Mia had somehow woken up, and was expected to recover fully, and that he could take his daughter home. Relief finally started to push the anguish of the last two days aside like when the sun chases away the darkness when it peeks over the horizon.

A woman with long black hair appeared in his path. "Frank," she said simply.

"Do I know you?" Frank asked, staring into the woman's bright, green eyes.

"You know of me. Of that, I'm sure. But no, we haven't met. I'm Xtina."

A wave of recognition swept through Frank. Mia had spoken of the mysterious Middle Eastern woman who led The Sisterhood. This must be her. Reaching forward simultaneously, they grasped hands. Warm energy shot up Frank's arm and startled him and he let go of her hand. "Oh my god."

Xtina raised an eyebrow. "Well, not exactly."

Frank was momentarily stunned by the captivating presence of this woman, but his awe and puzzlement were forced aside by his main reason for coming. "Do you know where my daughter is?"

"Yes. Happily, Bella is here and coming quickly to see you." Xtina nodded her head towards the other end of the hallway. "Come with me to the back entrance to wait. She'll be here soon. But first, I wanted to speak with you for a moment about her, and about my dear Mia."

"Yes. Yes. I want to see Mia also. Last night my daughter called and said she was hurt or maybe even dead, but then miraculously survived."

"Yes, I felt your concern for Mia when I touched your hand," Xtina said, smiling warmly, "just as I have sensed her love for you. She is alive but will need another day of rest and medical treatment before she should see you."

"But I—"

"I know," Xtina said. "You will see her soon, I promise. For now, I just wanted to tell you how important both Mia, and now Bella, are to me. We are now connected in ways that would be difficult for you to understand." Xtina paused. Frank sensed she was waiting to ensure his complete attention.

"I think I understand."

Xtina cocked her head. "Do you?"

"I think so. I believe that what you mean is that you expect me to love and protect them. And I assure you that I will."

Xtina nodded. "You are a rare man, Frank Bravo. You did understand what I meant, at least in part. And I will trust you to take care of them. Let me tell you though that Mia, although she is strong, still requires your kindness and support. And when your daughter received my…." Xtina paused, appearing to reconsider her words. "And your daughter, while injured deeply now, will someday become stronger than you can imagine."

Frank didn't understand all that Xtina meant, but before he could ask for clarification, she spoke again.

"Here she comes now."

Frank turned to see Bella across the courtyard. Their eyes met. Frank started quickly down the stairs as Bella pushed off her back foot and started running. He opened his arms as she approached, and she leapt. He caught her under her arms and spun her all the way around before easing her to the ground. Both burst into tears in each other's arms.

He took a step back but didn't let go of her hands. "You haven't jumped into my arms like that since you were eight years old."

She held onto his hands tighter than she ever had. And through her tears, all she could say was, "Daddy. I thought I'd never see you again."

"Oh, my sweet Bella," he cried. Her father pulled her close and squeezed her tightly. "I'm here. I'm here. I'm so sorry. I'm so, so sorry."

"No, I'm sorry. I should've listened to you about Johnny, and this never would've…" she struggled to speak through her tears, "this never would've—"

"Hey," he said firmly, "this was not your fault. You hear me? This was not your fault, Honey."

Bella buried her face in her father's chest and sobbed. Every emotion that she had been holding onto for the last few days was coming out. In her father's arms, she finally felt safe again. She never wanted to let go again.

"I'm just so glad that you're okay," her father said as he stroked her hair and held her tight.

Bella thought to herself how complicated that word seemed to her now. She was alive. For the most part, she was physically unharmed. But okay? She wasn't sure if she'd ever really feel okay again. And Sally warned her the euphoria of the rescue would wear off. But her dad was here and that was the most okay she'd felt in days. Not that she could say any of that to him. She didn't dare describe everything she had seen. All she could do was sob into her father's chest.

CHAPTER 35

THE NEXT DAY, Mia woke with renewed energy and voracious hunger. She went with the rescued girls to the buffet at The Refuge and gobbled down a plate of scrambled eggs and toast and then went back for seconds, this time a blueberry pancake stack with lots of maple syrup and a side of fresh fruit.

Zena showed up at The Refuge's dining room and said, "Wow, Mia, you look fantastic, especially for someone who just took a bullet. How are you feeling?"

"I feel better than ever. Ready to rock and roll."

"Yes, that's what I've heard happens afterwards."

"After what?" asked Mia.

Zena studied Mia for a moment and then slowly shook her head. "After she brings you back, at least that's what some of the older sisters say. There's talk of another sister who was thought to be dead and then was revived after Xtina arrived. She was stronger than before, and she…knew things." Zena hesitated before finishing. And now there's you."

Mia looked down at the ground in thought.

Zena added, "Anyway, you apparently feel great afterwards, like more alive than ever. Stronger than ever. But eventually, that wears off, and you feel normal, like you usually feel. For a while at least, you feel bulletproof. I think that I'd like to feel that. In fact, I would love to go on a mission feeling like that."

Mia replied, "I don't know. Think about it, Zena. I mean, if you have to die, then it's probably not worth it."

Zena shrugged. "Today's a good day to die." She glanced around and then gazed into Mia's eyes with an encouraging smile. "But it doesn't look like we're going to battle today, we're just going to debrief Xtina about the Bella kidnapping. She's waiting for us. So, unless you can stuff any more food into your gut, come with me now."

Mia eagerly crammed the last few bites of pancake into her mouth and chugged the rest of her orange juice. With renewed energy, she pushed her chair away, maybe too forcefully based on the way the other girls stopped in mid-bites and looked her way.

Mia and Zena arrived at Xtina's office where Sally was already speaking. "What about the yacht?" she asked the group as she skimmed their faces in the room. "The yacht was motoring southwards toward the Cayman Islands. The billionaire who bought Bella might have been on that boat."

Sally acknowledged Mia and Zena with a nod. "The billionaire's name is Jason Edgarton. If he was on that yacht, then he escaped on the helicopter after the shootout with Zena and Mia. Unfortunately, we lost that helicopter. But he is a well-known public figure, a businessman who goes to all the best parties of the rich and famous. I have a photo of him with one of the British royal family and other photos where he and his friends are surrounded by beautiful young girls. He'll be easy enough to find; we won't even have to look for him. Some paparazzi will take a photo and plaster it on the cover of a supermarket tabloid next week."

Zena asked, "What's his business anyway? I've seen him in the news, but the reporters are always vague about what he does, something about him being an investment advisor. Apparently, lots of the rich and famous give them their money to invest."

Sally commented, "Regardless of how he gets his money, the bigger question is, what do we do about it? What do we do about him? I mean, he's the one who bought Bella at an auction after Big D's guys kidnapped her. Do we take all our information to the FBI and hope they'll charge him?"

"Well, let's talk about that," Sally responded. "Whatever we do, I don't want to put Bella at risk. She would be the FBI's prime witness. Edgarton obviously has a small army of mercenaries available that he tried to use to eliminate any witnesses to his transgressions."

She paused and focused her attention on Mia and Zena. "Plus, he probably thinks you're all dead. From what Zena told me, all three of you were down when the helicopter took off. Maybe we should keep it that way."

"Come to think of it," Mia said, entering the conversation, "Zena and I would have a lot of explaining to do regarding all those dead bodies on the farm and on the boat."

Sally looked around. Since no one interrupted her, she said, "Okay then, I suggest we take care of him ourselves. First, we do some investigation…an international investigation. I'll contact some of our sisters overseas. We can decide what to do about him at some later date."

CHAPTER 36

FRANK WAITED EAGERLY to meet Mia for lunch at the family-owned Thai restaurant she liked. When she returned from rescuing his daughter, they thought she was dead.

Eager to see her alive, he had arrived early. He checked his watch over and over, but the seconds seemed to tick off more slowly than usual. Frustrated by the delay, he turned his head toward the door with fresh anticipation each time anyone entered, only to be disappointed each time.

Finally, Mia arrived. Frank glanced at his watch one more time. She was right on time.

He stood to greet her with his arms open. She rushed straight into them, and he wrapped his arms around her and squeezed her tightly.

After a moment, still holding her, he pulled back to arm's length. "Mia, I've been wanting to see you, to thank you in person for bringing my baby back home."

She beamed. "You're welcome, of course. In case you hadn't noticed, though, she's not a child any longer. She was emotionally mature beyond her years before all this happened. And now...," Mia gazed into Frank's eyes, "now, she has been through more extreme trauma in a few days than most people experience in a lifetime."

He stepped back, holding both her hands in front of him. "Please sit." He guided her to the bench seat and then sat down across the table. Reaching over, he took both her hands again. "Mia, I don't know how to thank you. Last night, Bella told me what happened. Well, not everything.

She said there were some things that she didn't want to speak about." He grimaced and swallowed hard. "But she said that you were fearless."

He choked up and could barely speak. He let go of Mia's hands to grab a napkin and wipe a tear from his eye. The server interrupted the emotional moment by laying two glasses of water on the table. "Your waiter should be by soon with a menu," she announced.

Frank took a drink of water to calm his throat. "Bella said you never quit even when it seemed to her that all was lost. She said that you didn't give up. You kept coming. And that it was you who saved her in the end."

He wiped away another tear. He shrugged his shoulders and raised his hands in front of him. "I'm okay now, but when I thought I had lost Bella, I... I felt like curling up in a ball. I couldn't think straight. I couldn't move." Frank took a deep breath. "Then after you called me from the farm, I called back but couldn't reach you. I thought I had lost you too."

Mia reached across the table and took Frank's hands in hers.

He wiped another tear from his eye, but this time he was smiling. "But then you came back. And you brought me my Bella. So, now, I am fine. I am good. I am perfect. I owe you everything. I don't know how I can ever repay you. I...I'm yours to command."

Mia took a deep breath and didn't speak for a long moment. She took Frank's hand. "I forgive you that debt. You don't owe me anything."

Frank smiled, then frowned, not sure what Mia meant to imply. He had just declared himself, in essence, her slave for life. He had opened his heart, no, more like opened his chest and handed her his heart. And she... she had waved the gesture aside like a fly over her plate.

Mia must have seen the question in his eyes because she added, "I mean, if we're going to be together, I don't want it to be because you feel you owe it to me."

"Oh!" Frank's face flushed with emotion. Stunned by the impact of Mia's words, he couldn't find his own. Maybe one. "Together?"

The waiter arrived, and Mia raised her hand. "Not right now, thanks. We won't be staying." The waiter nodded, collected their menus, and left.

Mia met Frank's questioning gaze but did not speak for a long moment. Finally, she squeezed his hand. "I want to tell you something." She gazed off into the distance for a moment before continuing. "After what I went through with Bella, not knowing if either of us would live through the day…I know now what is important in life. It's the people you love."

Frank's eyes moistened. He opened his mouth to speak, but Mia wasn't finished.

"And after Xtina brought me back…I can see. I mean, it's like the clouds over my mind parted and the bright sun cleared my view. I don't know how long it will last, but I can see the future. My future."

"Wow." Frank still was having trouble forming sentences. "What… what do you see?"

"For one thing, I see myself with The Sisterhood. It's my calling. To help the helpless, like with Bella, you know, to balance the scales of justice." Seeing she had Frank's full attention, Mia didn't pause. "The other thing I see in my future…the other *person*, is you. I'm not sure exactly what our relationship will be, especially with my commitment to work for The Sisterhood. But you are there."

"Mia, I…"

"Shhhh. Just come with me. Follow me home."

• • •

Frank parked and followed Mia up the stairs and into her apartment and closed the door behind him. Mia reached behind him and locked it.

Not sure exactly what Mia had in mind, Frank met her dark eyes and waited. She moved behind him and slid the sportscoat he was wearing

241

off his shoulders and laid it over the arm of the couch. Turning back to him, she moved close and put her hand on his chest. He felt electricity run through him. Then she moved her hand to his heart. He was sure she could feel it speeding up. She spread her arms, and he moved forward as she cradled him in a tender embrace.

After a moment she pushed back and met his eyes. He thought he saw a spark in her dark eyes. And intention. Yes, that's definitely what he saw. Then, Mia reached out and took him by the hand. She nudged him behind her, towards her bedroom, just as she had the night cruel fate and evil men interrupted their passion.

Frank recalled the feverish intensity of the last time they were together like this, the eager way they had kissed and touched. But she moved slowly this time. Deliberately. This time a calm serenity enveloped him as they entered her room and stopped by her bed.

She turned and met his gaze again. Her lashes parted and her eyes opened wide. She reached out and started unbuttoning his shirt, tugging it off with an eagerness that more than aroused him. Mia trailed a finger down his chest as Frank clasped the bottom of her blouse, pulling it gently upwards.

"Hold your arms up."

Mia obliged, finding his belt buckle when her blouse was on the floor. Frank's thumbs slid across the tops of her breasts, and Mia's breath caught when he found the front clasp of her bra and unhooked it, her breasts spilling into his hands.

"God, Mia, you're so beautiful. I love you."

"Then, show me."

Frank slid Mia down on the bed, wanting to commit her body to memory. She turned a bit to face him, their eyes meeting and breaths quickening. Acceptance. Mia focused on his lips and Frank brushed his mouth along her cheek, her soft moans hitting his ears like sweet music. He captured her bottom lip first, tenderly tugging it with his teeth. When her lips parted and their tongues mingled, the pent-up passion of their separation broke loose like a flood.

When he leaned back to catch his breath, Mia reached an arm around, urging him towards her, their arms and legs threaded together as if a blanket were being woven. His hand moved back to her breast, giving her nipple a gentle squeeze. She took in a breath, then rose to meet his hand, cradling his cheeks as she guided his mouth to her swollen peak instead. When Frank's lips captured her nipple and tugged, she cried out, squirming and lifting her hips off the bed. She urged him to stop, taking his hand again. She slid it downwards across her belly. He caressed her middle as she moaned softly. She coaxed his hand lower until it rested on the soft mound between her legs. Frank could tell she was ready for him, didn't need more foreplay. She didn't want to wait for him a second longer either. Mia grasped his manhood and squeezed, its stiffness filling her hand. Frank was more than ready too. He centered his square man hips on top of hers. She cried out when he entered her, pushing up against him until he was all the way inside her. Their eyes locked when they were one. No words were spoken, but they weren't needed.

Mia rocked her hips beneath him, pushing and pulling. They started slowly but the beat increased until their rhythm matched like they were singing a duet. The melody of the song sped up and then slowed down as they sang verse after verse in harmonious unison. Eventually the beat increased, building to its final crescendo. Frank slowed momentarily and caught Mia's eyes. He saw the answer to his question there, but she spoke it anyway.

"Don't stop. Give yourself to me."

They grasped each other firmly as their passion crescendoed to its intense climax, and they continued to hold each other close as the rhythm of their breathing slowed, like the fading echoes of the symphony's last chord, and their bodies finally relaxed. Their lips were almost touching as they lay together. He inhaled as she exhaled, and they shared their very breaths.

They held each other until sleep found them.

CHAPTER 37

BELLA LAY IN BED and stared blankly at the stuffed animals bulging in a net hanging from the ceiling in the corner, and the stack of Barbie dolls, the collector's type, stacked in boxes on the floor in the corner of her room. These toys reminded her of her happy childhood. That was over.

She had no idea what time it was, but she figured it was late. Finally, she got herself out of bed. She dragged her feet to the closet, pulled open the folding doors, and silently contemplated the clothes hanging there.

Her mother knocked on the open door. Bella hadn't heard the wooden stairs creak. She didn't know how long her mother might've been standing in the hallway, observing her.

"Are you alright, Honey?"

"I'm okay."

"Are you going to school today?"

She shrugged. "It's the last day of school for the year. There's no homework to turn in. It's mostly just a chance to say goodbye to my friends for the year. You know, sign each other's yearbooks. Take a bunch of selfies together."

Bella hadn't seen any of her friends since the night she had been taken. The thought of facing them or her school, knowing there would be all kinds of rumors floating around about her made her stomach twist. And the thought of seeing Johnny made her skin boil.

Her mother paused, pondering the meaning of Bella's silence, then pointed into the closet. "If you want to go to school you could wear that dress. It's warm out today, and it's lightweight, and pretty. Maybe good for a special occasion?"

Bella's gaze was drawn to a short blue dress. Some sequins that circled the low neckline of the bodice caught the light and drew her focus, reminding her of the sequins and glitter on the red dress she had worn to the prom. She gasped in a breath as the memory of being taken flashed into her mind.

"Honey, are you okay?"

"Mom, I don't want to wear that dress."

"That's fine, Honey. Don't worry, you have so many pretty dresses that—"

"Mom, no. I don't want to wear *any* of these dresses. I…I don't want to go to the school at all. Okay?"

"Oh, Honey. No. After all you've been through, of course you don't have to go."

Bella met her mother's eyes. Kind eyes. Caring eyes. She remembered with regret the argument they'd had several days earlier when she was leaving for the prom. Her eyes involuntarily started welling with tears.

"Yeah, I might…I might not…"

Her mother rushed to her, tears in her own eyes. She wrapped her in a warm, strong hug.

Bella hadn't been able to tell either of her parents any of the details of what had happened to her. She barely wanted to admit them to herself. But in her mother's arms she felt like somehow her mother understood everything intuitively. She didn't have to say anything. Her mother knew.

It was both the best and the worst feeling in the world.

CHAPTER 38

FRANK PUSHED DOWN THE LEVER on the toaster and reached to pour himself a cup of coffee. He had slept in at Mia's and was late for work but didn't care. The daily grind of being a criminal defense attorney weighed on him, more heavily than ever.

He was reaching for the coffee pot when his cell rang. *Maybe it's Mia.* He sat the pot back on the heating element and grabbed his phone, checking the name on the caller ID. *Detective Gooden?*

Puzzled, he answered. "Hello, Detective. What's up?"

Gooden didn't waste any time. "I got your message about your daughter being found and coming home. I have a few questions."

"Yes. She's home. She's safe." *No thanks to you.* "You can close your case."

"Nope. I can't close the case yet. I have some questions I need answered before I can file my final report."

Frank wasn't interested in answering any of Gooden's questions. "As far as I'm concerned, you can close it. Just write that she's been found and brought home. Period. End of story."

"Well, here's the thing, Mr. Bravo, FBI reported finding a bunch of dead bodies at a farm in Nebraska that they believe your daughter might know something about."

"I spoke to my daughter when she got back. She's too traumatized to talk about what happened. You've got daughters. Imagine yourself in my shoes. Would you put one of your daughters in the hands of FBI interrogators to be grilled over every detail of her trauma?"

Gooden was silent again. Frank figured he'd touched a nerve. No caring father would put his child through that. Eventually, he continued. "I get your point. But if she won't talk to me, she may still have to talk to the FBI. There weren't any other live witnesses to question at the farm. And there are FBI agents who are single. No daughters. Just diligent law enforcement officers trying to do their job."

Something Gooden said caught Frank's attention. "If there were no witnesses at this farm, why do you think my daughter was even there?"

"They found Chacho. And a white van that matches the description we got from a girl at the bar where your daughter was taken. They called me because, *at your request*, I sent out a nationwide ATL for the van, and for Chacho."

Frank was silent this time. Both Mia and Bella had mentioned being at a farm. If the FBI was investigating the dead bodies, Frank worried that anything he said might lead the FBI to Mia and The Sisterhood. That was something he couldn't do. No way.

"Great, so if Chacho's dead, then it's case closed as far as I'm concerned."

"The FYI wants to know who killed everyone. They want to know who found your daughter and where. Even if I close my case, they may not close theirs."

Frank didn't answer. Every detail he thought he could possibly give might open the door to information about The Sisterhood.

Gooden paused as if pondering how to deal with Frank's refusal to speak. "Don't you want to know who kidnapped your daughter? I mean Chacho's real name? His criminal record maybe? I'd think you'd be curious."

That got Frank's attention. "Yes. I guess I would. Tell me."

"I help you. You help me?"

"I don't know how else I can help you, Detective."

"I don't get it," Gooden said, changing his tone of voice. "It's strange to me that you either don't care where your daughter was taken, or that for some reason you are hiding information from the police. I could get you for obstruction for that. Plus, I checked gun registration records and found out that you recently purchased a gun."

Frank was taken aback by the mention of the gun.

After a brief pause, Gooden continued, his tone accusatory. "By the way, where were *you* the last few days?"

"Aha," Frank said, changing his tone now too. "Now *there's* the cop attitude I'm familiar with. Threats. And blatant disregard for the feelings of the victim. Look, I don't know shit about what happened. And my daughter isn't talking."

Both men were quiet now. Eventually, Detective Gooden cleared his throat. "Well, look. I'm not a monster. I'll give you Chacho's information. Hell, you'd get it from my final report anyway. The kid's real name is Carlos Martinez. He's from Texas."

"Thank you," Frank said. "I appreciate that. Really." Something about the name raised a red flag in Frank's mind. *I've had clients with that name.* "Carlos Martinez, you say. That name sounds familiar to me. But it's a common name. Do you have anything else? Maybe a middle name or something?"

"Give me a minute," Gooden said. "I'll try to pull it up."

What if he was a client of mine? Frank grabbed the pen he used to make his grocery list and the envelope from his utility bill to write down any additional information Gooden might have.

"Here it is," Gooden said. "His whole name is, was, Carlos Higoberto Martinez Sanchez."

Frank dropped the pen and fell into a chair. *No. It can't be.*

"Bravo, are you there?"

"Yeah, yeah. Ummmm, thanks. Hey, I, uh gotta go. Sorry I couldn't be of more help to you. Ummm, good-bye."

The memory came rushing all at one. Higoberto. He remembered because he asked his client if it was a typo. *Isn't your name Rigoberto?* It was less than a year ago. Guns, and drugs. Lots of drugs. Stolen guns. And even though the kid was young, he already had a record for aggravated assault and aggravated exploitation of prostitution. He was looking at prison. Three to five years at least.

Frank recalled the motion to suppress evidence he had filed. He had argued that the stop violated the client's Fourth Amendment rights. There was a valid traffic stop. Speeding or something. But he argued that police improperly extended the scope of the stop. That they lacked probable cause to search. It was a close call. The courts rarely suppressed evidence when there was a valid traffic stop. Especially this kind of evidence. This quantity of evidence. But Frank remembered researching the hell out of the law on point. And argued it hard. Sometimes the judges went your way if they saw you were passionate about a point. And he won the motion. The evidence was suppressed. So, the case was dismissed. And Carlos Higoberto Martinez Sanchez was released to the street.

The realization hit Frank like an unseen truck in an intersection and left him reeling. He collapsed against the back of the chair, stunned. As his mind slowly cleared, he realized, painfully, that if Chacho had gone to prison, he never would have had the chance to take Bella.

Frank put his head in his hands and wept uncontrollably.

CHAPTER 39

A WEEK EARLIER, Xtina had summoned Mia to the ceremony to induct her into The Sisterhood. Filled with anticipation and questions, Mia slept little during the week.

Mia was eager to arrive on time, so she pressed harder on the accelerator and hurried along Interstate 80. She turned off the freeway at the exit to The Refuge, but the directions to the ceremony sent her down a small side road to an outwardly plain building. It was the same place where she had met The Sisterhood's board of directors a few months earlier and asked for their help with the Kala Tausinga case she had worked on with Frank.

When Mia first met the secretive members of The Sisterhood, their existence and mission were strange to her. Xtina said even then that she believed Mia would join them. Xtina introduced her to the members of the board and let her observe a special ceremony.

But Mia had worked for years in the Salt Lake District Attorney's Office as a victim advocate, and she valued the rule of law above all else. So, when she learned that The Sisterhood took actions outside the law, it frightened her. When some of the board members challenged her commitment to their cause and questioned her about whether she would be willing, whether she would be able to step outside that law for the sake of justice, she was reluctant to agree. In her mind, it was black or white, so she balked at the opportunity.

But since then, Mia had come to realize that The Sisterhood was not a band of mindless vigilantes. They acted to get justice for women only when the legal system failed to protect them. They were just…balancing the scales, which as a general concept, she was able to accept. But then on that day when Bella was taken, all those general concepts evaporated.

They didn't wait for a police investigation to begin. They didn't wait for court hearings and a jury to decide the fate of those men. They didn't wait for the system to bring those men to justice. Before she knew it, she found herself part of "they." She not only came to understand their reasons, their mindsets, but she also embraced them too. Like them, she didn't wait either.

Mia parked her car and entered the building. The same brunette receptionist she had met the first time greeted her. "Hello, Mia. They're waiting for you downstairs. Let me call the elevator for you."

Mia's heart started to beat harder as she waited for the elevator and what could be waiting for her. She wondered if she would be ready this time.

When the elevator door opened, Xtina was there waiting, which eased Mia's nervousness. Xtina accompanied Mia down to the large board-room. Instead of the bright, modern recessed lights from before, flickering candles in ancient holders surrounded the entire room, creating shifting shadows on the table and on the faces of the women in attendance.

Three of them sat on each side of the ancient oak table. Xtina directed Mia to sit in the single chair at the head of the table, and she took her place and stood at the other head. She scanned the group, which signaled to them to be silent because the meeting was about to begin.

"Welcome my sisters. Today we are here to perform the Ceremony of the Rose for Mia Montes. You all know Mia. She lived in The Refuge as a child. She has come back to us as an adult. Long before today, I sensed in Mia a heart filled with compassion and the spirit of a warrior. I foresaw the possibility that Mia would eventually become a member of The Sisterhood. In the recent rescue of Bella Bravo, Mia demonstrated uncompromising commitment and extraordinary bravery. She proved herself to be worthy of becoming an official member and agent of The Sisterhood."

Xtina paused, and Mia looked into the eyes of each of the women at the table. Immense love emanated from each of them, love for each other and love for her.

Then Xtina continued. "We now invite Mia to join this table as a sister in our search for complete justice for the harmed and the voiceless, the shamed and the silenced, those lost to us at the hands of careless cruelty, and those taken before their time. We now ask her to help us in the work we do to return balance to the scales of justice."

Xtina moved a small shelf on the wall and selected a metal bowl with the markings of an ancient language on it and returned to her seat. She pulled a wooden mallet out of the bowl and said, "Let us focus our intention and be mindful of the significance of this day."

She slowly circled the side of the mallet around the top of the bowl until a pure, vibrant ringing filled the room. Everyone closed their eyes until the sound subsided.

Then she gave the bowl a soft tap on the side. "Now I ask brave Zena, our own warrior princess, to assist in the ceremony."

Zena walked into the room dressed in a simple white flowing gown tied over one shoulder. She carried a large vase full of roses and handed one to each of the women. Then she placed the vase in the center of the table, selected one more rose and walked over to Mia.

"Please stand with me, Mia," she requested.

After Mia stood up, Zena selected a large thorn on the long stem of the rose and pressed her thumb onto it, causing a bright red drop of blood to emerge on her thumb. Then she met Mia's eyes. "And now you."

Mia took a deep breath and then firmly pressed her thumb onto the thorn until the thorn broke through her skin as well. Zena held her own thumb up and pressed it against Mia's.

Zena smiled and kept her eyes on Mia. She announced, "Mia, we are now of the same blood. Now, we are sisters."

The women at the table clapped and took turns welcoming Mia and saying other kind words to her.

Then Xtina stood. "We are women. We can be beautiful and gentle like the petals of the rose. But, if necessary, like the thorns on the stem of the rose, we can draw blood. Finally, let us repeat The Keeper's Creed together. The women all spoke in harmonic unison:

I cannot stand idly in the presence of evil. I cannot remain silent in the face of injustice. I cannot be passive in the light of corruption. I will act. I will strike. And I will never give up. I will be my sister's keeper.

An electric wave of energy filled Mia from head to toe. Any lingering doubts she had felt before the ceremony fell away and disappeared. She met the eyes of each of the sisters at the table again and sensed commitment to their shared cause. Xtina's vision for Mia had come true, she was a member of The Sisterhood. Xtina's words about Mia's power to serve others echoed in her mind. Mia stood committed to serve The Sisterhood, with all her heart and might.

After a moment of silence, Xtina said to the group, "Since we are all here, shall we discuss which case we will take on next?"

"Yes," Mia quickly responded, feeling the responsibility that came with her new authority as an officially accepted Sister. "After all the things Bella told me she learned while she was on the farm, there are several cases that we should investigate."

Xtina said, "Sit down, sisters, and let's decide what wrong we will make right next."

ABOUT THE AUTHOR

RALPH DELLAPIANA was a long-time public defender who has handled thousands of cases and dozens of murder cases. Now, he writes compelling fiction inspired by the human drama of real cases. His award-winning first novel, Twice a Victim, is available on Kindle and paperback.